SHADOWS
OF SIN

R.C. HARTSON

Black Rose Writing | Texas

First printing

This is a work of fiction. Names, characters, businesses, places, events, and incidents are either the products of the author's imagination or used in a fictitious manner. Any resemblance to actual persons, living or dead, or actual events is purely coincidental.

ISBN: 978-1-68433-440-7
PUBLISHED BY BLACK ROSE WRITING
www.blackrosewriting.com

Printed in the United States of America
Suggested Retail Price (SRP) $19.95

Shadows of Sin is printed in Gentium Book Basic

*As a planet-friendly publisher, Black Rose Writing does its best to eliminate unnecessary waste to reduce paper usage and energy costs, while never compromising the reading experience. As a result, the final word count vs. page count may not meet common expectations.

For my wonderful wife, Lynie. Without her encouragement, understanding and love, this book would not be possible.

Also, to Dean Kuch, may he rest in peace.

SHADOWS
OF SIN

CHAPTER ONE

Gerald Albers crawled out of his Mercedes Maybach and checked both ways before he sprinted across Clark Street and jumped into the front passenger seat of the shiny black Escalade.

He was meticulously dressed this morning in a blue suit and starched white shirt. His face looked honest, but it appeared to be pinched by stress and worry. His rough complexion gleamed red with sweat and a fresh shave.

The September air was turning brisk. The heavy rain had stopped, but a mist was sweeping down from the north on a blustery wind. The leaves had started to turn red and gold, like Technicolor on the dull, wet Chicago Street. It was seven a.m. and the morning was starting to throb.

Once inside the Escalade, Albers pulled out a pack of cigarettes and lit up. He didn't blink or nod as he glared at the driver, and he removed a stray bit of tobacco from his tongue and cleared his throat. His mouth opened and closed like a marionette.

"I'm Gerry Albers. You've got a package for me?"

"Maybe," said the man.

Albers' eyes widened.

"Maybe? What in the hell does that mean?"

The sweaty, red-faced man shrugged. "'Maybe' means just that . . . maybe. It all depends on you, partner. Now...you got something for me?" His flesh seemed to ooze grease and his suit smelled like a locker room. He had the build of a weight-lifter.

Albers studied the man's concave face for a beat. "What do you mean?"

The other man smirked. "Come on, that's easy enough . . . you either brought the money or you didn't."

Albers eyed him warily as he nodded and fished a brown envelope from inside his suit coat.

"I've got fifty thousand here."

When the other man reached for it, Albers drew back. "I have to see the pictures first. Sorry. I have to be certain they're legitimate before I give you anything."

The man sighed and eyed the passing traffic. Then he looked back at Albers and squinted.

"Are you serious? That wasn't the deal. You only brought fifty grand?" He grabbed the money and shuffled through it. "Shit! You're in no position to demand anything, Senator. We told you the deal was two-hundred and fifty-thousand. You knew that."

He glared at Albers with eyes that looked like balls of lead, and his New York accent grated like a man whose voice box had been injected with Novocain. "Okay. Go ahead and look at the damned pictures." He pointed. "They're right there in the glove box."

He watched as Albers retrieved a Manila envelope and tore it open with feverish hands and then slowly sorted through a small stack of glossy, five by eight pictures. He gasped.

"How . . . I mean who took these? How . . . how could they? I just don't understand."

"You know I can't tell you that . . . and I wouldn't if I could." The big man cleared his throat, rolled down his window and spat. Then he looked at Albers and grinned.

"Ya know, I sorta like seeing big shots like you squirm. It's like watching you standing in the middle of the street bare-ass- naked with nowhere to hide your junk."

Albers glared at him.

"I could have gone all day without hearing that bullshit." His head jerked from side to side in disgust as he continued to thumb through the pictures. He was both pensive and appalled. "This is terrible. I . . . I just don't get it. Why me?"

The man shrugged. "Who knows? Probably for the money, don't you think? Pay up and you won't have to sweat it, Ace."

"I don't have all of the money. Two-hundred and fifty-thousand may not mean much to you people, but it's a small fortune to most people, myself included." He shook his head. "I don't know what to do here." He slumped back in the seat. "Why can't you just keep that fifty-thousand for now and give me the pictures?"

"Don't be stupid, Senator." The man's expression turned flat and he pulled a cigar from above the visor. He bit the tip, lit up and plugged it into the corner of his mouth. "You'll get that naughty picture collection when you come up with the rest of the money, not before."

He exhaled a plume of smoke and glanced at Albers. "The boss is gonna be real disappointed. He don't like waiting for his money." He paused, admired his cigar. "I guarantee you wouldn't be missed, Senator, if you should just disappear, you know." He snapped his fingers. "Overnight, your seat in the senate would be taken by some Democratic hard-charger . . . probably a card-carrying member of the NRA. And that horny wife of yours would be wearing him out every night in the sack."

"Shut up!" yelled Albers. "You don't know anything about my wife." He went silent as he continued to look through the pictures.

"You know we could just feed them pictures to *The Enquirer* or one of the other rags." He chuckled and leaned over until he was merely inches away from Albers' left ear. He lowered his voice. "I'm betting your constituents would love those photos, too.

Imagine your people seeing their squeaky-clean senator, his wife, and that other broad, all in one bed, doing the nasty in unbelievable positions. Ha! Picture them plastered all over the front pages, right there at the check-out lanes of your friendly Walmart."

Albers snapped his head to the left.

"You fucker," he spat out, his voice feral, low in his throat, as anger burned away his control. His bony frame became painfully erect, his gray eyes and thin mouth fierce and disapproving. "You wouldn't dare."

"Oh, we'll arrange it alright. Make no mistake. People who have underestimated my boss before have found out the hard way. I don't think you want to take the hard way here, little man." He paused and blew a puff of smoke. "But then, we won't do anything at all as long as you play ball. You wouldn't want to explain those photos at one of your black-tie dinner parties, would you?"

Albers slowly shook his head from side to side. "Damn you!" He cracked his window and flipped his cigarette butt out, then raised his hands.

"Okay. Okay, I get it." He glared at his tormentor. "Bullshit. Stop right there! I can't do this and I won't let you bully me with your gangster tactics. Tell your boss—whoever he is—that I said no way. I'm out of here."

He started to pocket the envelope with the pictures, but the thug grabbed his wrist and twisted. "Oh, no, you don't, pal. We get the rest of our money or no pictures."

"But, you're asking the impossible."

Albers groaned now and wrenched his hand free. He tossed the envelope carelessly at the man. It bounced off the steering wheel and landed in his lap.

"You can't get away with this. I won't put up with anymore threats. I simply won't allow it." Albers knew his words were due only to his anger, not to any confidence in what he was saying.

The man turned his head with the stiffness of a ventriloquist's dummy and let his eyes focus on Albers' flushed face.

"You won't what? You won't *allow* it? Ha! Just who in the fuck do you think you're dealing with here, Ace? Some weak damned amateurs?"

Like a magician, the man suddenly produced a .38 caliber pistol from inside his suit coat and jabbed it into Albers' ribs. He leaned to within inches of his face.

"Maybe you should have your doctor check that connection between your ears and your brain. You're not hearing me. You have to get your head tuned in to the right station, hot shot. Get your shit together and come up with the rest of the boss's money . . . pronto."

"I just don't know how," Albers moaned.

"Bullshit, Senator. We know your wife has got more money than God, so knock off that 'poor me' bullshit so we can put this deal to bed once and for all."

Albers began shaking.

"Okay. Alright. But I need to know you're not going to ask for more money after that." He buried his face in his hands, but stared down at the gun through his fingers. "Please, just put that thing away. Guns make me nervous."

"Sure thing, my man." He casually slipped the gun back inside the holster under his coat. "But the boss is not going to wait ten or twenty days for his money. I'm guessing he'll do five days, no more. Five days means this coming Saturday morning we'll meet to finish this business. You got that?"

Albers' voice quavered. "No, I'll need more time. For one thing, I simply can't let my wife know any of this." He lowered his head more and muttered, "It would kill her." He glanced sideways at the man. "You tell that to your boss. Tell him I'll get his fuckin' money as fast as I can, but leave my wife alone." He paused, looked at the envelope. "How do I know this is all of the pictures? Where are the negatives? I want the originals. Are they on a flash drive or a hard drive? I need the original source, too, whatever that may be." He studied the other man's face. "I'll need everything. You understand?"

The man sighed and shifted in his seat. He looked confused for a beat, but then grinned and cocked his head like a dog hearing a high-pitched sound. His grin tightened, but soured as he leaned forward and rubbed his temples. "Of course, Ace. I'll pass that along."

Sitting back, he added, "I should warn you, the boss doesn't like any changes or demands. It gives him the jitters. And when he gets jumpy, he takes it out on me. I still don't know how to handle it when his temper runs crazy like that. Know what I mean?"

Albers' eyes widened. He looked as though someone had just stepped on his foot. Silence permeated the air inside the car for the moment that followed.

"You just go to the bank, right? That's it?" He searched Albers' eyes. "Don't tell me you're one of those pansy-asses who lets his wife handle the money and can't withdraw anything without her okay."

"No, no. It's not like that, but the bank might want to hold the disbursement of that much money for twenty-four hours after the request or something. Hell, I don't know." He pounded a fist into his other hand. "Damn you! I have to cover the withdrawal somehow. My wife's no dummy. She'll eventually have questions." He paused for what seemed to him like an eternity. "I have to go. She will wonder where I am. It's not like me to be gone so long just for a few groceries."

Albers opened the door and started to get out.

"You got five days to get the rest, Senator. You'll be getting a call next Friday night telling you where and when this will go down on Saturday. We won't be meeting here again. And you damned well better be ready this time. No more games."

"Right," Albers croaked as he eased out of the Escalade and reached for his pack of cigarettes. "I'll be waiting for your call."

Before the man drove off, he grinned and said, "Don't worry, Senator. You won't have a problem with wifey being pissed. She'll be fine. Just keep giving her your hot meat injection."

CHAPTER TWO

Albers drove the few blocks to Cornelia Avenue and pulled over to the curb to unwind. The heavy silence in the car felt suffocating to him and a sick feeling of embarrassment and failure churned in his gut. He had acted like a coward, he thought. How had his comfortable life suddenly slid into these surrealistic threats from a blackmail scheme?

How had somebody gotten those pictures in the first place? His mind raced from one question to another as he fumbled in his coat pocket and retrieved a pack of Marlboro Lights.

Glancing in the rearview mirror, he lit up and inhaled deeply. Slamming the heel of his hand hard on the steering wheel, he growled loudly at his predicament. "Motherfuckers!"

He rested his arm on the wheel, drummed his fingers on the dash and pondered his next move. He couldn't shake off the ugly face of the thug he'd just been with, but now it felt good to chew down hard on a big "fuck you" as he exhaled a huge plume of smoke and talked out loud to himself.

"Why me? God knows there are so many dirty politicians who really *deserve* to be exposed and ruined. I'm damned sure they have a hell of a lot more money, too."

He stared vacantly through the windshield. His thoughts became jumbled. *There has to be a way out of this mess. But how? These people are definitely pros.*

He realized his life was in danger, not to mention his career in politics. He remembered he'd nearly shit his pants when that bastard jabbed the gun in his ribs. *I think he really meant business.*

This isn't something I can tell the police. That would open a whole new can of worms, that's for damned sure. And I can hardly ask the government for special security to watch over me day and night, as if I were running for VP or something. How would I explain why I need bodyguards?

Albers continued to puff on his cigarette as he wrestled with the barrage of worry overpowering his mind. He was all alone in this, and it was his own doing. He felt as if he were attached to his world by a single thin tether, like an astronaut walking in space, and the line was in danger of being severed. He felt powerless to stop it.

What else? What about Trish? Yeah ... what about my wife? What would she say ... after she screamed loud enough to wake the dead, that is? He inhaled deeply and allowed the smoke to drift slowly out of his nose. *I don't dare mention any of this shit to her. She simply couldn't handle it. She'd die of embarrassment or end up back at the hospital in Park Ridge—and most likely with a nervous breakdown this time.*

He stabbed his cigarette out in the ashtray. *No, I'll handle this somehow. I just have to. I'll take the money out of our savings. That's right. She has always been so lax with money—she won't even notice—for a while at least, until I figure something else out. Yes, that's it. Damn.- I hate to go behind her back ... but what the hell, I have no other choice.*

He continued to search his mind for options, but after twenty more agonizing minutes had passed and there still didn't appear to be any worthwhile answers, he pushed his mind into a completely different direction. Pulling out his cell phone, he scrolled through his contacts, found what he wanted and pressed "Call."

The man who answered had a voice that sounded like gravel being shoveled from the bed of a truck. Too much whiskey and cigars, Albers thought.

"Corky?"

"Yeah. Who's this?"

"Gerry, Gerry Albers, Corky. I know it's been a long time since we touched base, but listen, buddy, I need to talk to you right away. It's very important. Can I come by the bar?"

"Yeah, sure. But, Jesus, where have you been? I mean I haven't heard from you in ages, Gerry. Ever since you became a big shot, anyway." He laughed. "Don't tell me. Let me guess . . . you decided to become a bleeding heart liberal and you didn't want me to know. Right?" He laughed again.

"No, Corky, nothing that stupid."

"It must be pretty damned important, you calling me after, what's it been, about six months, at least, hasn't it? That senate seat must keep you jumping, eh?"

"Yeah, I've been pretty busy. Sorry about that, partner. Springfield has had me tied up in knots what with just coming back from summer recess and all. Hey, listen, Corky . . . are you real busy right now? I'd like to come by for lunch and buy you a drink. Sorry for the short notice, but this is... really important, buddy."

"Nah, I don't drink anymore, Gerry, but sure, you can stop by anytime. It'll be before the lunch crowd, so I'm not too busy this time of day. Hell, yeah. It'll be good to see you, buddy."

"Good. I'm on my way, Corky. See ya' in a few."

●　　●　　●

Charles "Corky" Hulce had attended school with Gerry Albers in Skokie, Illinois, twenty-five years earlier. His father owned The Last Resort Bar & Grill on Belmont Avenue until he died of a massive heart attack—the same year Corky was preparing to graduate.

To keep his family afloat after their loss, Corky took over running the bar, but failed to graduate as a result. He never went back to wear his cap and gown. Albers, on the other hand, finished high school, studied law at Northwestern University and went on to run for the Illinois senate.

In the years that followed, Hulce served three years hard time in Joliet for helping a friend boost a car from a prominent doctor's home in Elk Grove Village. Unexpected complications had erupted during the theft. Corky punched the doctor's gardener in the face and fractured his nose. A relatively simple car theft suddenly became much more when a felonious assault charge for Corky was tacked on.

Albers parked a block away, locked his car and walked down West Belmont to the bar. When he entered, the country song "Crazy Arms," by Ray Price. was playing from a radio somewhere in the back.

The place appeared empty with the exception of one man parked on a stool, watching the replay of a Cubs game on a TV set crammed onto a shelf above the bar. A bottle of Bud Light sat in front of him along with an ashtray that held a smoldering cigarette butt.

The whole place smelled of stale beer, pizza and disinfectant.

A petite blonde, who Albers figured to be the waitress, sat in a booth near the front of the place smoking a cigarette and rolling silverware. She fiddled with her makeup and got up when she saw Albers come in.

Her face reddened as she passed him and he caught a whiff of her sweet flowery perfume. Her blonde curly hair, now freed from its bonds, bounced as she walked. The way it moved and framed her face reminded him of a lion's mane.

Corky had spotted Albers as soon as the senator had set foot inside the door. He had a hangdog expression, and as thin as he was, his jowls and the skin of his neck appeared to have succumbed to gravity long before. He wore his wispy red hair in an unattractive comb-over. He sat on a stool, stoop-shouldered, and sipped a cup of coffee until he brought up the rag he was wiping the bar with and patted it against his double chin like an old matron trying to ward off a fainting spell.

"Hey, here is my man, Gerry Albers. Gerry, get your stranger's ass up in here, buddy."

Albers approached the bar and Corky met him and shook his hand.

"Shit, man! You look just as ugly as the last time I saw you, my friend." He chuckled and pumped Albers' hand. "Otherwise you're looking good, though. I'll give you that. How are you, buddy?"

"Fine, fine, Corky." Albers looked back over his shoulder, intuitively. "The place looks the same and you haven't changed a bit, have you, Corker?" He tapped him on the shoulder with his fist. "How you doing?"

"Great, just great. Come on. Let's go back in my office . . . a little more private for us, eh?"

"Good," said Albers. He followed his friend beyond the bar and through the cafe doors to the kitchen. The office was a small room off to one side of the cooking area. A black and white sign on the door read "No Parking."

"Quite a setup you've got back here, Corky. Having this kitchen has paid off, I guess."

"Yeah, we sell quite a bit of chow, believe it or not." He guided Albers to an uncomfortable looking chair in front of a metal desk. The top was cluttered with waitress checkbooks, menus and indistinguishable paperwork.

Corky dropped into a beat-up swivel chair behind the desk, tilted his head, and then shook a cigarette out of the pack from his shirt pocket and dangled it from his lip without lighting it.

He tossed the pack across the desk to Albers, who shook his head. "Not right now. Thanks anyway."

Corky lit up. "So . . . what's going on?" He tilted back in the chair and draped one foot over the edge of the desk, exhaling a cloud of smoke. "On the phone you sounded like it was a matter of life and death, pal. What did you do? Knock up your secretary or a student?"

"No. I only wish that was my problem right now." He leaned forward and spoke in a conspiratorial tone. His voice was calm, but his mind continued to race. "I need help, big time, Chuck."

Corky dipped forward in his chair and leaned in. "Okay, so shoot. What's up? You need money . . . what?" He clasped a hand over Albers' extended arm. "Give it to me straight. How in the hell can a nobody tavern owner help a big cheese like you, Gerry?"

Albers slouched back in his chair and let out a heavy sigh. "They're after me."

"What? Who?"

"I'm not sure right now. The fuckin' mob, I guess."

"What?" Hulce paused briefly, then grinned. "You're shittin' me, right?" He drew back a bit. "Come on, Gerry."

"No, I'm dead serious...and I do mean 'dead.' These guys mean business."

"Okay, so now comes the sixty-four-thousand dollar question . . . why do you think *the boys* want you all of a sudden?" He grinned. "Some bootlegging bill you won't help push through the senate or some such shit?" He paused and clicked his tongue. "I mean really, Gerry. Come on. You're acting paranoid."

Albers got up and walked once in a circle around his chair, then stopped.

"No, Corky, you've got me wrong. I really am in deep shit." He leaned both hands on the desk and got into his friend's face. "Look, didn't you tell me one time that you have some friends who are connected? You said you met people while you were doing time in Joliet, right?"

Silence, a long silence. Neither man spoke and they stared at one another for a beat.

Corky wobbled his head, but didn't speak. He dropped his cigarette butt in a dirty coffee cup, blowing smoke out his nose as he did.

"Yeah, maybe I know a guy. So what?" He leaned back in his chair. "What's going on, Gerry?"

Albers sat back down and exhaled a noisy gush of air. He paused, then lit one of Corky's cigarettes. Exhaling a cloud of smoke, he said, "I need your solemn promise that what I tell you here won't go any further." He studied his friend's face. "I'm serious. I need your word."

Corky nodded and locked his lips with an imaginary key. "These lips are sealed, Gerry. Now shoot already, will you? Jesus!"

Albers sighed. "Alright, here's the deal . . . somehow . . . someway, and I still don't know the how of this yet, mind you, but some bad actors have gotten their hands on some very personal pictures of me and Trish and they're putting the squeeze on me. They want two-hundred and fifty grand by next Saturday or they'll go public." His eyes met Hulces' for a split second, then wandered away. "So, there. Now you have it."

There were seconds of uneasy silence.

After a moment, a light seemed to snap on behind Corky's eyes, and a smile came across his lips.

"Damn! I am assuming these so-called *personal* pictures are of a naughty nature. Right?" His smile expanded into a grin. "What in the hell were you and Trish doing—or should I call you Mister Stud Muffin?"

Albers fidgeted, nodded and got up. "Maybe it's best if I just go away for a while. I should be back in Springfield after the recess, but for the time being, I'm still vacationing in Paris or something." He cleared his throat and gazed at his friend. "At least that will be the unofficial statement, if need be." He drew air quotes around the word *unofficial*.

"No. Hold on. Just hold up now. I'm in, okay? So, what is it exactly that you want my connection to do?"

Albers sighed, ground his cigarette out in an ashtray and clapped his hands together.

"Okay, first of all, I want to know who is behind this bullshit. And I also want to make sure that everything stops." He looked his friend in the eye. "I mean stops—one way or another, Corky. Got it? When . . . and if I pay them, I want everything they've got on me. I don't want anything hanging out there for somebody else to use to bleed me."

Corky relaxed in his chair again and stared at the ceiling. "That's a tall order, Ger. I'll need to make some phone calls." He got up, rested his hand on the senator's' shoulder and squeezed. "Meanwhile, you need to chill a little, my man. I'll contact this individual, but I can't swear he'll even want to touch this. It will probably cost you pretty heavy too, you know, depending on how far he has to take it. Sounds like pretty high stakes, though, know what I mean?"

"Yes. I understand. But, like I said, at least it's a start. I can assume your friend has a locking device on his mouth, too?"

Corky nodded. "Of course, but he'll want a complete explanation of what he's getting into," he warned in a meaningful whisper.

"Oh, he'll get all of that . . . the whole sordid story. Time is short, though. Like I said, they're expecting me to come up with the two-hundred thousand by next Saturday."

"Yeah, well, good luck with that," said Corky. He checked his watch. "I'd better get moving now. My customers don't get much time for lunch and I try to oblige them." He grinned. "You know what that's like, right, Senator?"

CHAPTER THREE

The sunlight that streamed through the window was brittle and swam with motes of dust. The stink of cigarettes, sour sweat and bourbon permeated the room. Cleve Hawkins rubbed the sleep out of his eyes and rolled out of bed.

He stumbled to the kitchen window and peered at the clouds. The storm had passed. The thunder was rolling away to the north, leaving behind only the gentle sound of rain. Ordinarily it would have been a perfect morning to pull up the covers and stay in bed, but such was not Cleve's fate today.

He thought about his homeless friend, Deckle, laid up in St. Joseph's Hospital. He had been hit by a car when he was crossing the street at Wells and Division. Cleve knew he should visit the poor guy. It was for damned sure Deckle had nobody else.

But right now, Cleve's temples throbbed and he felt like his brain was swelling and pressing against the inside of his skull as he stumbled into the bathroom and checked the mirror. His eyes were puffy and red, like a boxer's, and encircled by pale skin, a contrast he saw giving his face a resemblance to an inverted raccoon.

He jumped in the shower and let the water beat down on him in an attempt to pound out the numbness of sleep and to put the brakes on a miserable hangover.

Hawkins was no longer a Chicago cop, but he still hung out with a few of his cohorts on occasion and one of the things he missed about his old job in Robbery-Homicide was the camaraderie with his partners. The job had entailed long hours of stakeouts, waiting around the courthouse, hours filled up with chatter.

In those days, after hours, he went to the bar across the street and drank boilermakers until he was feeling good and mean. At least it seemed that way. A successful precinct day meant he and his partner had collared a burglar, a rapist or a high profile killer. Despite what Hollywood glamorized, rarely, if ever, was an actual murder solved in one day.

Days off were also rare, but sometimes he'd catch a break and see a day when he could scoot over to Wrigley Field, catch a Cubs game and hang out with a couple of his pals.

Indeed, yesterday had been like old times when he and his buddy, Sean Brophy, took in a double-header between the Cubs and Cincinnati. The Cubs lost the first one, but jumped all over the Reds in the second game by scoring nine runs in the fourth inning and never looking back. Afterward they beat it across the street to the Cubby Bear Lounge and continued to drink Old Style draught for a couple of hours. Everybody did. It was a tradition.

Later, they had migrated to a place over on Waveland Avenue, a dive called The Rockin' Robyn, an oasis of amber lights and Coors signs that reflected a glowing welcome out the windows to any passersby.

Cleve's last solid memory was himself paying for a Yellow Cab and fumbling for the keys to his apartment. Now, several hours later, he was suffering with an alcohol-induced, post-game let down.

There had been problems over the years for Hawkins in dealing with his penchant for alcohol. He had sworn off more than once. The strange thing was that he could stop the physical act of drinking. He had stopped for weeks at a time, for months at a time. His girlfriend Maureen had helped replace his hours of bar time, but she could not complete him. He had even seriously thought about getting married. He had been thinking about Mo a lot lately. He was in love with her, but marriage was out of the question. It just wasn't for him.

The truth was that at age forty-eight, he still liked to sleep in the center of the bed, to clean up only after himself, to earn and spend his own money, to come and go as he pleased, to pursue his career without worrying about hers, to plan evenings with input from no one else, to cook or not to cook, and to have sole possession of the remote control.

The alcohol problem, his thirst—the desire—never left him, but he knew he had to quit for himself, not to prove something to the world.

His attempts were like someone trying to see how long a time he could hold his breath for. It didn't mean he was actually going to stop breathing. Eventually he was going to have to take another deep breath.

After his shower Cleve brushed his teeth and dressed for the autumn day with dark trousers and a brown suede jacket over a camel cashmere sweater. He wasn't happy with the face reflected in the mirror, but then again, he frequently looked like he hadn't slept in a night or two.

He glanced at his Walther PPQ gun on the nightstand. I probably won't need it today, he thought. It was the same .40 Smith and Wesson caliber as the Glock pistols issued while he had been a cop. He still had one of the Glocks, but didn't like it and carried it infrequently.

He stepped outside. The weather had turned from crisp to damp and raw, and the cold wind that just one day earlier had felt fairly mild now cut through his exposed skin to the bone. He shoved his fists deep into his pockets and hunched his shoulders against the wind. He would need to flag a cab.

His 2017 Lexus RF was in the body shop after an accident that had left the passenger's side caved in. The drunk that T-boned him that day on Milwaukee Avenue had been booked and hauled away in a blue and white. Cleve subsequently learned that the driver's liability insurance had lapsed. Perfect, he thought. Nothing new.

He hailed two cabs, but both passed him up. He shrugged. Life wasn't fair—and more often than not, it was a real bitch. Cleve had learned that the hard way. Life could be exceedingly cruel, but he had developed a survivalist's perspective, for the most part.

He hadn't finished high school. He tried to join the Green Berets—a completely different path than his father, or his father's father before him. He ended up in the Marines, though, and was in Nam too long. Way too long, maybe killed too many people, including civilians – even women and kids. He wasn't proud of that now, but he hadn't given a shit about anything at the time. That attitude pushed him out of the Marines. He had killed one too many people who didn't actually need it. Even the Corps frowned on that, but they still gave him an Honorable Discharge.

As a Chicago cop he killed three or four men, and some of those killings were questionable. He dwelled on that much too often, still, he thought.

He lit a cigarette and expelled a huge puff of smoke. *In a few days I'll be getting the Lexus back, or at least that's what Teddy Chavez at the body shop promised. We'll see.*

He finally flagged down a checkered cab and crawled into the back.

The cabbie was clean-looking and eager.

"Where to, mister?" He started the meter.

"Take me to St. Joseph hospital on Lakeshore."

"Right you are," said the cabbie, a retirement age man, gray-haired, large-nosed, with a pair of cheap-looking sun glasses pushed up on his forehead. He watched Cleve in the rearview mirror. "You want the emergency entrance or the front door, sir?"

"The main entrance is good."

It was only a ten minute ride before he dropped Cleve by the front door of the hospital. Cleve knew where his friend Deckle was and took the elevator up to the ninth floor. He found him sharing a room with a beefy-looking black man whose leg was in traction. The man nodded when he saw Hawkins.

Deckle was watching an Andy Griffith rerun. Gomer had just exclaimed, "Gawlleeee!" and Deckle, all excited, was clutching the remote with both hands. He failed to notice Cleve until he felt the bump against the railing of the bed.

Deckle flashed a crooked smile full of nasty teeth at Hawkins and quickly clicked the TV off.

"What are you doin' here, buddy? Somebody musta blew the whistle on me, eh?" He raked his stubby fingers through his hair. He was unshaven and the side of his narrow face was swollen and black and blue.

"Good morning, Deck. I came by to check on you." He grinned. "That's what pals are supposed to do, right? Be there to help, ya know, when a guy needs it."

Deckle was basically homeless, but Hawkins had allowed him to hang around his office on Wells and serve as a combo clean-up man and gopher. Cleve knew little about the man except that he liked cheap red wine and sometimes camped on the front steps of his office. Deckle always aimed to please in any way possible.

"Yeah, you sure are a pal, Cleve." Deckle's smile widened. "I'm glad too, cuz' I ain't got that many real good friends, you know what I mean?" He gestured for Hawkins to sit. "Grab that chair over there and stay a while, Cleve. Yeah, I'm sure glad to see you. The doc says I'll live, but I'm lucky I don't gotta' have a new hip. I just got bruised up real bad. I'm sure happy about that, you know what I mean?"

Cleve nodded. "Sorry about that." He squinted. "Damn, partner, you were lucky." He leaned in and studied Deckle's bruised face. "You did have the light, right? I mean you didn't jay walk out there in front of traffic, did you, buddy?"

Deckle shook his head. "That's the same thing the cops asked me when the ambulance brought me in here. In fact, even the doctor and nurses asked me the same question. Weird, huh?"

His head wobbled like a bobblehead doll.

"Well?"

"Well, what, Cleve?"

"Well, did you stumble out into traffic?"

Deckle held up his palms and shrugged. "Wait a while, wait a while." He scratched his head. "I don't rightly know. Darn." He shook his head and squinted his eyes. "I don't think so. That would be crazy, you know?"

Cleve waved his hand dismissively. "It's okay, Deck. I didn't come here to grill you. Is there anything you need? Something to read or snack on, maybe?"

Deckle smirked and lowered his voice. "Yeah, I sure could use a stiff belt right now, but I know you can't help me there."

Cleve shook his head no. "Anything but booze, partner. Did the doctor say how long before he'd spring you?"

The black neighbor in the other bed looked at Cleve and said, "I heard that, and I sure hope it's not too soon." He smiled and it was obvious that he also had dental issues. He snickered as he addressed Cleve. "Your friend is damned good company. When he starts talking, I forget my pain and fall asleep."

Deckle, after following their conversation, said, "I don't know about getting out of here yet, Cleve, but I'm sure gonna ask as soon as I see the doc because I feel good and I need to get out of this place. The walls drive me nuts."

"Well, you don't want to rush things. Just do what they say and you'll be okay to go soon, I imagine." He stood, edged over to the bed and squeezed Deckle's shoulder. With his free hand, he slipped his friend twenty dollars. "I'd better be going, Deck, but promise you won't get antsy, okay? When they do say you're good to go, have them call the office and let me know. I'll come by and pick you up as soon as I can."

"Thanks, man." He grabbed Cleve's arm. "You're sure a good friend, you know that?" Tears welled up in the corners of his eyes.

Cleve patted his hand. "Take care, Deck."

On the way out he waved at the man in the other bed. "Good luck, friend."

* * * * *

A sullen cloud layer had moved in and a soft drizzle had taken over. As he exited the cab in front of his office, Cleve noticed a huge man sitting in the driver's seat of a new, red Dodge Ram.

Spotting Cleve, he slowly crawled out of the truck and strolled over to where Cleve stood.

"You Hawkins?"

"Could be . . . who wants to know?"

CHAPTER FOUR

The Eagles' *Hell Freezes Over* album played from hidden speakers on the Albers' eighteenth floor balcony. Don Henley and Glen Frey had been Trish's favorites since she and Gerry first began to date, back in the days when her future husband studied Political Science at Northwestern University. Gerry Albers had had no specific, long range goal in mind then. He was only focused on two things. He wanted some kind of lucrative career in government and he wanted the chance to get into Trish's pants.

Now forty plus-years old, Trish had become his wife and a Republican Party moneymaker in her own right. She was slim, tanned and freckled, with short blonde hair so expertly colored one couldn't see the occasional strands of gray. She had a square chin that made her look a bit like Jackie Kennedy.

It was now late Saturday afternoon and she sat on their balcony and sipped a ridiculously tall Sea Breeze in a frosted glass. Ignoring a traditional autumn wardrobe, she wore a white silk blouse and an ankle-length white skirt, both with cutouts that looked like lace and that offered peeks at what lay beneath. Trish called them her "mood makers."

At times the Senator's wife liked to wallow in extraordinary sexual fantasies while her husband was away, and those thoughts erupted more freely than when he was home for some reason. Sometimes she even had time to masturbate to orgasm before he returned. She felt guilty doing that, sometimes, as though she was cheating on him. She tried to stay occupied with other, less adventuresome thoughts that required much less effort to subdue, like crocheting.

She caught herself pondering the potential of their upcoming dinner party with Democratic Representative Kent Collier and his wife, Jill. That get-together was slated for mid-September, a bit after the congressional summer recess was over, yet before the annual holiday exodus. Trish smiled.

Ah, yes. Jill Collier. Well, I simply cannot afford to dwell on that beautiful woman too long, can I?

She quickly abandoned that thought and began to focus on her husband. She had been married for nearly sixteen years. He was good for her and to her. God knows, he had always been faithful. True fidelity, especially in political circles, was a rare trait indeed. Trish counted herself lucky that Gerry was safe, imaginative and best of all, open-minded in bed.

Lately, though, managing play time with him had become as difficult as arranging a confession with the Pope.

Financially, the Albers were well off. They owned a mansion downstate, in Bradfordton, Illinois, and leased this spacious, three bedroom apartment on Lake Shore Drive, near Chicago's Loop. The apartment, on the eighteenth floor, had a breathtaking view of the Lake Michigan shoreline and their guests often marveled at the wonder of witnessing the waves teasing the shore during the day, or the plethora of twinkling city lights at night.

The privacy was wonderful, Trish thought. Even though it was still possible to hear traffic from down below, it wasn't loud by any means, and although Gerry's job as a senator sometimes attracted the tenacious wolves of the media, most cameramen and talking heads were relegated to snooping for comment downtown in hotel hotspots.

Now, Trish wondered, where is that husband of mine?

. . .

After Gerry had met with his friend Corky that day, he was anxious to get home. He had stopped by Costco for a few things, including his cigarettes and more Absolut Vodka for Trish before heading to the apartment. He looked at his watch and realized the hours had slipped by and wondered whether she would be upset that he had been gone so long.

Yes, I'd better start considering a believable story to satisfy her inquisitive mind, he thought.

While he drove, his brain was muddled with the threats he'd gotten that morning. The realization of the depth of his troubles grabbed his insides and he suddenly felt himself trembling. *Damn, it's impossible to shed the reality of that thug's face. He was the epitome of mean and ugly all rolled into one. A genuine mob guy, if I ever saw one.*

Gerry fumbled around for a cigarette. *I've got to find out who that sonofabitch works for. Yeah, that's the key alright. And who took those damned pictures anyway?*

He located his lighter just as he turned left towards Michigan Avenue.

What the hell am I going to do if Corky lets me down? What next? Jesus! I'm thinking I'll just have to make the payoff next week like the guy said. Yeah, that's right, Ger. You just have to do it. No choice, but to man up. Then I'll have to keep the huge withdrawal hidden from Trish for a while. Just till I can figure out something for cover.

Dammit, I hate this shit!

As he approached Michigan, he located his pack of cigarettes. Doing a smoker's balancing act, he held the wheel with his arms and managed to stick a cigarette between his lips and light up without running over either of the two pedestrians in the crosswalk.

But how do I know that the money I give them will be the end of it? What if they decide to keep bleeding me? That's just it, Ger . . . you won't know, will you?

As he turned on Oak, he barely noticed that the grass was still a vibrant green or that new shades of red and orange rippled through the fig trees. Fall was in the air, but he could care less. Now the sky had turned heavy and lead-colored, threatening more rain, and an early nightfall.

The sun had been shining when he left the apartment early that morning to meet the thug on Clark Street. He told Trish he had a few errands to run. She was, of course, her typical blasé self, so unaware of the clandestine meeting her husband was to have with bad actors.

By the time Gerry got home and turned his car over to the doorman, the sky was lit up with a network of yellowish-white lines, and thunder boomed like cannon fire. Thick, rolling storm clouds were illuminated in the fluorescent glow of the lightning and they looked black and swollen like enormous sponges.

"Carl, do you mind parking it? And have those other two Costco bags brought up, would you?"

Carl grabbed the door handle and glanced in the back seat.

"Of course. No, worries, sir. I'll see to it that someone brings them up directly."

Then the rain hit, a downpour that would have given Noah a hard time, Gerry thought.

"I gotta run," he said as he turned up his collar. "Thank you, Carl. Much obliged, my friend. Try to stay dry tonight."

Gerry carried one large bag upstairs and started to key the lock, but before he could use his card, Trish swung the door open.

"There he is!" Ignoring the fact that that his arms were full, she snaked her arms around his neck and planted a wet one on his cheek. "I was so worried about you, dear. What in the world took you so long? My goodness, do you realize you've been gone most of the day?"

Gerry edged past her and heaved a sigh.

"Just taking care of loose ends, honey. Loose ends and important issues take time, you know that."

He headed for the kitchen while Trish stood aside and closed the door behind him. He spoke to her over his shoulder.

"And I stopped by to see my old pal, Corky. You remember Corky? I wanted to get a feel for the pulse of local tavern traffic. Know what I mean? We shot a game of pool and shared some lunch." He paused briefly to search her eyes. "After that I picked up a few things at the store as you can see."

There was an air of proud defiance in his voice and he shoved the bag over onto the counter.

Trish made no effort to inspect the contents of the bag or to put anything away. She grabbed her drink off the bar, glided across the living room and curled up like an Angora cat in her favorite overstuffed armchair. She caressed her drink with both hands and casually pressed the glass to her breast, moaned as she leaned against the back of the chair, and brought her hand up to push her hair back.

"Hmmmm. I was thinking, darling . . . what with tomorrow being Sunday, and since we have nothing on the schedule, maybe you'd like to take me out to dinner tonight." Her voice contained a lilt of anticipation. "We could make a night of it, you know? Maybe go to Harry Caray's for some of their scrumptious Surf n' Turf first, and after that perhaps we could stop by and visit some friends for a nightcap."

Gerry remained silent.

Trish paused for a beat then stood up and closed in on him. Tracing her fingertips over his bottom lip, she said, "What do you say, sweetie? Sound good?"

He searched her provocative face for a moment.

"Visit somebody? Like who?" When he spoke, his tone was a low, throaty response that stroked her senses like velvet.

He turned his back to her and wandered over to their trophy wall, filled with plaques and keys to Illinois cities and with photos of himself and the president, governors, other senators, and assorted, rich, clique citizens including politically conservative celebrities. His eyes wandered from one side to the other as he waited for the other shoe to drop.

"Oh, I don't know. I was thinking maybe Jill and her husband. How would that be?"

Gerry whirled around. "Dammit, Trish! I don't need to hear *anything* about Jill Collier today...of all days."

"What? Why, Gerry?" She moved to his side. "What's wrong with Jill? What are you saying about today?"

Gerry waved his hand dismissively.

"Ah, it's nothing, I guess. I'm just really not up to going out at all, tonight, to tell the truth. I'm not feeling well." He scrunched up his face. "I think I must have eaten something that didn't agree with me over at Corky's place. We got any Alka Seltzer in there?" He nodded towards the bathroom.

Trish folded her arms across her chest. "Yeah, sure. The bottom drawer, your side." She dropped back in her chair and stared through the balcony door at the dark sky and suddenly appeared to be in a world separate from his.

Gerry continued. "Maybe some other night, okay? It's terrible thunder and lightning out there and the rain is really coming down hard. I hate this weather. It just sucks the joy out of everything."

Trish glared over her shoulder as she rose from her chair. Rolling her eyes, she made a face and crossed her arms in front of her again. She heaved a sigh and pictured what might have been on this perfectly good Saturday night if her husband wasn't being such a wet blanket.

His voice grew quieter as he crossed over and caressed her shoulder. "Honey, to be honest, I just think we had better keep our distance from the Colliers for the time being."

She whirled around. "Why? What do you mean?"

"Nothing. I mean . . . " He put both hands up in a pushing back gesture. "I just think it would be a good idea, especially because of the vote on Collier's Wheat Bill coming up as soon as we get back from recess. I mean . . . it just wouldn't look right for us to be seen socializing with Kent and his wife right now. Understand? He's on the other side of the aisle, after all."

"Jesus, Gerry! Since when did any of that crap matter? Please don't speak to me in riddles. What are you really trying to say? What is it about the Colliers all of a sudden that's got your jockstrap in a knot?

Gerry dropped down onto the love seat. I'd better shut up before I screw everything up, he thought. He rolled his eyes and his shoulders slumped.

"Look, Trish, you and I both know real life can be stranger than fiction." He paused for what seemed like a long moment. "Fiction has to make sense in the end. There's plenty of shit that goes down in the real world no book editor would ever believe in a novel."

Tilting his head back, he stared at the ceiling and raked his lower lip with his upper teeth. Sighing heavily, he stood and paced in a circle. He brushed a hand through his hair and his eyes searched hers.

"Listen Trish, it doesn't matter how impossible, improbable or coincidental anything might be in the real world, shit still happens, Honey. I just want you to realize that...and be cautious. That's all."

Trish narrowed her eyes and glared. "I still don't understand, Gerry. You're still talking bullshit. This is not like you. What in the world is going on?" She stood up. "Why are you acting like Billy Graham all of a sudden?" she said with a laugh in her voice.

Gerry heaved another sigh. "I don't know what to say here, Trish? Dammit, I think you'll have to agree we have had rather unusual relationships with a few of our friends. I'm talking relationships some might consider abnormal and bad for our reputation if word were to get out because of some reckless gossip." He threw his arms in the air. "There. That's it. That's all I'm saying."

Silence, a long silence.

They sat and stared at each other for a while.

"I see. So, what we are really talking about here is our sex lives, is that right Gerry?"

He stared at the floor and nodded.

She grinned and slowly drifted over to sit next to him on the love seat. Draping her arm over his shoulders she whispered, "My dear Gerry, could it be that you are actually jealous?"

"What?" He turned away. "No. No. I've never been jealous when it comes to . . . to our private lives, and you know it."

Trish shrugged. "Well, you sure seem to be upset about something. Listen, you know as well as I do, this kind of stuff happens all the time these days. Sex, adultery, everything." She tugged at his ear lobe and nibbled at his neck. "Nobody wants to talk about it because too many powerful people are involved, including politicians, staff and lobbyists. We are not odd, by any means, my sweet."

He turned his head towards her, smiled, hesitated and then kissed her on the lips. "Thank you, my love."

She squeezed his hand. "The fact is half the newsies are sleeping with somebody they shouldn't be sleeping with so a lot of stuff doesn't get reported. We know that."

Gerry caressed her thigh absentmindedly and nodded as she continued.

"If word got out, in the papers, to the public, it might get a little embarrassing at senate cocktail parties, with all the senators wives from Podunk, Idaho or Bird Shit, Mississippi, and such, but that would be about it."

He turned. "I guess you could be right. I worry too much, don't I?"

She squeezed his package. "You sure do, my dear. You sure do."

CHAPTER FIVE

Concho Martinez had an incorrigible, lopsided grin and the reputation of a man who sensed trouble a second before he saw it.

He knew his boss would be pissed off when he heard that Senator Albers had not done as he was instructed regarding the two-hundred and fifty thousand dollar payoff. The fifty thousand would infuriate him, if anything.

As Jake Caldwell's enforcer and right-hand man, Concho had been surprised to witness Albers' uncooperative attitude regarding the blackmail pictures. He didn't believe the Senator was the least bit rattled—perhaps he wouldn't even be cooperative in the future without some sort of immediate physical pressure. No money next Saturday from Albers just wouldn't fly with Jake Caldwell.

Concho attempted to relay that negative report to his boss by cell phone that Saturday morning, after his meeting with Senator Albers. He was told that Jake was out on the links at the Orchard Valley Golf Club in suburban Aurora and wouldn't be available until nine that evening. According to Jake's secretary, Bev Porter, the boss didn't want to be bothered with anything whatsoever. She added that Jake might call in to get his messages that evening, but nobody was going to count on it.

Just before eight, Bev called Concho on his cell and told him Caldwell would meet him at ten o'clock that night at one of his favorite haunts, Griddle 24 on Chicago Avenue.

At nine that night Concho huddled in a booth at Jackie's Hamburger Joint on North Avenue. He was with his current squeeze, Debbie Guilcrist, a tall and strongly-built woman with long hair dyed the color of orange soda and braided. She looked every bit of thirty-seven and then some. Concho was admiring the feathery bangs looped over her sun-seamed forehead and the earrings that dangled from both ear lobes.

Pulling his ball cap low over his eyes and hunching his shoulders up around his ears, he cleared his throat and wiped his nose with the back of his hand.

"Them earrings are pure sex, baby." He lowered his voice as he caressed her arm. "But I can't be having you with me when I go to meet the boss. You know that, right?"

Deb nodded and lowered her eyes. "Yeah, sure." Caressing his tattooed hand with her long, tanned fingers, she cooed, "I'll be waiting right here for you, honey. Anyway, why would I want to be anywhere near that big prick unless I have to be?"

Concho squeezed her hand. "Shhhhh! Don't be so damned mouthy, little girl." His eyes narrowed. "Jake is damn good people. He's always been right with me. You should know that by now."

"Yeah, okay. I'm sorry."

There were times when Debbie's incessant jibber-jabber seemed to soothe Concho, especially when he was wound too tight. But at the moment he didn't need her diarrhea of the mouth. He sipped his fourth cup of black coffee and eyed her as she baptized her fries in a puddle of ketchup.

Deb was always a bundle of nervous energy, but Concho understood her better than anyone else. He could be brutal with his frequent and personal insults, but she still wanted and needed him.

She was still legally married, but her husband was a sleaze, the kind of government official who owned a high-end specialized razor that kept him in a permanent three-day-beard mode and who wore custom silk dress shirts open at the throat to show off the mat of his dark chest hair.

Deb had written him off when she met Concho.

The waitress drifted by with a Bunn coffee pot in one hand, a green order pad in the other. A short bottle-blond woman with thin, black arched eyebrows, she looked like she might work hard to avoid anything resembling a gymnasium.

"More coffee, sir?"

Concho shook his head. "I'm good."

"Me too," Deb murmured.

The waitress shuffled off to a nearby table.

Debbie leaned in closer to Concho. "Did I say something wrong, honey?"

"No, but you should hear yourself. You been yakking a mile a minute. Just shut up, okay?"

Deb cringed, then twirled a fry and popped it in her mouth.

Concho folded his hands and slid back into deep thought, but Deb wasn't finished.

"Okay, baby, but I was just gonna tell you about that new chick, Jennie. She is too damned pushy. She's got one hell of a nerve, setting herself up to cartwheel over all the rest of the girls. She's only been with us for a couple of months and we're tired of the bitch already. Know what I mean? I wish you'd take it to Jake. I mean when he's not busy, of course."

Concho nodded. His thoughts were still elsewhere.

Deb continued. "Ain't no way you oughta bug Jake while he's busy, I know that."

Concho studied her and shook his head. "Just forget about it, okay? I'll handle it. Jake doesn't need to hear any petty bullshit right now. Dammit! I've got enough to tell him without you or anybody else laying more shit at his feet. Tell the other chicks to cool their heels, too."

He saw the frown creeping across her face. His grin tightened, then soured.

"Hey, I appreciate you passing that shit along, baby. Okay? But, just shut up and let me handle it." He swiped his lips with a napkin and glared before continuing to sip his coffee and mull over the events of the past twenty-four hours.

He knew he had let Jake down. He had always lived with a certain puppy dog loyalty to the man and had followed his orders to the T. He had been Jake's personal gopher since he was a pimple-faced kid stealing hub caps in the Bedford Stuyvesant section of Brooklyn.

In this Albers deal, his hands had been tied by Jake himself when he'd said, "I don't want no rough stuff with Albers, under any condition."

Concho thought to himself, I just did what I was told. Didn't I?

• • •

Griddle 24 was crowded and noisy, the air thick with conversation and the warm, spicy smell of home cooking. Concho was sitting by himself in a back booth of the all-night restaurant when Jake Caldwell sauntered in the front door at precisely one minute to ten.

He was known for his punctuality, but he was not a patient man. He thought of nobody but himself. At forty-seven, going on sixty-two, his body was pickled and aged by alcohol and bitterness. His face was hard and carved with lines leathered from the sun. He thrived on Captain Morgan and had the gin blossoms on his nose and cheeks to prove it. He had salt-and-pepper hair, was as wide as he was tall, and he had the face of a bulldog.

He fist-bumped Concho then slid into the opposite side of the booth and acknowledged him with "Amigo."

"Hey, boss."

Concho had a bottle of Miller Light sitting in front of him and had been picking at a courtesy bowl of pretzels. A waitress came out of nowhere and swooped down on their booth. She looked at Jake.

"And, what can I get for you, sir?"

"Ahhhhh, give me a Captain n' Coke, light on the Coke, okay?"

"Yes, sir."

After she'd pranced away, Concho said. "How was your golf game?"

Caldwell folded his arms over his chest and shook his head from side to side.

"It was bullshit. I was in a foursome and it turns out the bum I was paired up with didn't have a lot of arrows in his quiver. A tad off plumb, ya know, and he was a friggin' survivalist to boot."

Concho looked at his boss like he had suddenly sprouted antlers.

"What the hell is a survivalist?"

Caldwell waved a hand. "Ah, survivalists. They believe in doomsday, when all manner of shit will hit the fan." He grinned. "Mexico will invade Arizona, gasoline will run out, all of the chickens will be eaten and anybody who doesn't have a root cellar fully stocked with AR-15s, hunting bows and pistols will be history."

"Damn, homes. You believe that shit?"

"Hell, no. And he was a fuckin' cheater, too. The jerk must have toe-kicked his ball out of the rough at least a half-dozen times when he thought I wasn't looking."

Concho shook his head, but stayed silent, knowing his boss needed to vent without interruption.

"That asshole's idea of a gimmee was to take one stroke on every hole." He paused for a beat and fumbled around in his pocket.

Concho nodded his head knowingly.

Caldwell blew a gust of air and his brows plowed a deep V above the bridge of his slightly crooked nose.

"Fuck him. The next time I play any course with him will be never."

There was a long moment of silence as Caldwell checked his cell phone for messages, then snapped the phone shut and looked in Concho's eyes.

"So? I take it you have stashed the senator's payment someplace safe, amigo?"

Concho glanced around as if others were listening.

"Yeah, well, I stashed all he gave me, boss. The senator didn't have all of it."

Caldwell sat forward and concern creased his high forehead as his brows pulled together. He shook his head and blinked like a man in deep physical pain, then rubbed his hands over his face, and swore a litany of curses under his breath.

"What the fuck? What does that mean, 'he didn't have it all'? You mean he was short a few thousand...or what?"

"Well, yeah, but more than a few thousand." There was a long pause while Concho gave Jake time to digest that before he continued.

"I don't think he believed me when I told him how much the pictures would cost him. And he said he couldn't come up with that much money without robbing their piggy bank."

Caldwell glared. "Piggy bank?"

"Yeah, well, you know, their joint savings account at the bank. He calls it their piggy bank. He doesn't want his wife to know about the pictures or the payoff. He's afraid it will upset her, so he has to steal it on the sly."

Jake laughed. "No shit? Upset her?"

He had the habit of jerking his entire head when something caught his attention, looking like a chicken pecking in the barnyard, and as he did that now, his chest and belly tugged at his starched white shirt.

The waitress came by with Caldwell's drink and the men went silent.

"Put that on my tab," said Concho.

After she left, Jake said, "So you were left with your dick in your hand and he just took off...still owing us how much?" His brows came together in a look that now seemed more confused than curious.

"He gave me fifty thou, saying it was all he could get his hands on right now. He said he has to rob the big bucks from that savings account without his wife knowing."

Concho smirked. "I know . . . fat chance, right, boss?" He paused. "But she does have it. We know that . . . right? I mean the broad is loaded."

"Yeah." Caldwell heaved a sigh, raked his hands through his hair and laughed, but it was a hollow laugh. "I have to admit the senator has got steel balls coming to the meet with just fifty grand." He lowered his eyes and shook his head. "Jesus!"

"He didn't seem to be one bit scared until I mentioned giving his pictures to the rags. He really perked up when I mentioned that possibility."

"When are we getting the rest of our money? Can we even depend on getting it at all?"

Concho nodded. "I gave him until next Saturday to come up with the other two-hundred thousand. All of it. He says he'll have it by then." He lowered his eyes and his voice. "I believe him, boss. Besides, you told me no rough stuff with Albers, so I had no other choice, did I?"

Jake gave Concho a cold stare. "Is that yes or no in asshole-speak?" He tapped his knuckles on the table. "You got balls too, Concho. You taking a jack-off politician at his word?"

Concho snickered. "Only because his old lady has the money. It's a wonder she married a pussy like Albers. She's a damned gorgeous woman, by the way, and she doesn't live with a stick up her ass. With her, it's more likely to be the entire fucking tree . . . with branches."

"Just tell me you didn't give him the pictures," said Jake.

"No, boss, of course not. I ain't that stupid."

Jake took a long swig of his drink and shook his head. "Okay, look. I don't want this deal to turn messy. There's no reason it should. If we play our cards right, we'll be able to milk this cow for a hell of a lot more up the road. Go see our friend, the senator, on Saturday. Even sooner, if you can figure a way. Get our money and give him the pictures. Tell him that's it. There are no more. He's got them all."

"How do I know he'll believe me?"

"Who gives a shit? He's anxious. He'll buy it, trust me."

"Okay. I'll handle it, boss."

Caldwell tossed a fifty on the table and got up. "Get yourself another drink and keep me posted, eh, compadre'?"

CHAPTER SIX

The man who had approached Cleve in front of his office that afternoon had on aviator sunglasses and an expensive Armani suit. He was an anxious-looking individual with a red face and a redder nose.

"You Hawkins?"

Cleve stepped back. "Depends. Who wants to know?"

The stranger handed Cleve a card. "My name is Glick, Bentley Glick. If you have a moment, I'd like a word with you."

Cleve examined the stranger from head to to. The man was a rotund individual with close-set eyes who used too much gel in his dark hair, so much so that Cleve could see the tracks left by his comb. His suit was also dark, like something out of GQ, Cleve thought.

Cleve eyed the card and searched the man's face.

"A word about what?" he asked.

The man edged a bit closer and spoke in a conspiratorial manner. "Can we talk inside?"

He didn't look threatening and it wasn't the first time Hawkins had been approached in such a way.

"I guess so. You're not carrying, are you?"

Glick squinted. "Carrying?"

"Yeah, you know, a piece? A gun?"

"Oh, goodness no. I don't believe in violence of any sort, Mr. Hawkins."

Cleve nodded. "Follow me. My office is just inside to the right."

He paused a second and glanced over the man's shoulder.

"You'll probably get a ticket if you leave your truck parked there, though." He pointed. "It's a No Parking zone."

"Well, I don't plan on being here that long, sir." He grinned. "I'll take my chances."

"Suit yourself."

Cleve advanced up the small flight of concrete steps and turned a key in the door. He couldn't help but notice that the man carried himself with disdain in a kind of round-shouldered skulk.

After flicking on the lights, Hawkins pocketed his keys and nodded toward the chair sitting in front of his desk.

"Have a seat, Mr. Glick. It is Glick, right?"

"Yes, that's correct, Glick." He smiled. "Dutch, you know."

He appeared to squint at everything once he was inside. Craning his neck, he took in the entire three hundred and sixty degrees around him.

"So, these are the trappings of a private detective, eh?"

"They are for *this* detective, yes."

Glick pulled the chair back a foot or so. He sat down and studied Cleve for a moment. At the same time, Cleve edged around the desk and sat in his executive-style armchair.

Glick grinned. "You're sort of a tough guy, huh?" His voice was raspy and rough—from too much whiskey and too many cigarettes, Cleve surmised.

"I have my moments," said Cleve.

A few awkward seconds passed, long enough for each of the two men to get the message that any notions of politeness had already gone out the window.

Cleve took the initiative. "So, what are you selling . . . or do you actually need my services?"

Glick shifted in his chair and fumbled around in his coat pocket. "Do you mind if I smoke?"

Cleve shoved an ashtray over to him.

"Go for it. Just try to flick the ashes where they belong, if you don't mind. My cleanup guy is hospitalized."

A smile crept over Glick's face and his eyes appeared to twinkle. "Yes, I know." He dug a cigarette from the pack he had retrieved and lit it, taking a deep drag.

"Oh? And how's that?" Cleve asked.

"You know a man named Harold Gladstone?"

Cleve leaned back in his chair and laced his fingers behind his head. "No, I don't believe I do. Why?"

There was another long gap in the conversation.

"As a matter of fact, we think you may know Mr. Gladstone. We understand his associates call him Deckle. Does that name sound familiar?"

Cleve eased forward. "Deckle? What kind of name is that?" He shook his head. "No, I don't believe I know him either. Why?"

Glick pulled on his cigarette and exhaled twin jet streams through his nose. "Mr. Gladstone listed you as a reference. He gave your name to my client after that unfortunate incident that took place two days ago."

Cleve's eyes narrowed. "What incident is that?"

"The one that occurred when Mr. Gladstone walked in front of my client's car at the corner of Wells and Clark Streets. And, I might add, he appeared to be severely inebriated, according to my client and three witnesses."

Cleve felt his gut muscles tighten. "And this Gladstone guy gave my name to your client?"

"I don't think it's too late. I could still request a police report if you would like, but my client feels remorse for striking Mr. Gladstone and simply wants to pay any medical expenses and incidentals until he is back on his feet." Exhaling a stream of smoke, he grinned. "Pardon the pun."

Cleve tilted back in his chair and eyed the halo of smoke forming around Glick's head.

"Well, sir," Cleve said, adding some distance between them with the little formality, "I think you had best discuss this with Mr. Gladstone. I'm certain he would be glad to hear about your client's offer. I don't think this is something I want to get involved with."

"I think I understand, sir. Like I said, we can get a copy of the police report and . . . "

"And nothing, Mr. Glick. I used to be a cop and I know how they work. If credit and congratulations are being handed out, the Chicago Police could step to the front of the line. If it were hellfire and damnation, they would pass and pretend they were in the cafeteria buying Ding Dongs when the shit hit the fan. That's where I usually get off the bus."

A minute passed, though it seemed like much longer.

Glick stabbed his cigarette out in the ashtray and stood.

"Very well, Mr. Hawkins. However, I should tell you, my client considers this a serious matter and intends to follow up in the near future. In the meantime, if you should remember anything regarding Mr. Gladstone, you have my card."

Cleve stood and circled the desk.

"You'll pardon my saying so, Mr. Glick, but I have all sorts of people drifting in and out of that door with some of the most ridiculous stories you've ever heard. There are a lot of people in this town who get up in the morning, eat breakfast, get dressed and go out to look for some way to play and win the con. It's a profession...like any other."

Glick fidgeted. "Really?"

"Yeah. Those weasels are bullshit artists. My old cop buddy would call them crap-a-holics."

"Well, I am not a part of that ilk, I assure you, sir."

Cleve raised his hands. "I'm not saying you are, but over and over in my life I've found that people are amazing . . . and seldom in a good way. So you'll pardon my skepticism."

"Yes, I can appreciate you're feeling a bit wary about this, Mr. Hawkins. I'll report back to my client and see where he wants to go from here. Thank you for your time. I'm sorry I bothered you."

Cleve extended his hand. "No bother. I'm sure Mr. Gladstone will be happy to hear from you and your client."

Glick nodded. "Good day, sir."

Hawkins perched on the edge of his desk. He absentmindedly swung his foot back and forth, dangling a loafer, while he stared out the window and pondered Bentley Glick's story.

I wonder if that guy was legit? Maybe it could be a good thing for Deckle. Hell, I don't know. It's probably just bullshit. What good would it do for me to get involved?

He looked at the two empty coffee cups turned upside down on top of the filing cabinet and glanced at his watch. *It's late. I'd better make some coffee.*

He stepped over to the bathroom and filled the pot with water.

The hospital wouldn't bill Deckle anyway, would they? So, the offer to pay medical bills is no big deal. Deck will be considered a vagrant and homeless. The taxpayers will pick up the tab. Poor little guy doesn't need anything that might cause him more trouble—even if he is the one at fault.

His musings were interrupted with the ringing of his landline phone. After three rings, a message began to record.

"Hi. This is Sherill at Credit Card Services. Did you know you are now eligible for a new lower interest rate on your Mastercard. It can start with your next billing cycle. Just call…"

Cleve jabbed the delete button, then pushed "play" to hear the other messages, signaled by the blinking red light.

One was from Sgt. Gil Fillmore of the Police Athletic League wanting Cleve's annual donation for the kids' football league sponsored by his old precinct.

Chaz, the bump man from Teddy's Body and Collision, had also called. "Hello, Mr. Hawkins. This is Chaz at Chavez's Body Shop. Your Lexus is ready, anytime you want to pick it up. See you soon."

A third call was from Mo. She had a pleasant lilt in her voice, but wanted a return call as soon as possible. Cleve had to ponder that one.

I know she's pissed. I can't put off calling her anymore, that's for sure.

Another call was just a dial tone followed by a hang up.

He stared at the phone and thought about finally making the call to Mo.

It's Monday. She'll be at work. Must not be too upset though. She called.

He punched in the numbers. "Hi, it's me. I'm sorry I missed your call."

"Well, hello, stranger," Mo said. "Did you get lost last Friday afternoon? I was ready to ask a couple of uniforms to stop by to see if you were okay, but obviously you're fine."

"Yeah. I know I missed our date Friday, and to tell the truth, I just chickened out on calling you back on Saturday and then, well, again yesterday. Guilty as charged. I felt bad every minute of the weekend. I am really sorry, Mo."

She lowered her voice. "I can't talk right now, but know this. I'm not pissed, Cleve." She paused. "I'm just hurt. I thought we were done with lost dates and everything that goes with them."

"I know, baby. Look, I feel terrible about this. My car was still in the shop and, well, it was just a chain of things that rolled up into a ball. Bottom line, I screwed up bad and I'm sorry."

There was a moment of silence.

"Mo?"

"I'm still here."

"Look. I want to see you and explain, if you'll let me."

More silence.

"When will you get your car back?"

"As a matter of fact, I just got a call. It's ready and I'm going to pick it up after I hang up. Can I come by after you get off?"

She spoke in a whisper. "I called to see if you were dead or alive, Cleve Hawkins."

He thought he could hear tears in her voice. "I'm so sorry, Mo."

After another exaggerated pause, she said, "Stop by at seven, okay?"

"Sure, babe. I'll be on time. Maybe we can do dinner, huh?"

"Cleve . . ."

"Yeah?"

"If you're going to be late, don't bother to call about it. Just don't ever call me again."

The dial tone that followed was like a knife in his heart.

CHAPTER SEVEN

Cleve's phone conversation with Mo had invigorated him. Maybe there was still a chance with her after all. He thought she would be through with him after he broke their date that Friday night and went on his alcohol-induced baseball bender.

Now, the old rush of adrenaline was there, speeding up his metabolism, making him feel a hum of electricity running just under the skin. Making him feel alive again.

He hoped he wasn't spinning his wheels. Maureen was the only woman he had cared anything about in the past fourteen years, and more and more it became obvious to him that he had to start making the right moves or he would lose her.

It was around three-fifteen by the time he had finished picking up the Lexus from Teddy's Bump Shop and had driven back home. It had been raining for about fifteen minutes when he decided to stretch out on his bed and relax. He dimmed the lights and closed his eyes.

The ceiling fan was all but silent as the paddles rotated above his head. It felt good to have a window cracked in the bedroom for a change, with no humming from the air conditioning. A late summer breeze poured in and he could smell the rain striking the hot sidewalk.

He realized there wouldn't be time for a decent nap, but there were several tangled ideas stalking around in his mind, and he needed space to meditate and get right with them. He checked the time on the clock radio. It was almost four o'clock.

I can't just lie here. Hell, I should get over to the gym right now and punch the bag for a while. Maybe pump some iron, too. The gym will be empty this time of day. I'll still have plenty of time to get back here and clean up before it's time to be at Mo's. I damn sure can't be late again.

He got up and slipped into a pair of shorts and grabbed his Chicago Cubs sweatshirt. Pulling it over his head, he rushed outside, got into the Lexus, and headed out.

His brain rumbled with dread and anger as he drove toward *Gold's Fitness and Spa*, located in a plaza just a few miles away. He couldn't seem to shake the guilt about Mo which festered inside.

He considered how he had missed his date with her Friday night. *Damn me! How in the hell did I manage to pull that crap? Do I have a personal vendetta here and intentionally fuck up just to see how far I can go before the shit hits the fan. My friends get away with it. They don't give a damn. They'll do it all the time and cruise right along without any problem. But, that's them, not me. I know better, so why in hell do I pull stunts like that . . . especially with Mo? Her, above all people. She's the only one who has taken the time to see who I really am. Inside and out. She's the only one who accepts me for who I am.* He slammed the wheel with his fist. *She doesn't deserve an asshole like me.*

His emotions were in full boil by the time he reached the gym. *Maybe I'll luck out and meet some bastard bruiser working out. Some muscled giant who I can deliberately pick a fight with and let him kick my ass.*

Pulling into the rear parking lot of the shopping center, Cleve got out of the car, breathing hard, his heart pounding. He ran to the side door and raced inside. Being a lifetime member, he had no thought of checking in at the desk. Pulling the sweatshirt over his head, he balled it up and flung it against the wall.

His pace quickened as he crossed the main floor until he was running at the old heavy leather punching bag that hung from the ceiling.

He launched himself at the bag from five feet out, slamming his shoulder into it, absorbing the pain, welcoming the pain, as it exploded through his chest and neck and down his back. The bag swung away, and returned to swish past him like an angry bull sidestepped by a matador.

Cleve turned and came back swinging, bare knuckles connecting hard with the cracked leather and the patches made of duct tape. Left, right, left, right. One, two, one, two. Left hook, right hook, left hook, right hook.

Asshole!

He grabbed the bag in a clinch and drove his right knee into it as hard as he could, again and again, then switched his stance and brought the left knee up, once, twice, three times, four times.

You dumb shit!

With every punch, his breath left him with a hard guttural sound. He sucked in oxygen tainted with the smell of sweat and leather. His pores opened and sweat beaded on the surface of his skin. As he worked the bag, sweat began to run down his back and soak the back of his shorts.

He continued to throw his hands until the muscles of his arms were bulging and heavy, the veins popping. His emotions poured out of him like poison steam, bitter and pungent. He tasted it, like metal, in his mouth. His feelings came up from the depths of him like bile.

Selfish sonofabitch.

When his body was spent, and his knees had given out, he fell into an exhausted heap. Only then did he decide his penance was complete—for the time being at least. He took a swallow of water at the fountain, grabbed his sweatshirt and headed back to his apartment.

After he'd shaved and showered, there was still plenty of time to kick back on the sofa with a can of Old Style and watch some taped DVR episodes of The Three Stooges before he had to get going. At five-thirty he got dressed. He decided on black slacks, a black shirt and a grey sport coat. Adding a purple tie for pizzazz, he checked himself in the mirror and was almost out the door when he heard his landline phone jangle.

He tensed up, wondering who it might be, and hoped it was nothing important. He realized if it was serious, they would be calling him on his cell. He waited until the answering machine took the call.

"Hello, Cleve? It's me, Deckle. Hey, they say I can go home anytime now if somebody comes to get me." There was a long pause filled with raspy breathing before he spoke again. "Cleve? You will pick me up like you said, right?" Another pause. "Well, I guess you're busy. Call me back when you get this though, okay, buddy?"

Cleve sighed and exhaled a deep breath. You'll have to chill a bit longer, Deck. I'll pick you up tomorrow, he thought.

On the way, he stopped at the La Fleur Flower Boutique and bought a bouquet of six red roses. He hesitated for a moment and then nervously signed the card.

"Please forgive me, Mo. Love, Cleve."

Maureen was the head secretary in the Major Crimes Division where Hawkins had been assigned before he retired. The special investigative group was based in the Chicago Police Administration Building along with the other elite detective groups. MCD caught the hot, fast, headline cases ranging from multiple homicides to celebrity victims, and they were assigned any crimes with the potential to threaten public safety.

Mo, as she was fondly called by her close associates, was the private secretary for Lieutenant Kris Branoff before his demise in a good-cop-gone-bad situation two years earlier. Branoff had been Cleve's immediate superior at the time, but Hawkins quit the department when Branoff was finally exposed. Ironically, it had been Cleve's bullet that had killed Branoff in a showdown-style gunfight in suburban Wheeling, Illinois.

After an investigation by Internal Affairs, Cleve's action was found to be a "good kill" and he was cleared, but he didn't return to the department. Mo had stayed on for the new section head, Captain John Bowden.

Now, the clouds broke open a final time as Cleve drove over to Mo's apartment on the near North Side. The skies hammered with a downpour so fierce the wipers were useless, but just minutes later, as he found a parking spot for the Lexus, a soft wind barely rustled the wet leaves of the black oaks between the porch and the sidewalk on Mo's street.

Her place was in a stylish apartment building swallowed in ivy, all red brick, with ample windows and a front door painted funeral black. Flower boxes still bloomed with petunias and ivy.

Cleve checked his watch. It was exactly six-forty-eight. He was early.

He pushed the outside buzzer to gain entrance and once inside, found he knew the grey-haired security guard on duty in the lobby. Sitting at a small desk with his legs out and his arms crossed, he watched Cleve come in as if he'd already had a long day and he knew it was going to be longer.

Cleve remembered. Rich Kriesel was his name. He was an odd looking duck who had a throat like a bullfrog, a sack of flesh wider than his head, spilling over the collar of his shirt. He wore the blue security uniform with a couple of extra pins on the chest. No doubt for meritorious ass-sitting, Cleve had always thought.

"Hello, fella." Kriesel said.

"How's it going, Rich?"

"Oh, okay, young man. How about you? You letting any grass grow under those flat feet?"

"Nah. Same old, same old. You know. Just stopped by to see my lady on the fourth floor. It's been a while."

"Yeah, I figured as much." He eyed the flowers. "It's the only time I ever see you, Cleve. You must be in the doghouse again, huh, bringing her flowers and all?"

"No, not really, Rich." He nodded towards the elevator. "I'll just go right up if you don't mind, pardner."

"Nope. Just sign the sheet here, like always. Job security—you know how it is." He winked.

Cleve took the elevator up and walked down the carpeted hall. Maureen answered her door after the third knock.

She looked distressed at first, her brows tugging together in her forehead, digging a deep furrow. She eyed the flowers, then looked at Cleve with those eyes that had seen—and could see—so much about him. Her full lips were glossed glassy and looked like they were begging to be kissed.

"Right on time, detective," she said.

He handed the bouquet to her.

"And here I thought I was a few minutes early." He shook the wrist that held his watch. "Damned cheap watches."

Mo smiled. "Beautiful flowers. Thank you, Detective Spade."

He grinned. "I prefer Phillip Marlowe."

She was dressed in a white peasant blouse with a flowered skirt, and a black patent leather belt circled her waist. She wore strappy sandals and her flaming red hair was put up in a loose bun. She never seemed to need or use much makeup, Cleve thought, except for the lip gloss.

"Come on in then, Marlowe."

Cleve eased past her into the apartment, then turned to face her, but she turned away.

"Just go ahead and have a seat," she said. "I'll put these beauties in some water. I want them to keep as long as possible."

Cleve rubbed a hand across his mouth and made an impatient gesture as he lowered himself onto the couch. He sat and leaned forward, elbows braced on his thighs.

From the kitchen, Mo called out, "Can I get you something to drink? Beer, coke, lemonade?"

He stood up.

"Hmmmm. Lemonade? Haven't had any of that in a long time. Yeah, lemonade sounds great, thanks."

In a few minutes Mo brought him a tall frosty glass.

When she handed it to him, he reached a hand out to touch her cheek, but she gently pushed it away.

Cleve winced. He narrowed his eyes in speculation, surprised, not sure about how to react.

"Jesus, Mo! Look, I told you I'm sorry. Can't we get past this somehow?"

She looked at him with a raised eyebrow.

His eyes met hers and in a much lower voice he said, "I swear, I'll never hurt you that way again, baby."

His face was pensive, expectant, his dark, deep-set eyes locked on hers, studying, waiting.

He caught himself moving closer toward her, close enough he could feel the familiar electrical field come to life between them, close enough that she narrowed her eyes as if in subtle warning. But she didn't back away. She couldn't.

He was standing so close his heart beat a little harder with the thought of having her in his arms. He ached to hold her.

As he edged even closer, Mo backed up ever so slightly until the back of her knees touched the couch. She kicked off her sandals as he wrapped his strong arms around her. He parted her lips and slid his tongue between them, into her, as if he had every right, plunging deep and retreating slowly in a rhythm that was primal and unmistakable, blatantly carnal.

She was into his kiss, answering with a hunger of her own. She moaned.

He could wait no longer and gently pressed her back down onto the couch and buried his face in her hair. He held her there for a long time, saying nothing, then placed his head against her breast and listened to the rapid beating of her heart as he caressed her lovely neck.

Mo trembled at the feel of him hard against her, perhaps at the mental image of the two of them together, naked in the bed in the next room.

But she whispered, "Please, Cleve. Not tonight, okay?"

Moments passed in silence until she finally pushed him away and spoke again.

"Try to understand. We need to stop before this goes any farther. Not that it isn't tempting." She grinned as she trailed her fingertips over his lips. "Let's just go to dinner. We need to talk, but it can wait for a bit."

"Hold up, Mo." He held her close and gazed into her eyes. "I need to know that you forgive me, baby. That's all."

She smiled, ran her fingers through his hair, sighed, then nodded. "Let's go eat, big guy. Like I said, we need to talk."

CHAPTER EIGHT

Hawkins was wounded.

He wasn't prepared for the way Mo had acted when he showed up at her apartment for their date. He knew she was probably still ticked off, but he'd thought surely she had been looking forward to some make-up romance with him that evening.

All afternoon he had been psyching himself up for their date with visions of her trotting over to him, throwing her hands on his shoulders, and jumping up to wrap her legs around his waist.

Instead, she appeared to be excited about having dinner with him . . . but not much more.

It didn't add up, he thought. Now her staunch assertion that she wanted to talk, before anything else, bothered him. It crushed his ego and gave him further pause to wonder about their bond. The bricks of their relationship were crumbling down around him and their date was starting out about as exciting as string-cheese night at Lambeau Field.

He had very little opportunity to speak about anything before she made herself ready to leave the apartment. The hurry up, the zippedy-doo-dah, let's go, and the flash were her choice. Cleve knew it would be counterproductive if he attempted to change her mind.

"Why don't we have a drink before we leave?" he asked when she came out from her bedroom.

Mo's makeup was scant as usual, but what little she did wear did nothing to hide the violet smudges beneath her eyes. He suspected she had been crying.

"No . . . if you don't mind," she said, "I'm sort of hungry. We'd better go."

There it was. Something told him this date was going to be a genuine payback for his Friday night mess up. Impatience pulled at his features and made him look petulant as he checked his watch.

"I guess you're right," he said. "We'd better go."

Outside, the air was damp. Even after all the rain, the night was hot and sticky and thick with mosquitoes.

The silence inside of the car was palpable. It was as if neither of them dared to speak for fear of starting an argument. Cleve smiled as he realized they were like small children tip-toeing to the water's edge and swirling their toes in the water to test it before wading in.

For Cleve, tonight felt especially strange. Even during the worst of their arguments, Mo would have forgiven him by now. The whole scenario had him wondering how the pure quiet of the car was affecting the way Mo now felt about things.

Is she really that pissed off at me? What can I say to convince her that I'm sincere when I say I'm sorry? What will it take to right this ship?

He pushed the button on the CD player to cue up Jackie Gleason's album Music *For Lovers Only*. "I Only Have Eyes for You," one of Mo's favorites. The trumpet solo by Bobby Hackett began playing and ended the silence in the car.

Cleve sighed. "Any place special you'd like to eat?"

Mo shook her head. "Not really. You've always been pretty good at choosing, so go ahead."

Hackett's trumpet again serenaded the silent couple.

"Okay, well," Cleve finally said, hesitantly, "I've been hearing good scoop through the grapevine about Rosebud on Rush, so I made reservations for eight-thirty, just in case. Is that okay with you?"

"Yes, that's fine. Italian food sounds good."

"How'd you know that, smartie?"

Mo shrugged. "Girls talk, you know."

"Yeah, I know." He paused, more to give her an opening to continue the conversation than anything else. She remained silent. He checked her profile in the semi-darkness.

"The gift of gab has to be good for something besides filling awkward silences, you know?" He paused. "So talk to me, Mo."

She adjusted his rear-view mirror and checked her hair.

A frown creased his mouth as he pulled into the valet parking lane.

"To be honest with you, I've been searching my mental files all night...looking for the right thing to say, Mo."

More silence as she continued to primp in the mirror.

He studied the side of her face and said, "Alright then. I'll let them take the car and we'll go in, okay?"

"Sure." She tilted the mirror back and looked around. "I think I'll enjoy this place. Val, in Robbery Division, said she and her boyfriend Scott come here all the time."

"Do I know him?"

Mo sighed as she prepared to get out. "No, I don't think you'd know this guy. To tell the truth, he's not your type." He heard her snicker. "He's been in some kind of trouble, she won't say what. He sleeps half the day and spends the other half on the sofa watching Judge Judy and complaining about his ankle monitor." She grinned and mused, "I think she's crazy to deal with it, but who am I to say?"

Cleve came around the car, helped her out and tipped the valet.

"I definitely don't know this guy. I wonder what they put the bracelet on for." He kept talking as they walked. "Speaking of guys with troubles, Deckle's got a whole new set of problems."

"You mean that little homeless guy? What's his problem?"

"He's in St. Joseph's. Seems he stepped out in front of a car over on Wells a few days ago."

Cleve didn't want to discuss anything except their own situation, but he was glad Mo was finally opening up just a bit to have a conversation.

As he guided her to the door, Mo asked him, "Is he okay?"

"Yeah, he's just a little shook up. Bruised here and there. He was lucky. Thing is, I had a visitor at the office, though. Strange-looking guy, trying to get answers from me about the accident. He wasn't a cop, or an insurance guy, either, as far as I could tell. He said Deckle sent him to see me. I didn't buy it."

"Hmmmm. That does sound a bit strange."

Cleve was glad to see her interested.

"Offhand," she said, "I'd say your pal has shit on his nose."

They walked into the restaurant and the maitre d' looked up their reservation and had a waiter take them to a cozy booth in the back.

Perfect, thought Cleve. After they were seated with menus, he snaked his arm around Mo's shoulders.

"What do you think, babe? This is kind of nice, huh?"

"Yes, very nice, really," said Mo and she smiled. "Thank you. Good choice."

A short blonde waitress with an inviting smile came over to their table with a pitcher of ice water, As her quick hands poured, she said, "Good evening, folks. My name is Crystal. I'll be your waitress this evening. Can I bring you something from the bar? We recommend Frangeleco on the rocks."

Mo shook her head. "No, I believe I'll have an Absolut Vodka martini, neat."

"Scotch and soda. Johnny Walker Red," Cleve said.

When Crystal was gone, Mo tilted her head back, closed her eyes and began tapping her forehead as if in a trance.

"Well, I'm glad you agreed we needed to talk, Cleve. That's a step in the right direction, I'm sure you'll agree."

"Sure. I know we need to talk alright, and I'm up for that, but it's hard to talk until you tell me you forgive me, Mo. I feel like I'm walking on eggshells here, to be honest."

Their drinks came. Cleve thought he saw the flicker of a smile on Mo's lips.

Playing with the little stirrer in his drink, he leaned on his elbows and asked, "So what are we doing, baby?"

Mo took a long swallow of her drink, as though she were drinking Pepsi, he thought.

Cleve sipped his drink then took in a big breath and blew it out slowly. He spoke in a low voice.

"Look, I'm sorry, Mo. I'm sorry, okay?" He held his hands up in surrender. "How many times do I have to say that before you'll believe me?"

Mo's expression was one of reserved caution. She shrugged and looked in his eyes.

"Mo, look, I'm sorry, but I am what I am. You must know by now, there are few creatures on this earth more pigheaded than cops. I can say this with surety, being one myself, and being around lots of them for nearly twenty years."

" . . . and I've been sleeping with one for fourteen years," Maureen murmured.

Cleve nodded and raised his hand to her. "Yes, of course. There is that, too. So . . . I know I no longer carry a detective's badge, but that isn't what being a cop means. Being a cop is in my nature, in my bones. A cop is a cop, regardless of status, regardless of uniform, regardless of agency, regardless of age."

Mo gazed over his shoulder. "I agree...so far. Go on. What's your point?"

"Well, I suspect you know me on that level as well as anyone could. At least you know where I stand on most things, don't you?"

She shrugged her shoulders and raised her finger.

"I've heard this same speech wrapped in a different package many times, Cleve."

There was another moment of silence between them.

"Now, let me talk," she said. "My turn, okay? You are selfish, Cleve." She spoke with conviction. "Do you realize you have never . . . I mean never... put me first in your life? Never made me feel like maybe, just maybe, I might have a chance at something more than a roll in the hay? No. I always come last, don't I?"

She finished her drink with one motion and continued.

"You say you love me, Cleve, but you certainly have strange ways of showing it. You love your buddies, the bar and a bottle a hell of a lot more than me, Hawkins."

He tried to hold her hand, but she drew back. He looked in her eyes and saw they were misted over.

"I have to stop this, now," she said. "I need another drink."

"Listen, baby, I try. I really do. I don't know what causes me to screw up every once in a while. I think it runs in the family. I don't know. Sometimes I believe you deserve a lot better than me. You need a guy more committed to you and maybe, just maybe, that's why I deliberately try to sabotage our relationship. Because I *know* you deserve better."

His gaze drifted away and lingered in space, trying to find the justifications he would need to keep going.

Mo exhaled with as much noise as possible, toyed with her silverware and said, "You don't really believe that, do you, Cleve?"

He looked at her as if she'd just suggested he put a lampshade on his head and dance the hokey-pokey.

"It makes sense to me. Why else do I manage to screw up the way I do?"

Crystal returned and he ordered two more drinks before they both ordered their food.

"I'll have the Calamari," said Mo. "Creamy garlic dressing on my salad."

"How are the meatballs, Crystal?" Cleve asked. "You make them here?"

"Our meatballs are delicious, sir. Yes, we make them in house. I love them, myself."

Cleve handed her the menu. "Alright, I'll have the spaghetti and meatballs then. Italian dressing for the salad. Thanks."

They waited in silence for their drinks.

Mo finally looked at him directly and said, "I'm really so tired of it, Cleve. You know?"

He nodded. "I never said I blamed you, Mo. I don't. You're a good woman."

"No. I mean I get tired of it all, Cleve. The job, the same old routine ... my life. I like my time off. I wish I could quit, but I have five more years to go in order to get my pension. I'll be damned if I'll let them screw me out of that, so I'll ride it out."

He nodded and reached for her hand. "I understand, Mo. I really do."

To Cleve there still seemed to be a wall of her silent anger between them, even while they ate their food.

They were nearly done a half hour later when Mo said, "I'm way too full for dessert. How about you?"

He nodded. "Same here."

Cleve still hoped for her forgiveness. A couple of times earlier, when Mo had laughed briefly, he had thought the big thaw was coming.

Maybe she's ready to forgive me after all.

Back in the car, on their way back to her place, however, the air was still thick with nothing.

Cleve parked and walked her to her door.

"Cleve, I know I haven't been the best company tonight, but I didn't want to mislead you any more than I had to."

He leaned on her door and edged ever so close. Their lips were merely inches apart when he spoke.

"What does that mean, baby? Mislead me...how?"

Her head was bowed and she held his hands in hers.

"We won't be seeing each other like this anymore, Cleve. I really do forgive you. And I care an awful lot about you ... about us, actually, but please don't call me anymore. I want this to be our last date. We need space from one another. Above all, you need time to sort things out and figure out what is really important in your life."

He started to speak, but she reached up and touched his lips with her fingertips.

"No. We owe each other that chance."

She unlocked her door, turned, and kissed him on the cheek.

"Goodnight, Cleve."

CHAPTER NINE

The sting of Mo's words gnawed at Cleve's pride all the way back to his apartment. It was still early, and although he had considered stopping at one of his favorite watering holes, he was emotionally drained. He decided to go home.

Sulking and camping on his couch with a fifth of Cutty Sark and pack of Marlboros was just what he needed to nurse him through the night with his bad boy blues.

Even though he had given up smoking six months earlier, there was a new pack hiding on the top shelf of his bedroom closet. At the time he'd stashed them, he'd sworn he'd only bust the pack open in the event of an unexpected crisis. Such was the case tonight, he told himself, as he kicked off his shoes and settled in for what would prove to be a long, empty and lonely night.

On Sunday morning a sliver of daylight crept past the living room drapes and Cleve realized he had fallen asleep watching reruns of The Twilight Zone.

By the time he showered, shaved and grabbed a quick cup of coffee, it was close to nine in the morning. Cleve drove over to St. Joseph's on Lakeshore to pick up Deckle.

He found a Burns Corporation security guard who had evidently nodded off behind a desk just inside the front doors. His name plate read Jacobs. Cleve stepped forward loudly and the guard, now a bit startled, said, "You need to sign in here, sir."

He was a well-fed guy who appeared to be in his early fifties, with a wide butt and a hairline that probably hadn't seen his eyebrows in years. The top of a Krispy-Kreme bag stuck out of a wastebasket by his desk.

Cleve checked over the sheet attached to the clipboard and filled in the pertinent information.

"You need to see my driver's license too, Jacobs?"

The guard grinned. "Yes, sir. Rules, you know."

"Yeah, I'm just here to pick up my buddy. He's a patient here. They're releasing him today."

"Good deal." Jacobs nonchalantly swung the clipboard back around so he could read it. "We just need to see that driver's license now, Mr. Hawkins. I have to log the number on here."

Cleve pulled out his wallet and showed him his license. His PI badge flopped over and was exposed at the same time.

A squinting Jacobs logged the information, then asked, "You a cop?"

"Sort of."

"What's that mean...sort of?"

"It's a private shield." Cleve moved his wallet closer. "Check it again, if you want."

"No, that's fine." He waved a hand dismissively. "What's your friend's name and what floor's he on?" He smirked. "You forgot to fill that part in."

"His name is Deckle and he's on the ninth floor, unless they moved him in the last couple of days."

Jacobs flipped through pages at the back of the clipboard and scrutinized a list.

"Okay, Mr. Hawkins, your friend is still on nine. Room nine-sixteen. The elevators are right around the corner." He pointed.

Cleve rode up to nine and stopped to check with the nurse behind the desk. She was in the process of stuffing her handbag into a desk drawer.

A tall, attractive woman in her mid-forties, her name plate showed "Crocker. RN." Her blonde hair was streaked with gray and she carried herself with an erect, no-nonsense manner, every inch a medical professional. When Cleve approached, she dusted her hands and asked, "Can I help you?"

"Yes. I'm here to take my friend home."

"Okay, and who might that be?"

"Well, I call him Deckle, but I'm not sure of his given name. I think he's considered homeless. So, who knows?"

She checked the computer screen, smiled and said, "You must be Mr. Hawkins. Is that right?"

"That's me." He pulled out his wallet to show his driver's license. "Cleve Hawkins. Will I be able to take him right now, nurse?"

"Well, let's see. Yes. We have him in the system as Mr. Deckle." She continued to check her computer. "And, I see we have no available home address here for him, either. Will Mr. Deckle be staying with you when he leaves us, sir?"

"Uuuh. Yes. Well, yes, I guess so."

Crocker stopped typing and narrowed her eyes as she studied Cleve.

"Sir, I have to fill out these papers if you want your friend to leave here with you. Is he going to be living with you? And if he is, your address please?"

Cleve gave her his driver's license. She noted the information. "Is this your current address then?"

"Yes, ma'am."

Her fingers danced on the keyboard for a moment longer. When she was done, she said, "All set, Mr. Hawkins. You can take Mr. Deckle with you now. We can give you a wheelchair for him, but he has been walking on the floor with a cane and seems to be doing fine. Here's a copy of his discharge papers. I know he's been very anxious, waiting for you."

Her tone left little room for skepticism.

Cleve's mouth felt dry. His tongue trailed across his lips, and he asked, "Should I go get him or will you be bringing him out?"

"He's in nine-sixteen. You can follow one of our helpers and she will assist you."

"Thank you," said Cleve.

A candy-striper went with him and they found Deckle dressed and sitting in a bedside chair. He was wearing his usual soiled Chicago Cubs cap and held a plastic bag containing some things Cleve couldn't identify in his lap. He was smiling from ear to ear while he watched Sesame Street.

"Deckle . . . you ready to get out of here?"

"Hey, Cleve, old buddy! Boy, am I glad to see you. Wow! I've been waiting for a week."

His widened grin showed he still had a dire need for dental work. Guess they don't throw in any dental freebies here, Cleve thought. The multi-colored bruising on his face had gotten decidedly worse since Cleve had seen him two days earlier.

They had given him a four-pronged cane to aid his walking. Otherwise, Deckle appeared to be Deckle. His hard blue eyes seemed very far away at times, staring at something that no one else could see.

The little man was homeless as far as anybody knew. He had been bathed during his stay in the hospital and no longer gave off his usual smell of old sweat, alcohol and smoke. He was also clean-shaven that day, when generally a razor wouldn't touch his face for months.

Cleve shook his head. "No, Deck, it hasn't been a week. In fact it's only been a day or so. Are you sure you're okay, partner? I mean, you're sure you're ready to leave here?"

"Yeah. Sure. I'm fine, Cleve. They said they was gonna take me to one of them shelters, you know what they meant? A shelter? I told them no way, Jose. I said my buddy, Cleve, would be picking me up. They kept on offering me that same thing every time they changed nurses. So I'm glad you came when you did, Cleve. You know what I mean? I don't want to go to no shelter. All kinds of crazies in them places. Somebody should clean them places out. Spray them good and start all over." He paused. "Right, Cleve?"

"Yeah, I agree, Deck. Here, sit in this wheelchair and we'll get you out of here, pronto. Did you eat breakfast yet?"

"Oh, sure. They feed you real early every day in this place. I ate eggs and toast at six o'clock this morning. Orange juice too. Yup, I ate then. I had coffee too. You can have all the coffee you want in here, Cleve. It's free, too!" He plopped down into the wheelchair.

Cleve looked him over. His once beige desert boots were now blackened and scuffed and they were held together with layers of duct tape. He wore a tattered fatigue jacket. It was olive-drab and had three faded marks where sergeant stripes had once been sewn on. Most of the snaps and buttons were missing or broken and the zipper pull was gone.

As far as Cleve knew these were the only clothes Deckle had to his name, although the man always swore he had a stash of brand new clothes tucked away somewhere on the South Side of town.

Cleve had left his car out front with the flashers on, per Jacobs. He opened the passenger door for Deckle, who seemed to be moving pretty good considering everything.

"Sorry about being late, Deck. I got your message yesterday, but I got a little tied up last night. Sidetracked, actually. Nobody gave you any static about it at the hospital, did they?"

"Nope. I gave the nurse your phone number. She told me they called you a few times, but when you didn't answer, they left a message. I sorta figured you were busy and I told them that. I told them you are a busy man. Right, Cleve? I told them you would probably be calling or coming today." He chuckled. "I just knew you would, Cleve. Know what I mean? I knew it."

"Listen, Deck, I don't know where you want me to take you." He looked sideways at his friend. "You can come and stay at my place for a few days, if that will help. I don't mind. You know, just until you get on your feet. You understand, right?"

Deckle raised his hands. "Oh, no, Cleve. I can't do that. I got my own place to go to, Cleve." He chuckled. "Yes, sir, I got a lot of friends who probably been looking for me too. You understand that, right, Cleve?"

"Yeah, sure, Deckle."

Cleve continued to drive until he got to his office on Wells and parked in the one spot he found right in front.

"Here we are, partner. Why don't you come inside and have a cup of coffee? I need to talk to you about a few things anyway. You don't mind. I mean you're not in a hurry, are you?"

"No, not in a hurry, Cleve. I'm not in a hurry. What is it you want to talk about, Cleve?"

"Just come in and have that coffee, okay?" He patted his friend on the back.

"Okay, buddy. I'll do that. Anything for you, Cleve."

As was always the way, he let Deckle make the coffee while he sat behind his desk and thumbed through the *Chicago Sun Times*. When the coffee was ready, they both had a cup and shared the silence of the room.

After a second cup, Cleve brushed the paper aside.

"Deckle . . . do you know a man named Glick?"

Deckle leaned forward in his chair and craned his neck. "Mr. who?"

"Glick, Mr. Glick. Do you know the guy, Deckle?"

Deckle shook his head. "No, Cleve. I don't know nobody named Mr. Glick. Why did you want to ask me that, Cleve?"

Cleve got up and paced the floor a bit.

"Ah, never mind, Deckle. It's not important, I guess. But listen, if anybody by that name approaches you for any reason, I want you to let me know right away. Okay?" He squeezed Deckle's shoulder and tried to look in his zig-zagging eyes. "You got that, my friend?"

"Yeah, okay. I sure do, Cleve." He was obviously nervous about the prospect and stood up.

"If you don't need something else, Cleve, I'm going to go see my friends and get settled in." He grinned. "They'll be glad to see me. I could have been dead for all they know. Crazy, huh? Well, I'll see you later on, Cleve. Okay?"

"You got it, partner. Catch you later."

Cleve tilted back in his chair and pushed his coffee a few inches away and clasped his hands behind his head.

His mind once again focused on Mo's last words outside of her door the night before. ". . . please don't call me anymore. I want this to be our last date. We need space from each other. Above all, you need to sort things out and figure out what is really important in your life. Goodnight, Cleve."

That "goodnight" really meant goodbye, didn't it?

"Damned right," he mused out loud. "I'm screwed,"

I sure as hell can't go begging her. I won't. Yeah, just let her miss me for a while. She'll call me. That's the best way.

He tried to switch gears and get her off of his mind, at least for the time being, but he just stood and began pacing back and forth.

I have to get busy doing something. Anything. I could go over to Butch McGuire's place, I suppose. Have a cold one. No. That's no good.

The ringing of the landline shattered the silence in the room. He picked up.

"Good morning. Hawkins here."

"Mr. Hawkins, have you got a few minutes? I'd like to stop by and see you about something pretty important, if you don't mind."

"Depends. Who is this?" He jammed the phone between his shoulder and his ear and grabbed a pad and pen.

"My name is Maclam. Russ Maclam. I need to see you about a job. I want to hire you."

"What kind of job?"

The man on the phone paused and cleared his throat. "Mind if I come by?"

Cleve looked at his watch. "I guess so...yeah. You know where I am?"

"Yeah. I know exactly where you are. I'll be by in about twenty. See you then, Hawkins."

CHAPTER TEN

Back in his apartment that night, Hawkins took a Heineken from the refrigerator, turned on the radio, and went out onto his balcony. He couldn't sleep so he stood in the muggy night air and drank the beer.

Off to his left, a dog barked and the lingering scent of a neighbor's barbeque hung in the air, not as strong as it had been earlier, but still it was sufficient to tease his palette with visions of slathered ribs.

The night was hazy, and the heat and humidity created halos of fuzzy light around the nearby streetlamps.

Cleve wondered what Maureen was doing right then. Was she miserable without him, as he hoped, or out on a date with some animal he knew from his old precinct? He had never known her to cheat on him, but if he was out of the picture, that scenario could become a reality.

Brooding about her would do no good, and sleep would come easier after a few weeks—or so he had heard. He thought about Mo and remembered the old adage, "absence makes the heart grow fonder." That was just propaganda, he thought, contrived by some lonely asshole in order to make him feel better. It just wasn't true as far as Hawkins was concerned. Absence simply made him more pissed off.

Standing there in his boxers, he realized he had to get going in the right direction if he was to put the past behind him. He'd accepted the two grand from Maclam that afternoon because the case intrigued him and he had to stay busy doing what he did best. Then, there was the money, of course.

He knew one thing for sure. In the morning he would get started, if for no other reason than it was something to keep him from dwelling on his failed romance.

He finally turned in, slept late but woke up feeling good, even though his mouth tasted bad. He was still groggy when he slipped into some gym shorts, a T-shirt and his Nikes, and went down to the gym and burned off the rest of his doldrums on the elliptical machine.

He worked out in the weight room and then spent a half-hour on the treadmill. After a shower, he changed into his choice of street clothes for the day. Levi's, black long-sleeved shirt, and a pair of tan suede desert boots. He grabbed his Cubs cap and the car keys and was on his way to take a piece of the day for himself.

The cool morning had shrouded the landscape in a thick ground-hugging fog that obscured his vision as he drove to the office. In the back of his mind he was anticipating Deckle might be camped on the steps in front of his office. But that proved not the case. The homeless man was not there. It wasn't unusual for the little guy to be missing for days on end. Cleve wasn't concerned. He unlocked the door and scooped up the mail at his feet. The heat was stifling inside and he opened a window.

After brewing some coffee, he sat down, leaned back in his chair, and planted his feet on the edge of the desk. He checked the mail, at the same time glancing around the room and admitting to himself that now, more than ever, he had to do something with the place. With just one window it was too dark and depressing. He thought a new coat of paint on the walls and ceiling would do wonders. Then again, maybe that wouldn't be enough.

The building was located on Wells Street, near the touristy section called Old Town. It was in one of the older buildings where landlords still spent a lot on themselves but little on the investment of their holdings. The surrounding area was a potpourri of blacks, Latinos and southern-bred whites.

In recent years, crime had gone on the decline and the inhabitants attempted to stick to their own business there. Before that Cleve had gotten a good deal on the lower floor, and he intended to keep his office for at least another two years, when his lease would expire.

His space consisted of two rooms, an extremely small bathroom and one big, open area that was his office. His large desk dominated the room, but there was also one filing cabinet, a landline phone, and two chairs, just in case a client came with their husband or their wife. Two attractive area rugs covered the floors and a water fountain and coat rack occupied the little space by the front corner.

The old iron radiator had no real controls, and the room, when closed for no longer even than a day, reeked with heat. The solitary window allowed a view onto Wells street.

Cleve's cell vibrated, and it broke his train of renovation thoughts. A quick check of the number and he didn't bother answering Carnival Cruise Lines' robocall. He shoved the phone back in his pocket. He realized he had wished the call was from Mo.

He decided he would begin his investigation of Senator Albers' blackmail by visiting Corky Hulce at The Last Resort Bar and Grill. Maclam had made it clear that Hulce was the friend who had asked for help. He was also the one who knew how to contact the senator.

Cleve fueled up his car and headed for the bar on Belmont Avenue.

He'd never been inside The Last Resort, but he had passed by it numerous times in his travels around the city, and it always appeared busy, if the lack of parking spaces was any criterion.

When he pulled up to the tavern that Thursday morning, he found both trucks and cars, mostly trucks, in the bar's parking lot. With no other bars in the neighborhood, it was easy to see why the Last Resort neighborhood bar might be a goldmine for Corky Hulce.

Inside, there was not much going on, some people in booths eating hamburgers and drinking beer, two or three more on barstools, and a couple of guys in the back were shooting pool at a coin-op table.

Cleve edged his way past a blaring jukebox playing Golden Earring's "Radar Love." He headed toward the bar, all the while trying to appear unobtrusive.

A waitress skirted past him and he caught her attention.

"Excuse me, miss. Can you tell me where I would find Corky Hulce?"

She was a large girl with a perfect complexion and a sweet country smile, dressed in black from head to foot. A five-pointed star hung around her neck on a silver chain.

"The boss? Sure, he's back there behind the bar." She pointed. "Not the bartender. He's the blond-haired one. The other guy."

The bartender had straggly blond hair and a skinny neck and was busy stocking beer. He had probably been a thin guy once, but as time had passed, he had gotten plump enough that the only remnant of his former self was his thin neck.

Cleve approached the other man behind the bar, who had to be Corky. He glanced up at Cleve as he finished signing an invoice for a truck driver wearing a Budweiser uniform.

"Thanks, Pete," he said to the driver, who turned and was on his way out.

Cleve stepped in.

"Corky?"

The man smiled from ear to ear. "Unless you're the Board of Health, that's me alright. What's up?"

His face was pallid, with the only color coming from the salt and pepper stubble of about five day's growth. He had piercing indigo eyes that lifted themselves fully from the Budweiser invoice as Cleve extended his hand.

"Cleve Hawkins, Corky. I need to talk to you when you're free."

"I'm not free, but I'm reasonable." He shook Cleve's hand and checked his watch. "I've got the lunch crowd popping in here pretty quick though, so what can I do for you?"

"Russ Maclam met with me yesterday regarding a friend of yours, Senator Albers? I think we need to talk when you've got a little more time. I can come back after lunch if that would be better."

"No. That's okay. I'll be alright. So, Russ stopped to see you, eh? Big sonofabitch, ain't he?"

"Yeah. He's a pretty impressive guy. I have to admit I haven't seen a man that huge since I left the Marines. We had a couple about his size...right in my outfit, actually."

"Yeah, Russ wears a size eighteen shoe. You tell me, but I wouldn't want that up my ass, ya' know what I mean?"

Corky's wore thinning red hair in a comb-over and he had a predominant double chin that jiggled when he spoke.

"Can I get you something to drink, Hawkins?"

"Nah. It's too early for me. Thanks anyway."

"Ah, hell, one won't kill you. What'll you have?"

Cleve glanced at the myriad of colorful bottles highlighted on the top shelf behind the bar.

"A shot of B&B then."

"You've got it." Corky called out to his bartender who was now stuffing empty bottles into their cases. "Jimmy!" He paused and waited for a response. "Yo, Jimmy!" He tapped his fingers on the bar while he waited to have the bartender's attention. "Hey, Jim, give this man a shot of B&B, will you?"

"Aren't you having anything?" Cleve asked.

"Nah. Years ago I discovered booze was tougher than me, so I gave it up. Mind you, I sell it by the shit load—but I won't drink. You go ahead, bottoms up, then we'll go in the back to my office. You can bring your drink with, if you want. It's already getting too fuckin' noisy out here for me."

"Thanks," said Cleve. He downed the amber liquid quickly and felt it trail heat down his throat then explode in his stomach. It mixed badly with a little guilt for drinking so early in the day.

In his office Corky shuffled himself around behind an old metal desk, sat and threw his feet up. He pointed to a wooden chair sitting in the corner. "Go ahead, cop a squat, Hawkins. Tell me what's on your mind."

"Well, suppose you tell me your side of this thing with Senator Albers first. We'll go from there."

"Okay. Well, Gerry Albers is an old friend of mine, you know. We go way back before he went into politics. Grew up together, but then we went our separate ways. I helped my old man run this joint and Gerry, well, Gerry disappointed nobody. Just as expected, he went to college and learned how to walk the walk and talk the talk. He became a lawyer, and a damned good one from what I hear. He put a lot of bad guys behind bars before he ran for office."

He paused briefly and slid his top drawer open. "We hadn't touched base in about six months until he stopped in and asked for my help."

"What did he want you to do?"

Corky retrieved a cigar from inside the drawer. Stripping the cellophane from it, he stuck it in his mouth and lit up. Puffing on it a few times, he took a minute to admire it burning in his hand, then blew a huge cloud and squinted through the smoke.

"Tell me, what do you do, Hawkins?"

"I'm a private detective, but I spent twelve years with the Chicago Police."

"Hmmmm. Pretty impressive. A cop who decided to do his own thing, eh?" He blew a wide smoke ring that held together for a few seconds and then dissipated. "Must be nice. Did you retire? You don't look old enough."

"It's not quite that cut and dry, but yeah, I'm my own boss now."

"You figure you can find the scumbag who's trying to bleed the senator?"

"I'll give it my best shot."

"Well, Russ must think you're a straight shooter if he brought you in. He's a pretty solid guy himself, you know. I met him a long time ago while I was doing time in Joliet. He was doing five to ten at the time." Corky paused. "See, he can't afford to get too involved himself because he's out on parole, but he knows how to get shit done." He grinned. "Where I come from they call that making chicken shit into chicken salad."

"I need to meet with Albers of course, but is there anything else you can tell me about him? Anything that he might have confided to you that might steer me in the right direction?"

"A guy phoned Albers a little over a month ago and said he had something he should see. He claimed he had compromising pictures of Gerry's wife, Trish, and said that if he didn't want them to be seen on the internet or the entertainment page of the Tribune, he should meet his man on Clark Street that next Sunday morning." Hulce paused to puff on the cigar again and reached for a slip of paper. "I think I'll give you the Senator's number and let you two take it from there. How's that?"

"Okay. How much were the blackmailers asking for? Do you know?"

"I'm not sure, but Gerry figured it was all just a scam. He figured he'd meet the guy and brush him off, but then he was worried because the guy threatened him with a gun."

"And what happened after that?"

"I don't know. I told Gerry I would see what I could do and he left. He was pretty shook up, though. I got hold of my friend, Russ, and now you probably know more than I do."

"I'm not sure. You say he was told to bring a huge amount of cash to the meet with this complete stranger?"

"I know it sounds crazy, but yeah. Gerry said the man sounded pretty sure of himself and he knew a lot of personal stuff . . . you know, about Gerry's wife. It scared the shit out of him and he didn't know which way to go. I guess he paid the guy fifty grand, but that wasn't enough and the asshole was pissed off. He threatened Gerry with a gun and that's when he came to me looking for help."

"Did the Senator say what this go-between guy looked like? Would he recognize him if he saw him again?"

"Hell, I don't know, Hawkins. I didn't think to ask him. He just wanted me to find somebody to tail him when and if he went to meet the guy. Maybe scare him off in the bargain."

Hulce stopped and scribbled a phone number on the slip of paper.

"Here's Gerry's private number. Give him a call. The two of you can take it from there. I'd appreciate a call to let me know how it all turns out, though."

Cleve stood and pulled one of his cards out of his wallet. He handed it to Hulce.

"Thanks for your help, Corky. If you think of anything I should know, give me a call."

Corky squinted and tried to read the card. "I left my friggin' glasses out by the register. This is where I can reach you, though, right?"

Cleve nodded, shoved the chair back into the corner and went to the door. Grabbing the knob he said, "You might want to keep an eye looking over your shoulder for a while, at least until this is cleared up."

Hulce flicked the card back and forth on his chin and laughed.

"Yeah, sure. We don't sweat the petty stuff as a rule, though. Good Luck, Hawkins."

When Cleve got back to the office, Deckle was parked on the front stoop, puffing on a cigarette butt.

Somehow, he had been able to change clothes and he now wore faded jeans and a blue tee shirt with the sleeves ripped off at the shoulders. Not cut, ripped, so that errant strings dangled against his thin, pale arms. The jeans were hanging off his hip bones so the brand name of his underwear was showing and a chain ran from one belt-less loop to his back pocket, where there was no doubt a big empty wallet.

Deckle smiled, or what passed for a smile. His eyes were glassy.

"Yo, Cleve. I figured you'd be coming back pretty soon. I was watching the place for you. Okay, Cleve? You know you can count on me to watch things, right?"

"Yeah, that's fine, Deck. Come on in."

Cleve opened up and Deckle made his way inside. He grabbed his usual chair sitting beside the water cooler. He slumped down in the chair and steepled his fingers, his bony shoulders hunched up to his ears, a pose like a vulture on a perch.

Cleve flicked the light switch, opened the blinds and parked behind his desk. He began to check through his mail, but eyed Deckle.

"You can make some coffee for us, if you don't mind, partner."

Deckle bolted out of the chair, went to the filing cabinet and grabbed the glass coffee pot from the Bunn coffee maker.

"There's still some coffee left in the bottom, Cleve. Should I save it or pour it out?"

"Pour it out, Deck. Make eight cups fresh, okay?"

"You got it, Cleve. Right now." He stuck out his lower lip like a pouting child and set about making the coffee while Hawkins continued through his mail.

A few minutes passed and fresh coffee was brewing and Deckle was pacing when he suddenly stopped in his tracks as if a cop had yelled, "Halt."

"Hey, Cleve?"

Cleve didn't hear him.

"Hey, Cleve?"

"Yeah, Deck?"

"I forgot to tell you something when you picked me up from the hospital yesterday."

Cleve tossed another piece of junk mail into the circular file. "Yeah . . . what's that?"

"I just . . . I mean, I just . . . well, I do remember about that Mr. Glick."

CHAPTER ELEVEN

Cleve was taken aback by Deckle's comment. It was completely out of character for the homeless man to admit to anything, much less something he had previously denied.

"I'm not sure what you mean, Deck. You already told me you didn't know anything about Mr. Glick. Tell me what's really happening, partner."

Cleve's eyes followed the man as he resumed his hobbling around.

"And, where's that cane St. Josephs' gave you, by the way?"

Deckle cast his eyes down as red roses bloomed on his pale cheeks.

"I . . . I um, I lost it the first day I got out of the hospital. Must've been after I left here, Cleve. I sure didn't mean to. My knee still hurts a lot, too," he said, as he rubbed his leg, then shifted from one foot to the other. He scowled so hard, he looked to Cleve like he might be passing a kidney stone.

"What's the story, Deck? What were you supposed to tell me about Glick?" He closed the blinds with a twist of their plastic wand and circled around behind his desk, then stepped back and crossed his arms.

"Well?"

Deckle pressed both hands against his mouth and shook his head soundlessly. With his head still down, he was able to squeeze out the words "Mr. Glick."

"Yeah, I know. That's what you said. That's what we're talking about here. Now I need you to tell me about him. Where do you know Glick from, Deckle?"

Deckle's eyes widened. "Saw him do it." He shrugged like it was the easiest thing in the world.

"Saw who do what?"

Hawkins could see that the little guy had already become a nervous wreck just telling as much as he had.

"Okay, sit down, Deck. Let's talk about it."

Deckle slid the wooden chair over and put it in front of Cleve's desk, next to the two client chairs. He settled into the chair, his oversized field jacket creeping up around his earlobes, making him look like a turtle ready to pull his head back into his shell. He rocked back and forth nervously.

Cleve was silent for a moment and reached for his coffee. What felt like a full minute passed before either man spoke.

"Deckle . . . who did you see do what? What were you going to tell me, partner?"

"Mr. Glick." He fidgeted like he had to use the men's room.

"I know. You said that. I got it. What about Mr. Glick?"

"Tell you it was Mr. Glick who did it."

"Did what, Deck? Goddamnit!"

"I ran! I ran!" Deckle knotted his fingers together and rocked back and forth on the chair. "He saw me, but he couldn't catch me cuz I ran."

Cleve pondered what he had just heard from the man sitting in front of him.

"And...Glick did it?"

Deckle nodded. "I saw him. I ran." His voice sounded like a band saw, high-pitched and nasal. Angry veins on his nose became evident from his addiction to alcohol and perhaps high blood pressure. He crossed his arms and went into a sulk, refusing to speak at all. He covered his face with both hands and gently massaged his forehead with his fingertips.

Then a light seemed to snap on behind his eyes and he looked up. "I forgot him, but it was him, wasn't it?" he mumbled. "Saw him do it." He sat on the edge of his seat with his hands clasped lightly between his knees and shook his head. "I ran fast."

"You saw him, Deck?"

Cleve nodded and smiled as though he was dealing with a child who thought he was first in line. He watched as Deckle shrugged, then winced and rubbed at his stiff neck. He seemed to have the attention span of a moth.

Cleve let the foam settle for a moment then tried a different tack.

"You hungry, Deck?" He reached for the landline. "We can order a pizza if you want. I'm just about running on empty, myself." He paused, anticipating a reaction of some kind.

Nothing.

Deckle's nose began to run and he swiped it quickly with the back of his hand.

"It was Mr. Glick. That's right."

Cleve had a small box of Kleenex sitting on his desk and he handed it to Deckle.

"Deck . . . put some of those in your pocket while you're at it."

Deckle grabbed a fistful and blew his nose loudly then tossed the tissues into the wastebasket beside the desk. He pulled another fistful out of the box when his nose continued to drip and shoved them into his jacket pocket.

Hawkins picked up the pack of Marlboros that was lying on his desk. He pulled one out and lit it.

He offered one to Deckle. "Want one, partner?"

Deckle shook his head.

Cleve pulled on his own cigarette and exhaled twin jet streams through his nose.

"Where did this happen, Deckle? Was it right where you got hit by that car?"

Deckle's eyes widened. "I promise you," he said, holding up his right hand as though swearing an oath, his hand so white it looked like he was wearing a latex glove. "Mr. Glick saw me. I ran. I saw him and he saw me. I ran. I promise you."

"Okay, Deck . . . are you saying you saw this Glick character do something bad . . . and he saw you at the same time? That it?"

Deckle nodded his head vehemently.

"That's it, right?"

Deckle slumped back in his chair. When he let out a measured sigh between his teeth, his relief became obvious to Cleve.

Cleve inhaled his cigarette deeply and went back behind his desk. He fell into his swivel and locked his hands behind his head.

"Anything else? I'm not sure if we're getting someplace or not, Deckle."

We are, but we're not, he thought. This whole thing is crazier than a bucket of drunk rattlesnakes. I have to watch where I go with this. If it really is anything at all. Deckle is sensitive to publicity in the same way kittens are sensitive to firecrackers. But, what in the hell is he trying to tell me? Why now? I might as well take a shot. Maybe something will stick.

"Okay, Deck, let me see if I've got this straight. You were over on North Clark Street and you saw this guy, Glick, doing something bad. Just nod your head if I'm right . . . okay?"

Deckle swiped his nose and nodded.

"Trouble is, Glick saw you watching him?"

Deckle nodded.

"When you knew he saw you, you ran and then got hit by that car while you were running across the street. Yes or no?"

Deckle nodded again.

"Now we're getting somewhere, partner. Well, we know he didn't catch you. Then the ambulance came, right? Only one thing left, Deck. What did you see?"

"Dumpster."

"Dumpster? I'm not following you. What about the dumpster?"

Deckle threw his arms around as if trying to show somebody stuffing something into a bag.

"You mean Glick was cramming something into a dumpster?"

A slight smile crept across Deckle's lips. He nodded enthusiastically.

"What was he throwing away, Deckle? Could you see?"

He nodded again and his face became drawn and saddened at the same time.

"No, don't stop now, Deck. Tell me, was it a body?"

Deckle nodded.

Cleve simply stared at him. He saw the bleakness in a soul who had lived a long, hard life and had seen too much that wasn't good.

"You done good, partner. You done real good."

CHAPTER TWELVE

Two mornings later, Cleve threw back the covers and climbed out of bed. He walked like a man who had fallen out of a moving car and rolled to a hard stop in the gutter.

His boxers hung low on his hips and he hadn't managed to take his socks off before succumbing to unconsciousness. They drooped around his ankles. The rest of his clothes lay where he'd dropped them as he peeled them off on his way to the bed.

He had neglected to close the drapes and the sun beamed in through the bedroom window. The room stank of cigarette smoke and vodka sweat.

He shuffled off to the bathroom and splashed cold water in his face. Then, yanking off his boxers and socks, he stared at himself in the mirror before jumping in the shower and letting the hot water beat him severely about the head and shoulders. He felt like the water was being fired at his scalp in a steady barrage of pins, and it felt good.

As he soaped up, he thought about Mo.

I've done it again. Good thing she can't see me now. She'd have the last laugh for sure and might even say "I told you so." But, no, she wouldn't do that. Maureen doesn't judge does she, Hawkins? All she wanted was to be considered above some of the other things that have always come first in my life.

He thought about Deckle, who was currently sleeping on a cot in the office. He hadn't had time to sort the entire thing out that involved the homeless man, and what he claimed he had witnessed in the alley over on Clark Street. Letting it go for the day seemed like the best thing to do at the time, but he had to notify Lieutenant Ashbaugh at the police department.

The day after he had talked to Deckle, Cleve had gotten a call from Corky Hulce. The tavern owner informed him that a meeting had been arranged for him with Senator Albers for the following day. Cleve was to call back and confirm that he'd be there, and he did.

Now it was already quarter to ten in the morning, a couple hours before his meeting. Luckily Cleve had woken up fairly early, especially considering the fact that the cab dropped him off at his place around three in the morning, after a night out with his old detective buddy, Jeebers.

Damn you, Hawkins. When will you learn? You can't have a few drinks with your buds anymore, can you? Just because Jeebers wants to do the town, doesn't mean you have to hang out with him.

He turned off the water and stepped out of the shower. After drying off, he used his fingertips to smear the steam off the mirror and stared at himself again.

You don't know when to stop once you start, asshole. One is never enough and two is too many. I look like I've gone through a long night of bruising my soul.

After fluffing his hair, he looked worse. I need a shave. I must have skipped yesterday, he thought.

When he'd finished in the bathroom, he pulled a dark blue, fall blazer, dark trousers and celery-green shirt out of the closet. After arguing with himself, he decided to go tie-less and slipped into a pair of comfortable black shoes. He said to himself, "This will work," and he was out the door.

The October morning held a temperature in the upper sixties and the sun was nearly overhead by the time he found a place to park in the Loop.

Arriving at the senator's office just before eleven-thirty, he was a shade early for their meeting, scheduled for noon. The senator's driver stood just outside the outer office door, right next to the American flag draped so proudly above a gold-embossed plaque that read, The Honorable Gerald P. Albers, Senator - State of Illinois

Cleve had never met a senator and couldn't help feeling a bit anxious at the prospect, even though he realized the senator put his pants on the same way he did.

He smelled the familiar scent of Hugo Boss aftershave and realized it was coming from the senator's driver, who looked bored standing in the hallway. Wearing a dark blue suit and a red tie with a gold tiepin, his eyes were narrow, his eyeballs fixed in their sockets. Excess hair on the back of his neck appeared to be seeking a way to escape his pinching white collar.

"Good day, sir," he said to Hawkins. A slight smile creased his lips.

He checked Cleve's identification and let him pass. Cleve entered the reception area and he was immediately confronted by Albers' secretary, who had obviously been to smile school. The nameplate on her desk read Felicia.

"I'm Cleve Hawkins. I have an appointment with the senator at noon."

"Good morning, Mr. Hawkins. Yes, Senator Albers is expecting you. He will be with you in just a moment. May I bring you a cup of coffee?"

"No, I'm good, thanks."

Coasters and magazines were neatly arranged on a narrow coffee table and Hawkins took a seat, then thumbed through a recent issue of *Time* while he waited.

Albers had overheard the conversation and a moment later he emerged from his inner sanctum.

He was a short, fifty-something man, with a head slightly too large for his body, its size emphasized by a wild thatch of curly black hair shot through with silver. His face looked honest, but it appeared to be pinched by stress.

He wore a nine-hundred dollar suit and a seventy-dollar silk tie with a faint gravy stain two inches below the knot. Cleve noticed his

Gucci dress shoes and realized the good senator spared no expense with his clothing allowance. Albers smiled and extended his hand.

"You must be the detective, Cleve Hawkins? Good Morning, sir. Felicia, have we offered Mr. Hawkins something to drink yet?"

Cleve raised his hand. "She got me first thing, senator. I'm good."

"On the phone you said you didn't mind talking over lunch, Hawkins, so I've picked one of my favorite spots, if you don't mind. Nothing too fancy, excellent food, good atmosphere and privacy. I never need reservations for lunch. Now, if it was for dinner, that would definitely be a different story. Know what I mean, detective?"

Cleve nodded. "Yes, sir."

The senator looked at his driver. "Go ahead and wait outside, Cliff. We'll be right behind you."

Cliff pulled out of the slight slouch he had been in. "Yes, sir."

"We're a little early for lunch," said Albers. "Shall we go over to the little place around the corner and grab a quickie first?"

Cleve felt his stomach lurch. The last thing he wanted today was alcohol in any form, beer or cocktail, but for the sake of diplomacy he said, "Sure. Lead the way."

Outside, Albers lit up a cigarette, and after a few quick puffs, very purposefully dropped the half-smoked butt on the sidewalk and ground it out with the toe of his Gucci shoe before they got into his government issue black Lincoln.

"Cliff, take us over to The Gage." He glanced at Hawkins. "You'll like this place. I do, even though it can get crowded. About half of the people in there need another drink, the other half need an enema."

The words "slop chute" were gold-leafed on the door, otherwise painted entirely sand brown, glass windows and all. Inside, there were several ridiculously large color TVs, dark wooden tables and high-backed booths, a bar along one side.

"The place is usually pretty empty until noon. We shouldn't have a problem getting a table," said the senator.

Cleve had heard of The Gage. Bankers, brokers and other big shots met there for lunch and gulped beer in green bottles and sipped Swedish vodka. After a while they'd probably line the bar and gather around small tables to discuss the direction of the market and debate the future of the prime. Cleve felt uncomfortable.

Cliff had gone to park the senator's car, or do whatever it was a senator's driver did while the boss was hobnobbing and enjoying costly lunches at the expense of Illinois taxpayers.

"They've got fairly decent food in this place, Hawkins. Privacy is key, though." He lowered his voice. "Plenty of that here, you know. That's what I like about it." He leaned in to Cleve, just a bit. "Please . . . never forget that in our dealings, Hawkins, okay? Discretion is so very important as you can imagine."

"I've got that loud and clear, senator. So, let's get one of those booths in the back, if that's alright with you."

"That's fine." They went to the back, seated themselves, and Albers spoke.

"I guess we really could eat lunch right here, if that's okay with you, Hawkins?"

"This is fine." He knew he really had no appetite at all. He rarely wanted to eat after he'd pulled one of his drinking capers.

"So, I'm just curious Hawkins, why'd you quit Chicago's Finest? You come highly recommended as a cop." He grinned as though he had been clever. "I took the liberty of checking you out, big man. They're pretty tight-lipped over at the precinct, but I was told nothing but A-plus marks for Cleve Hawkins. Care to add anything?"

Cleve shook his head. "Every job has its drawbacks. Sometimes there's a lot of in-fighting that doesn't set well, and when a man has had enough of that, he knows. He moves on."

A waitress stopped by with tray and an order pad. She was a bit overweight, but attractive, in a Dorothy McGuire sort of way. Beads of perspiration were visible on her forehead when she leaned over to straighten up the condiments on their table. She was an older, handsome woman with perfectly cut, shoulder-length graying hair and striking blue eyes. Her name tag read Trudy.

"What can I get for you gentlemen, today?"

"Go ahead, Hawkins."

"Coffee for me...if it's fresh, Trudy."

Albers looked at Cleve and grinned.

"Coffee? Really? Don't tell me you're a teetotaler, Hawkins?" He grinned again and, looking at Trudy, said, "Give me a double Jack on the rocks, please. Twist of lemon. Thanks." He looked at Cleve. "Where were we?"

"You asked me why I quit the police force." He hesitated. "Somewhere in their careers, most cops come to a bad-tasting conclusion about themselves. They realize they are in danger of becoming like the people they have investigated and put behind bars. But when people lie to you on a daily basis, and lawyers work on behalf of killers and drug lords—or you investigate cases involving child abuse so horrendous your beliefs are called into question—you have to re-evaluate your own life and outlook in the ways normally reserved for saints. At that time you check your belief in justice and protection of innocent people or you don't. I still feel comfortable in my skin. I'd rather regret the things I do rather than the things I didn't do."

"That's a pretty deep philosophy, detective."

Cleve nodded. "So, not to change the subject, senator, but let's get down to it." He lowered his voice. "What's this about paying a quarter of a million to a blackmailer?"

Albers now seemed slightly off guard.

"Please . . . Call me Gerry, if you don't mind, detective. It's a pleasure talking with someone outside of the government surplus, by the way. I'm usually strapped to lobbyists or my senate cohorts day after day. This is truly refreshing."

"Okay, it'll be Gerry, for now at least," Cleve said. "If things go south for some reason, I may go back to calling you Senator." He paused. "So, what's going on, Gerry?"

Trudy brought their drinks. "You guys want to order, or do you want to wait a while?"

Albers said, "Give us a few minutes, please, Trudy."

"Yeah, sure. Whenever you're ready. Take your time."

Albers shifted just a bit in his seat and leaned in. Lowering his voice, he cleared his throat.

"So far I've given them 250,000 dollars. That's not chump change, by any stretch, but there's more to it with these evil bastards."

Cleve nodded. "There always is."

Albers took a sip of his drink. "Alright, I'll lay it all out for you, Hawkins. They're not just after money. That never was their deal. At least not entirely, as I found out when I made the last payment."

"Go on."

"There's an agriculture bill being put in front of the senate called the Collier Wheat Bill. I don't expect you to understand, but it's tied to subsidies that I've been trying to push through the house. It's been in the works for some time, and if it passes, a bunch of our Illinois farmers—indeed, farmers all over the country—should benefit."

"So what's wrong with that?" Cleve focused on the senator's eyes. "You haven't told me about the pictures of your wife that are floating around, Gerry. Let's start there, shall we?"

CHAPTER THIRTEEN

The senator had seemed jarred when Hawkins mentioned the blackmail pictures.

"Hulce told you about the pictures, then?"

"Of course, Gerry. But don't hold it against Corky. I make it my place to find out everything I can before I step in a pile of horseshit. Tell me about the pictures, okay?"

Albers glanced from side to side, then back at Hawkins.

"They called me five or six weeks ago and told me they had something I should see immediately...if I didn't want a huge fucking scandal on my hands. So I agreed to meet a guy over on Clark Street that following Sunday morning. It was a Thursday when they called me at my office."

Hawkins interrupted. "Why do you keep looking around like a spy from Interpol, senator? We're safe here, okay? Nobody's listening. So, you were saying?"

Albers rubbed his eyes and shook his head. "You don't understand, Hawkins. This whole thing could ruin me. Just the mere mention of blackmail tied to my name in today's world would do it."

"Look, I understand all that, but you will have to learn to trust me if we are going to stop these people. And you have to be straight up with me, too. No bullshit. Understand?"

Albers sighed and nodded. "I understand. It's just all new to me and I'm worried sick. I haven't had a decent night's sleep in weeks, for Christ's sake. These blackmailing bastards are out to get me."

"What do you mean?"

"Well, it's all part and parcel of the same package. I suppose you have to know it all."

He sipped his whiskey and chased it with water before continuing, still in a clandestine tone.

"It's not just the money they want from me. If they can get me to vote thumbs down on the bill, it would give their interests an opening to win the gubernatorial election next year. They're holding those pictures over my head in order to make me stop the legislation with my negative vote. The bastards want me to simply shelve the bill. I'm supposed to back it out of committee by arguing that we can't possibly fund such a bill for at least two more years. Of course, by then the elections will be over."

"And at the same time they rake in some big money from you for themselves."

"Yes." He nodded and lowered his eyes. "And I can't be sure they won't demand more either. God knows when they'll stop pulling my strings. And Trish . . . poor Trish, what will she do when she finds out about this?" He rubbed his forehead. "That's a stupid question. She'll blame herself, of course. They've got me by the short hairs."

"You've already given them the quarter million, right? Because your pal Hulce wasn't too clear on that." He paused and searched the senator's face for answers. "How do you know this tavern owner, by the way? How does he fit in the picture?"

Albers gave a heavier sigh.

"Corky Hulce is an old buddy of mine from school. He has always had a lot of connections. So, after meeting with the thug that Sunday, I was scared. The guy was pissed off because I only brought fifty-thousand with me that day. He told me he wanted the rest of the quarter million by the following Sunday. I ran to see Corky to ask for help."

"Go on. Tell me the rest."

"Well, then he brought Maclam in. I didn't have anything to do with that, but as it turned out it was a good idea. Maclam is connected with the mob, but he's a good man. I guess he heard about you somehow...and, well, you know the rest."

"Maclam is a jailbird."

Albers rubbed the back of his neck.

"Yeah, well, I can use a good bodyguard, you know. Especially now. Cliff is alright for pumping gas and using a GPS correctly, but he's not handy for the dirty jobs. If you get what I mean?"

"Yeah, okay. So let's get back to the pictures. What happened when you met the guy that Sunday? And who was he, anyway?"

"Hell, I don't know who he was. He looked like a thug and acted like one. He didn't give me his name, for Christ's sake. After I gave him a briefcase with the fifty thousand, he let me see a brown envelope full of pictures, but he wouldn't let me keep them. He gave me a week to come up with the rest of it." Albers shook his head and rolled his eyes. "They were five-by-sevens of Trish and another couple having sex." He paused. "Every position you can imagine, Hawkins. They were terrible, I tell you."

He took a big swallow of the Jack Daniels and coughed.

"I gave him two hundred grand the following Sunday. And by the way, my wife knows about absolutely none of this. Zilch. I had to be very careful in withdrawing the money from our savings." He shook his head. "It's her money. I mean, it's coming out of our savings account, but it's really her money."

"What's hers is yours and vice-versa, though, right?"

"Yeah, well, I keep the books and pay all the bills, but she would have a stroke if she knew I was paying blackmail to anybody, that's for damned sure."

"So, you feel like you're stealing from her, is that it?"

Albers nodded. "Trish doesn't know I made either of the payoffs."

The waitress came by. Albers looked at Cleve.

"You fellas want another drink or are we ready to order?" Trudy asked.

Albers held up his tumbler and tinkled the ice cubes. "I'll have another Jack, same way, please."

"Another coffee too, Trudy," Cleve said.

"Okay. I'll be right back. Our menu's right there in case you want to look it over."

Albers continued, "Like I said, I'd only brought fifty grand with me to the first meeting." He saw Cleve's sour expression and shrugged. "Hey, put yourself in my place. I had no idea who I was dealing with, or if he would even show up. There were too many 'what ifs,' know what I mean?" Albers' eyes widened. "Well, I couldn't very well go to the cops, could I? Imagine the scandal. I had no choice. I agreed to that second meeting in order to get the pictures in my hands and get the dirty sonsabitches off of my back once and for all, know what I mean? I don't think Trish realizes somebody has invaded her privacy. I'm still not sure how they did that, myself."

"So, I'm thinking you've got the pictures stashed away. Or did you burn them?"

"No, I have them in a safety deposit box at the bank."

" So, you actually believe that's the end of it, huh? You're probably thinking these guys have given you everything, is that it?" Hawkins dusted his hands and smirked. "Just like that. Bingo! You paid, you got the pictures, game over. Is that what you believe, Gerry, or is it what you want to believe?"

"What choice did I have?"

Cleve followed Albers' troubled eyes that still roamed from side to side.

"And, when did you plan on telling your wife about all this, Gerry? She's going to find out sooner or later." Cleve sighed. "How'd she come by all that money, anyway? Hope you don't mind my asking. It is important."

The senator took another sip of his drink and sat back, somewhat more relaxed.

"Trish's father left her a bundle in his will eight years ago. He died shortly after we were married. Hell of a guy. He owned a meat-packing outfit. Trish was his little girl, you know what I mean?"

"I get the picture."

"Anyway, the old man drank too much and died of cirrhosis. But he left Trish in good shape and, by the marriage, me."

"Tell me, Gerry. Do you and your wife have a good sex life? I mean are you into swinging, that kind of thing?"

Albers' face paled.

"What?" Guilt plastered his face like that of a teenage boy caught masturbating. "What do you mean? Hell, no! We have a good sex life by ourselves, Hawkins." He smiled. "Ha! I sure as hell don't need to invite anybody else into our bed." He sat back and took a big swallow of his drink. "Why would you ask me such a fool thing, anyway?"

"Pretty reasonable question, I think, Gerry, considering those pictures of your wife showed her having sex with a couple of your friends . . . friends to both of you, the Colliers. You know the Democratic Rep, Collier and his wife, Jill? You say why would I ask such a thing? Because I know for a fact that you have engaged in threesomes with Jill Collier. Isn't that right?"

The senator's face changed from chalky white to a telltale pink in seconds. His eyes lowered and he shook his head.

"Alright. Are you going to help me or not, Hawkins? At this point, it sounds like you're just going to needle me about my transgressions. I don't need that, especially now."

Cleve sipped his coffee and leaned on his elbows.

"Listen, senator. I personally don't care who you and your wife fuck, okay? It's really none of my business. But your lying to me damned sure is my business. I told you my requirements—most important thing being I need you to always be absolutely straight with me. You can lie to the cops all you want—perhaps even to your priest or your asshole lawyer, if you choose to get one—but do not, I mean do not, ever lie to me again or I am gone. Is that clear?"

"I...uuuh, I'm not sure exactly when I lied to you, Mister Hawkins."

"You're not? Well, that figures. The bit about you not being involved with swinging when you know damned well that's a lie. You told your friend as much, but just now you lied to me. Really, senator? You guys are so used to wading in bullshit, you don't recognize the truth."

Albers lowered his head. "Okay, maybe just now, but that's all. I apologize." He spoke into the table. "It's embarrassing, that's all."

Cleve nodded. "No more bullshit. Do we understand each other, Gerry?"

"Yes, of course." He raised his right hand in an oath-taking gesture. "No more lying."

Cleve draped his arm across the back of the booth and sighed.

"You're involved in a first class clusterfuck, senator."

"Oh, I know, and I'm just sick about it. Like I said, Trish doesn't know about any of this. She'll have a fit when she finds out, and it will break her heart if any of those pictures see the light of day. You understand, Hawkins? I have to keep her in check somehow, besides all the rest of the shit I'm trying to handle. I've paid them all that money, and they still might be holding something to make sure I stay in line for that bill."

Cleve sat up straight and patted Albers' hand.

"Alright, slow down, Gerry. Let's get your head screwed on straight. First of all, do you think you could ID the guy you gave the money to?"

"You mean like in a lineup or something?"

"Maybe. But, at first we'll just try to finger him using the mug shots at the police department. We'll see after that."

"The police?" Gerry shook his head. "Oh, no. Uuh-uuh. I can't get the cops involved, don't you see that?"

"Settle down, Gerry. The cops don't have to know why we are looking through those books. I still have friends at the department who won't ask any questions. Plenty of friends."

"Well, if you think it will be safe, fine. I guess so, yeah. There wouldn't be other cops watching me, right? I mean it would sort of be private and all?"

"It's all done in privacy. Quit worrying about your friggin' image, senator. You'll be fine. I'll handle it. I'll line it up and get back to you. I may have to see those photos, too, whether you like it or not."

Albers glared at Hawkins.

"Meanwhile, let me know if you hear from these assholes again. Call me right away, night or day, if you do. You are not to give these clowns any more money either. None. Zip. Nada. And say nothing to anybody from here on in. That includes your bar buddy, Hulce. Understand? It sounds like the mob may be behind this, so whatever you do, keep your mouth shut." He leaned back in the booth and looked the senator squarely in the eye. "And don't let your alligator mouth overload your hummingbird ass."

CHAPTER FOURTEEN

Truck was a big man with a fat stomach and thick arms. He had big head, as well, with a wide nose and a dimpled chin. His hair was black and close-cropped, with traces of silver on the sides, and something or someone had placed a nasty gash over what was once a right eyebrow, leaving him with a mean-looking, telltale scar.

He sat quietly on the porch, sipping lemonade and watching the sun slip lower toward the horizon, appearing and disappearing amid the gathering clouds of evening.

He plugged his cigar into the corner of his mouth. The stubble on his face had grown thick since shaving that morning.

"With any luck at all," he said, "we can take care of Albers, whether he wants to go along or not."

Big Jake Caldwell set his glass on the coffee table and watched the condensation forming around the edges. He'd taken only a few sips of the lovely caramel colored McMasters and water. He licked his lips, lit a cigarette and played with the cane at his side, stroking the silver handle. He grinned, tilted his head to the side.

"Since when do we need any luck—good or bad?" he said. "We just need the right man for the job, that's all. Don't you agree?"

He laughed, spilling smoke out of his nose before he waved the little blue cloud away with his free hand.

"I've met Concho. He's the same guy you sent to meet Senator Albers with our deal?"

"Yeah, that's him. But it wasn't Concho's fault the Senator only brought fifty grand. That wise-ass politician was going to screw us on the deal, no matter who you'd sent that day. Concho convinced him he'd better have the rest the following Sunday."

"No shit?"

"Yeah, I told you that before, boss. Remember? I went with him the second go-round and watched the way Concho operates. He's smooth. No problem. When we got our other two-hundred, we left him shitting his pants."

"Sounds like the senator is going along just about the way we planned then, doesn't it?"

"Yeah." Truck nodded. "I'd say he's all ours now, and we can twist him anyway we see fit."

"Good, let's make sure we keep him that way." He rolled his eyes and sipped the scotch while his leg rocked back and forth over his knee.

"No problem, boss. In fact, Albers was still shaking when we left him. Man, I tell you that fuckin' Concho...he don't just look mean, he smells mean. Know what I'm saying, boss?"

Jake shook his head and raised his hand. "I agree. After I met him, I was convinced, as a matter of fact. I'd rather have a colonoscopy with a garden hose than deal with Concho." He laughed, spilling more smoke out of his nose. "I'm still holding you personally responsible if any of this deal turns sour, though."

Truck nodded. "Now, if that's out of the way, I've got something else to bring to your attention, boss."

"Jesus Christ. What else?" He stood and started pacing the floor, as if he thought walking would make things better in some way. "Okay . . . go ahead. Spit it out." He'd finished his cigarette, coughed, and started a new one.

"Well, word is your friend, Albers, has hired a private detective to find who's blackmailing him. Albers knows it ain't no small-timer and he wants the name of the man behind it all, so he can hang him."

"Well, I find that hard to believe. For one thing, Albers ain't got the balls. And, anyway, just how did you come by that crock of shit, my friend?"

"I'm serious, boss. A couple of the guys picked it up while they were shooting pool over at The Dewdrop. I don't know the exact words or who said it, but it boiled down to this snoop had been hired to shadow us."

"Us? Who's 'us,' Truck?"

"You and me and Gwen, I guess."

"Gwen? Why in the hell would they want somebody to shadow my woman?" He waved his hands dismissively. "It's all bullshit, I tell you. Look at the greaseballs who hang out over there at that shithole. I wouldn't even trust them with my skivvies at the laundromat, much less a bullshit rumor like that."

He crossed his arms over his protruding belly as he paced, then stopped to face Truck.

"You hanging out with bums like that? Ha! Believe me, you need to put guys who spread that shit in your rearview."

"Just letting you know what I heard, boss. That's the word on the street."

"And I'm telling you, fuck that noise. Understand?"

"Sure, Jake. Whatever you say."

Feathery clouds had stolen into the sky and the wind had picked up. Leaves rattled across the street and gathered against the side of Jake's red storage barn.

"Jake, I hear bullshit like that all the time, where me and the boys hang out. I usually don't let it faze me, ya' know? But this sounded too real to be made-up, boss, and I figured you should know, that's all. Maybe some of it could be real."

Jake shrugged and sat down.

"So, Albers hired a snoop? Big deal. Why should we be worried about it? He ain't gonna find anything. We're squeaky clean." He rolled his eyes. "Unless there's something you haven't told me, Truck."

"No, Jake. You know me better than that."

"I sure as hell hope so. Let me remind you what's real and what's not."

Truck shifted in his chair. "You mean real like in The Godfather? The honest-to-God Mafia . . . like in the movies, only for real?"

"Yeah, my friend, the outfit. That's right. Look, when I was about twenty-five, me and a buddy named Jerry went with this Italian gumbah who was collecting for a capo." He glared at Truck, who looked anxious. "Yeah, well, you know, captain or capo, same thing. Anyway, it seems some tavern owner on the South Side come up short on his vig. He was skimming and the big boss knew it. So, when the owner was about to close, at three in the morning, he locked the front door and told me and Jerry to close all the doors and windows in the back room." Jake smirked. "When we were done, we got to watch while he slipped another greaseball in through a side door. That guy held the owner down on the floor while he proceeded to cut off most of the poor bastard's ear with a pair of tin snips. I can still hear the guy screaming."

Gwen had been inside the house making snacks. She stepped out onto the porch just as Jake was finishing the story. She was an attractive, forty-ish woman with natural blonde hair and rare green eyes, the narrow eyes of someone who blames everyone but herself for the bad times in her life.

"Honey, I wish you wouldn't tell that story no more. You promised me. People will think you're mean and cruel." She skirted around and, slithering past his hand holding the cigarette, plopped onto his lap.

Jake shifted to make room for her.

"No problem, babe. I just won't tell it anymore." He winked at Truck. "Did you make us some good chow, Baby Girl?"

She kissed the tip of his nose. "You're so cute, Jakey," she said in her two-pack-a-day voice. "Yes, I've got some stacked corned beef sandwiches on rye with pickles and chips...whenever you two are ready."

"We're ready. We'll be right in. You go ahead and give us a minute, okay?"

Gwen slid off of his lap. "Okay. You come in soon though. I don't want the corned beef to get cold."

Jake waited until she disappeared into the living room before he spoke again.

"Okay, so you keep your eyes open and your ears to the ground on this private detective shit. I'm not going to lose any sleep over it, but still, if there is somebody hanging around, I want to know about it." He paused before he added, "And let's just be sure we have our shit together. Kapeesh?"

"Yeah, boss. I'm all over it. I'll keep you posted, you got my word. If a detective is really creeping around, we'll un-detect him in a hurry."

Jake laughed. "Even if Albers did hire a private snoop, most of those guys who carry a private ticket couldn't find their asses with both hands and a flashlight."

•   •   •

Cleve stopped by his office to check on Deckle.

The homeless man was walking better. His cot was put away and he was drinking some fresh coffee.

"I'm glad you have some fresh stuff made, Deck. Anybody been here besides you?"

"Nope. Nobody came by and the phone only rang twice. Both times they hung up as soon as they heard that answering machine message thing turn on. I did what you told me to. I didn't go out of here and I didn't answer the phone. I stayed right here all the time, just like you told me, right, Cleve?"

Cleve watched the man's gait as he moved around.

"How's that leg feeling. partner? You seem to be moving around better."

"Yeah, It's feeling a lot better, Cleve. Thanks for letting me stay here, but I have to get moving along pretty soon. You understand?

My friends are going to wonder what happened, you know what I mean, Cleve?"

"I got it, Deck, but listen, I need you to come down to the police department with me."

Deckle stopped mid-step.

"The police department? Oh, no! Why should I go down there? I already told them I don't know who hit me with their car. I already did that, Cleve."

"Easy now, Deck. I didn't say this minute, but in the next day or so, for sure. It's just procedure, my friend. You are the victim of a hit and run and you can possibly ID that guy you saw in the alley. Did you tell the cops about him when you talked to them in the hospital?"

Deckle shook his head. "No, I didn't, but they didn't ask me nothing about that neither, Cleve."

"I understand, partner, but you'll have to make an amendment to your statement with the police and tell them about the alley and Mr. Glick, understand?"

Deckle shook his head. "No, I just want to go home and see my friends, Cleve. I'll come back, I promise."

"You just sit tight, partner. I'll take you wherever you want to go after we go to the police department, okay?"

Cleve stepped inside the bathroom. When he came out, a few minutes later, Deckle was gone.

Damn! I shoulda known better than to trust him. I left him alone here all that time and he stayed put, but after he sees me, he's suddenly in the wind. It's almost like he wanted my permission...or waited to see if I was alright before he split.

Cleve checked the answering machine just to be sure Deckle hadn't forgotten something, then poured a cup of coffee and nursed it while sifting through a few pieces of mail.

He decided to set up something as soon as possible to get the senator into the department to look at some mug shots. Maybe, just maybe, he might get lucky and Albers would make a positive ID. He realized he had no other practical leads in the case, and that seemed like his best shot.

Deckle was another matter.

Images of Mo had been prying into his thoughts more and more with each passing day. He stared at the phone in his palm and thought about making the call. What could he say? At times, especially at night, when he was alone in bed, the words seemed to come easy. He'd found himself preparing a little speech for her just in case he ever had the opportunity again. In other words, if she ever spoke to him again.

I'd be only half a man without you, Mo. I promise you will always be first in my life from now on. You're more than my lover. You're my confidant, my best friend, and all the good things that good women are. No one could ever take your place. There's a glow on your skin. You smell like flowers in the morning and I'll have sexy dreams about you every night for the rest of my life.

Remember that time, about three years ago when we went to that little place on Armitage for a candlelight dinner? It was called Geja's and you thought it was very romantic and we both felt something special that night. I think about that night all the time, Mo. Give us another chance, huh? I promise I won't mess up again, ever.

He said to himself aloud, yet whispery quiet, "Yeah, I'll call and tell you all of those things, Mo. . . just not right now."

CHAPTER FIFTEEN

The following morning Hawkins dressed in jeans and a wool vest over a white dress shirt. He also wore the lightweight Chicago Cubs windbreaker that hid his .30 caliber Smith and Wesson and shoulder holster.

After over fifteen years, he felt naked if he wasn't carrying for some reason. Better to have a gun and not need it than to need a gun and not have it, he thought.

He drank two cups of coffee, and at eight-fifteen called his old partner at Chicago Police Headquarters. Lieutenant Harvey Ashbaugh had been a Sergeant for eight years in the Robbery Homicide Division before Cleve left the force. At one time they had been partners. Now Ashbaugh was the man in charge of the entire robbery section in RHD.

Maureen worked in the same building with Hawkins and Ashbaugh, but had long since been transferred to the secretary pool over in the Sex Crimes Unit. Cleve considered the possibility of accidentally running into her while he was in the complex. That would be awkward, but he realized the probability of it happening was slim to none. He would not let it be an overriding concern in any event.

The two men agreed to meet in Ashbaugh's office at nine-thirty that morning.

Knowing Ashbaugh's penchant for donuts, Cleve stopped by the Dunkin' Donuts at 600 Wabash Avenue and picked up a dozen mixed. He arrived at headquarters on Michigan Avenue fifteen minutes early.

The Major Crimes Division was a special investigative group based in the Police Administration Building along with the other elite detective groups. MCD's hot, headline cases of multiple homicides and celebrity victims meant their detectives caught way more nightly news time than a divisional section head like Ashbaugh.

His office was on the first floor of the aging headquarters building. Cleve always thought the surroundings smelled faintly of sweat, old coffee and office chemicals. It held all the warmth of a cyanide factory. The hallways were already buzzing with suited civilians and uniformed officers just after nine-fifteen that morning. The lobby had twenty-four-hour security and Cleve had a pass.

Ashbaugh's squad room was large, bright, and filled with partitioned cubicles. Conference rooms lined an inner wall and offices with views lined the outer wall. The narrow, gray two-person cubicles could just as well have housed a bunch of accountants.

A uniformed officer at a nearby desk sat with his legs out and his arms crossed. He watched Cleve as if he'd already had a long day and it was going to be longer. He also watched a shapely blonde drinking water from the fountain, his eyes glued on her ass. His view abruptly changed direction when he spotted Cleve looking at him.

At nine-thirty on the dot, Ashbaugh opened his door. Spotting the Dunkin Donuts box under his old partner's arm, he said, "Damn, Sherlock. If I had known you'd brought donuts, I would have let you in sooner."

The two men shook hands.

"How the hell are you, Hawk?"

"Good. Real good. Hangin' in there, Harve. We both know there's not much other choice, right?"

"You've got that right."

The lieutenant wasted no time and cracked open the box, picked two coconut-laden donuts, and took a seat behind his desk.

As he took a bite of a donut, a few shaved sprinkles fell across his desk like snow. He carefully set them on his day planner and reached for his coffee. His mug read, "Go ahead. Make my day."

Ashbaugh swiveled in his executive chair, took another bite of the donut and said, "So, what's on your mind, Hawk?"

"So, nothing much, LT."

"Cleve, I know you better than that. You didn't come flittin' around headquarters after all this time to deliver donuts like the freakin' sugar fairy for nothing. So whaddya want?"

He smiled and took a sip of coffee.

Cleve raised his hands in surrender.

"Okay, you got me, Harve. I need a favor." He paused to pull a plain donut out of the box. "You know, sometimes I feel like a damned dinosaur. In the technological revolution, I usually feel like I have chosen the wrong side. I can make a computer do what I need it to do—which isn't much—but in the last couple of years with the rise of Facebook and other online media, I feel like I have been overrun on the information highway and just left behind. As far as I'm concerned, tweeting comes from birds and a post is something that holds up a fence."

Harve laughed. "Stop, already, Hawk. You're making my heart bleed for Chrissakes."

"Harve, you field sympathy as awkwardly as a shortstop with a catcher's mitt. But okay, yeah, I need a small favor . . . well, actually a big one, coming from you. If you can help me out, I won't make you pay for the rest of those donuts."

"It's been one hell of a long time since we've had a cup of coffee together, Hawk." He grinned. "We had some good times in those days, eh? Most of the time it was a big load to carry, but we handled things pretty damned good, I think. Yeah, and I have to admit I miss those stakeouts as much as I hated the long hours spent doing nothing, you might say." He shook his head. "So, what's up? What can I do for you, partner?"

"It's not too complicated, really, Harve. I need access to your mug shot books for a few hours. I have a client who needs to ID a perp for me. By his MO, I figure he must have been tagged for something."

"I don't see a problem there. Bring your client in and we'll give him the right of way. I can arrange that. Wait. Is this a case that my people should be made aware of?"

Cleve shook his head no.

"Good. Then it's no big deal."

"Thanks, Harve."

"How are you liking that gumshoe game anyway? I hear there's good money to be made."

"Business can be good at times. You know, most of my cases make their way to me by way of the grapevine or the underbelly off the street."

"Cheating husbands and wives club, I imagine, huh?"

"You got it. Things have gotten interesting at times, though. Remember the Kris Branoff deal a couple years back?"

"Hell, yes. How could I ever forget that whole serial rapist deal? Who would have guessed Branoff was dirty? I liked Kris. Most of us did. But, you know, I've never understood our collective unwillingness to question the authority of a predator who happens to acquire a badge or insignia or a clerical collar or who carries a whistle on a lanyard around his neck. Without our sanction, these pitiful excuses for human beings would wither and die like amphibians gasping for oxygen and water on the surface of Mars."

"Amen," said Cleve. "That's quite a spiel you've got there, lieutenant."

They laughed, and there was a brief pause in the conversation.

"You and Mo still an item?"

"Sometimes yes, sometimes no. You know how that goes."

"You two need to marry up, Hawk."

"Yeah, well, we'll see."

Another silence invaded the room for a beat.

"Well, okay. So, I can see where a few bucks could be made doing private jobs. Am I right?"

"Depends."

"Well, I wouldn't begin to ask you what you're charging for your services...but how much?"

"Let's just say you're probably still pulling down more than I am a year, Ash. Plus you get that pension when you turn over your badge."

"Yeah, there's that." His voice dropped off as he said, "You want to come back, Hawk? I think that could be arranged...anytime. You know that. Like I told you before, you might take a dip in salary, but so what? There would still be the pension."

Cleve shook his head.

"I appreciate that, Harve, but not right now."

"You don't want to wait too much longer. I don't need to tell you you're not getting any younger."

"I know, but listen, Harve, there is one little hitch to the favor I'm asking."

"I knew it." He tilted back in his chair and locked his fingers together behind his head. "Okay. Now, let's have it all. What do you need, exactly, Hawk?" He plucked a jelly donut from the box, took a bite and a swallowed it with some coffee.

"My client is high profile and most likely recognizable, so we need to let him have access to those books at night, when traffic isn't as heavy around here. He expects privacy and, besides, you don't need the hassle of explaining his presence in your squad room."

"Hmmm. Now you've got my curiosity aroused, partner. Mind telling me who this client is? You have my word, it won't go any further."

"You know, I am supposed to respect client privilege, but I also know you can spot my guy anytime you want with your squad room cameras, so what the hell...it's Senator Gerald Albers."

Ashbaugh whistled softly. "Damn! You do get the big fish, don't you, partner?"

"Well, this one actually fell in my lap, to be honest."

"Yeah, well I won't put you on the spot by asking any more questions. Maybe someday you'll be able to fill me in."

"Thanks, Harve. I appreciate it."

"I've got your back, Hawk. If anybody questions you about being back there in records after hours, you tell them they can call me at home. How long do you figure you'll be, anyway?"

"Well, I'm not sure. I want him to take his time and go through all the books...if need be. I already have our suspect compartmentalized by age, race, the usual nullifiers, so that trims it down a little. We'll get it done in one night, hopefully, if he spots the guy we're looking for. I don't know. No guarantees, but we'll do the best we can, I can promise you that. In and out, I hope."

Ashbaugh settled back a bit and eyed him. One knee crossed over the other, and he tossed his foot for a moment while he studied Cleve.

"When do you want to do this?"

Cleve stood up to leave. "Believe it or not, I'm thinking tonight, Ash, if that's okay. I think I can line the senator up. He's as anxious to nail this guy as I am."

Ashbaugh stood and the two men shook hands.

"I'll alert my night shifters. I'm just glad we could help. Good luck, partner."

Cleve thought about reporting Deckle as a missing person while he was at the police department, but he didn't see anything to be gained by doing so. Without Deckle's statement he had nothing to go on. Instead, he would wait the little man out and go from there when he turned up.

He stopped for lunch at Flo and Santos Pub and Pizza on South Wabash and called Albers' private number. The senator was in agreement for that night and would meet Cleve in the Barnes and Noble bookstore at State and Division at seven o'clock.

Later, when Cleve went to retrieve his car from the parking garage, the autumn sun had turned into a red ember inside a bank of maroon-colored clouds above the Chicago skyline.

CHAPTER SIXTEEN

Hawkins waited for Senator Albers inside the bookstore on the corner. It was ten after seven and Albers was a no-show. Cleve had gone through one grande black coffee and was working on a second.

At seventeen after the hour, Albers strolled in the front door with an air of nonchalance. He spotted Cleve at the magazine racks and sidled up to him.

He whispered, "Sorry, I'm late. I was tied up at the office."

Cleve nodded and motioned for him to follow him to a table in a corner of the cafe where they took seats.

"Maybe we need to get one more thing straight between us, senator. I swear by dependability. I expect you to do the same as long as we're working together."

"Yeah, I know and I'm sorry, but . . ."

"No 'but's.' There are phones, and I know you have one. You could have called. This is serious business. When I have people lined up to help us out, I cannot expect them to understand why we're late. Understand?"

Albers' voice was just above a whisper. "Okay, I get it. I'll be prompt from now on. You have my word. I'll make it work."

Cleve nodded. "That's what I want to hear. Now, where are you parked?"

"I'm not. I have to call my driver when I'm done and he'll pick me up." He gave Cleve a sidelong glance. "Is that alright?"

"Yeah, sure. Must be nice," he murmured as he glanced at his watch. "Okay. It's getting late. Let's get moving. Traffic is still going to be a pain in the ass."

"Fine. Mind if I grab a quick latte?"

Cleve glanced at the line of five customers at the checkout counter and his eyes widened.

"You can't be serious."

Albers saw Cleve's face redden.

"No, of course not. Sorry. I'm ready. Let's go."

After overcast skies for the better part of the day, the clouds now broke open and hammered them with a downpour so fierce, Cleve's wipers were useless.

They drove in silence for the first few blocks before Albers spoke.

"In all of my time as a senator, I don't believe I have ever been to the Chicago Police Department. Where is it exactly?"

Cleve glanced over at him.

"You're shitting me. Never?"

Albers shook his head. "No, I haven't. Where is it located?"

Cleve sighed. "On South Michigan Avenue."

Another block of silence passed between them before Albers spoke again.

"Can I tell you something, Mister Hawkins?"

"Shoot."

"Well, quite frankly, you seem to be a nice enough guy, but you also seem to come off like, I don't know, a hard ass. Are you always, I don't know, so hard to get along with?"

Cleve glanced over at him and cleared his throat.

"Listen, senator, there are few creatures on this earth more pigheaded than cops. I can say that with surety because I was one. I may no longer carry a police department badge, but that isn't what being a cop means."

"I'm not sure what you are saying."

"Just this. As a cop you never let your guard down. The ones who did are not with us anymore. Understand? That instilled discipline rubs off on you all through your life. So, a cop is a cop, regardless of status, regardless of uniform, regardless of agency and regardless of age. Being a cop is in my nature. It's in the bones. If you take that to mean I am a hard ass, as you call it, then I am."

"I see."

"Do you?"

"Yes, I think I do." He paused. "I know you better than you think. I had you checked out. People say you're a straight shooter."

"Maybe. Tell me, senator, do you know anybody who would want to harm you or your wife for any reason?"

Albers turned sideways and faced him. "You don't think somebody would come after me, do you?"

"Anything is possible. If these people want something badly enough—as you say they do—they could turn to any measure imaginable."

"Oh, my God, Mister Hawkins. You're scaring me."

"Good. A little bit of that won't hurt you. Keeps you on your toes. But take what I tell you to heart, and you can avoid a lot of problems." He paused and looked at Albers. "Understand?"

"Yes, I think I do."

"Now, we're almost there. When we get inside the complex, with all due respect, senator, I want you to keep your mouth shut. I will do the talking. Are we clear?"

"Yes."

Cleve parked in the on-duty officers parking lot. He turned off the ignition and looked at Albers in the dim lighting provided by the few light poles in the parking lot.

"What if somebody recognizes me? I mean I would be hard-pressed to explain what I am doing in the police department—much less being here during at night."

"That part is taken care of. As I told you earlier, on the phone, the traffic here at night is minimal. Working officers are on the street for the most part. We may run into a few desk officers, or maybe even some civilians who work here, but they won't bother us."

"You seem pretty sure, Mister Hawkins. I'll trust you."

"Hold it. Before we go any further, I want you to stop calling me, 'Mister,' sir."

A look of surprise came into Albers' eyes. "What? Why?"

"You calling me 'Mister' is making me uncomfortable. 'Mister Hawkins' died almost eighteen years ago. From now on call me Cleve, or Hawk, or even Hawkins, but save the 'Mister' for your constituents, okay?"

Albers shrugged. "Sure. Whatever you say, Mister Hawkins."

Cleve stopped walking and glared at him. "Are you trying to be a smartass, senator?"

"No, sir. Just forgot."

Once inside, Cleve led the way to the elevator and from there they went up to the Records Section on the fourth floor. Locks clinked and clunked before the door labeled "Records & Archives" buzzed and opened.

Hawkins approached the service desk with Albers at his side.

The officer on duty was a slugger, a corporal who weighed perhaps three-hundred pounds, his chin sunk into the folds of fat around his neck. He had the body of a Greek god who lived on pasta. The officer shifted in his chair, ducking his head as he looked up distractedly from the papers on the desk. He shoved his glasses up on his nose, then took them off as he walked to the counter. "Fletcher" his name plate read,

"Can I help you, gentlemen?"

Cleve pulled his creds and showed them to Fletcher. "Yes, Lieutenant Ashbaugh gave us clearance to look through the mug books tonight."

He referred to his notes, licking the tip of a thick finger and paging through them. He had noticeably big hands, and even though everything seemed to fit him fine, his hands were so big that it made him look like his sleeves were too short.

"Ah, yes. You're Hawkins, right?"

Cleve smiled at him. "Yes, that's right. And, this is my associate, Bill Ford."

"Yeah, the lieutenant said you might have a guest with you. No need to see his ID as long as he's with you." He slid a clipboard in front of them. "Just sign in here, please, and I'll take you back." He chuckled. "Good luck finding everything you want. Johnny Cushman is the civilian in charge of that section. He's a good man, but he's got the organizing savvy of a junkyard falling down a spiral staircase."

He glanced at the clipboard after the two men had signed in. "Okay, follow me, gentlemen." He led the way, waddling like a pregnant woman, his belly preceding him down the hallway.

Once back in the shelves with the mug books, Fletcher said, "As you can see, there are one hell of a lot of books." He pointed along the shelves. "They're supposed to be in alphabetical order. Help yourselves, and good luck."

"Thanks, Fletcher. Hopefully, we won't be too long."

Fletcher waved a hand dismissively. "I've heard that a few times. But it makes no difference to me. Take all the time you need. Hell I'm here until seven am."

He started to leave, then turned. "There's a pot of Joe up front if you want, Hawkins. Feel free to help yourselves."

"Thanks. I think I will."

He pulled one of the books for Albers. "Go ahead, Bill. Take a seat and dig in. I'm going to get a cup of coffee. You want one?"

Albers sat down at the wooden table and opened the book. "Yeah." He smiled and looked up. "That would be great, Hawk. Thanks."

Time seemed to drag by for Cleve. Two and a half hours later, Albers had his suit coat hanging on the back of the chair and his sleeves rolled up. He was studying one page for an unusual amount of time, Cleve thought.

"You haven't got time to read histories, champ. Just look at each page and move on, okay?"

"But, these information charts with each mug shot are very interesting, you know?"

Cleve sat with his feet up on a desk. "Just stay on point here, senator, okay?"

Cleve went back to reading yesterday's copy of the *Chicago Tribune* he'd found on top of a filing cabinet. He yawned and headed up front to get another cup of coffee for both of them. It was his fifth cup, Albers' third.

At five-forty-five in the morning, Albers said, "Here he is!"

"Oh, yeah? Let's see." He went over to look at Albers' selection.

"Hmmmm. Jesus Martinez, eh? Are you sure, senator?"

Albers eyes widened as he continued to jab a finger at the mug shot he had singled out. "Oh, yes. I will never forget those mean, dark eyes, or that rough-looking complexion. I'd swear on my mother's life that's him. You think you can pick him up now?"

"Easy, Gerry. This is just a start. A good one, I'll grant you, but still it's not going to be that easy." He pulled a small notepad from the inside pocket of his windbreaker. "Do you think for one minute a punk like that is going to be standing in the middle of Michigan Avenue, waving at us?"

"Well no, of course not, but I just thought . . ."

"Stop thinking."

Hawkins knew that by checking with local records and those of the National Crime Information Center database, it was possible to track this man, and thanks to Harvey, the rap sheets would readily become available.

Hawkins jotted down everything he thought pertinent to aid him in finding Martinez. The mug shot book noted that names the perp had used in the past were Gonzalez, Rodriguez and Samboro. Nicknames were Pedro and Concho.

Cleve noted Martinez was Hispanic, thirty-four years of age, and had spent eight years total in the Illinois prison system. Two years of a four-year sentence he'd served in Joliet Correctional Center, for aggravated assault. He was incarcerated again in Stateville in 2012 and had served five years of a twenty-to-life sentence for manslaughter. Interesting, This guy was a lifer waiting to be caught, Cleve thought.

He had been paroled for good behavior, with eight years probation, less than a year ago. His last known address was on the west side in Humboldt Park. He'd missed appointments with his probation officer for the last eight months.

Albers put his suit coat on. "Are we ready to go, then?"

"Yeah, we're out of here. Come on."

Fletcher met them on their way out of the section. "Did you strike gold, Hawkins?"

"I think we might have gotten lucky, Fletch."

"Good. I hope it works out for you."

Outside, the storm had passed. Thunder was rolling away to the north, leaving behind only the gentle sound of rain as Hawkins and Albers made their way to their car.

Albers immediately got on his cell and called his driver, Cliff, and told him to pick him up in an hour at Wildberry Pancakes on Randolph Street. Cleve was lucky enough to find a parking spot on the street there.

"May I buy you breakfast, Hawk?"

"Thanks, but no thanks, senator. I'll wait with you until your driver shows up, though."

"Sure. Thanks." He cracked his window. "I really do appreciate you guiding me through all of this, you know?"

"Yeah, well, I need you to do something for me, too, Gerry. I want you to tell your wife what's going on. Just level with her. It is very important at this juncture. What was her name again?"

"Her name is Trish."

"Yeah, well, like it or not, my friend, I need to meet Trish as soon as you can arrange it."

CHAPTER SEVENTEEN

When Hawkins got home, he found he had company.

After he had turned his key in the lock and stepped inside the foyer, he saw Big Russ Maclam sitting on the couch in the living room, looking like a huge, misplaced Buddha.

Hawkins quickly pulled his gun and pointed it with two hands, wrists locked, the stance of a pro shooter at the pistol range.

"What the fuck are you doing in my apartment, Maclam?"

"Whoa! Slow down, champ. Don't let that thing go off."

He raised his hands in surrender and grinned.

"I haven't touched a thing. Just making myself comfortable waitin' on you, Sam Spade."

Cleve slowly holstered his gun and tossed his keys in a bowl on the kitchen counter.

"My guests are generally invited before they come in, Maclam. Tell me, what gives you the right to break into my place? I should call the cops, asshole."

"Hey, you weren't home. I wasn't going to stand out in the hall all night. I figured you would want me to be comfortable."

"Bullshit! I don't appreciate bad manners, especially from jailbirds."

"Okay. I hear you. Maybe next time I'll knock before I pick the lock. Can we move on, Hawkins?"

His sarcasm slid off Cleve like oil on Teflon as Hawkins moved to the kitchen, reached in the refrigerator and retrieved a bottle of Old Style. He uncapped the beer and asked, "Okay, so what's up?"

Maclam pulled out a pack of Camels and after sliding one out of the pack, lit up and expelled a thick cloud of smoke which drifted above his head like a halo.

"What's going on with our boy Albers?"

Cleve took a long swig of beer. "What's it to you?"

"Let's just say I have interested parties who are anxious for answers. Besides, I figured on giving you a heads up."

Cleve sat on the arm of his favorite stuffed chair.

"Really now...about what?"

"You've got a shadow."

"Is that so?"

"They're on to you, pal. I'm actually surprised you didn't spot the tail yourself, being the smart snoop you are."

"And how in the hell do you know this?"

"That's not important, Hawkins." He stood up and yawned at the same time. "You need to concern yourself with your back, as well as your front, from now on. Word has it these people are pissed and don't take kindly to interference in their business."

"That's too damned bad because I haven't even begun to stick my nose in things yet." He put his beer on the coffee table and stood up. "I'm just getting started as a matter of fact. And, while I appreciate the heads up—and should probably appreciate you looking out for me—I don't."

He paused and strolled back towards the kitchenette. Turning back around, he said, "By the way, what's in this for you?"

Maclam grinned and shook his head back and forth. "I told you. I have to even up some scores. Certain people owe me a hefty chunk of change, too. I plan to collect."

"Yeah, well, it's time for you to leave. I've got things to do, but I'm warning you, if you bust in here again, I'll rip off your head and shit down your neck."

Maclam moved slowly forward and closed the gap between them. He towered over Cleve. He frowned, and huge wrinkles creased neatly across his mammoth forehead.

"I'll let that go, Hawkins, because I realize you don't know what you're saying. But don't you ever threaten me again."

He edged past Cleve and opened the door as he looked back.

"I was trying to do you a solid, you ungrateful sonofabitch!"

"I don't like threats, big shot, so back off." Cleve walked over to the door. "Good night, Maclam."

The big man kept his eyes glued to Cleve's, then turned and left.

The apartment suddenly felt calm, the tension gone. Hawkins polished off his beer and retrieved another. He dropped into his armchair, relieved that Maclam was out of there.

"Dammit! What next?"

He took a deep breath and tried to relax.

Your plate is getting crowded, Hawkins. Time to regroup and get your shit together. He put his head back and stared at the ceiling. *Deckle? Where in the hell is he? If he doesn't show pretty soon, I'll check the morgue.*

He swallowed more beer.

I've got to call the Senator and line up that interview with his wife. That should be a real grin. What in the hell did Maclam really want? What's his angle?

And Mo. What she's been up to? Is she alright? She probably doesn't even give me a thought. Maybe I should stop sweating the whole dea, and just call her. Call her? Yeah, why not? What have I got to lose that I haven't already lost?

He pulled out his cell. There was one ring. Then two and three. On the fourth ring, Mo picked up.

"Hello?"

The sound of her voice sent chills racing down his spine.

"Hi, Mo. It's me."

Silence took over for what seemed like a full minute.

"Hello, Cleve."

"I just thought I'd check in with you."

"That's nice. It's been quite a while."

"Yes, it has. I wasn't sure you'd take my call." He paused. "Are you okay? Not sick or anything, are you?"

"I had a bad case of the flu right after I got a shot at Walgreens. That was a couple of weeks ago. I'm good now."

"Good. It hasn't hit me yet. I guess I should get that shot."

"You really should."

Awkward silence dominated the conversation for another moment.

"How's everything at the department? Anything special going on?"

"Same old, same old, you know." She paused. "Did you need something, Cleve?"

"Yes, well, as a matter of fact, I do." After a slight pause, he added, "I need you, Mo. I miss you something terrible and I need to talk to you. I'm ready."

"Really?" She hesitated. "Ready for what?"

"Well, I really need to see you in order to explain, if you'd let me."

Another long pause prevailed and Hawkins was afraid he'd scared her off.

Now I'm really done.

"Mo?"

"I'm here." Another long pause. "Why don't you swing by for a while? I guess it wouldn't hurt to talk."

"When?"

"Now, if you want, I guess. I'm just watching reruns of the *Golden Girls.*"

"Okay. Yeah, sure. I'll be there in about forty-five minutes. Is that alright? I just want to jump in the shower."

"Okay. See you then. Bye."

•   •   •

The night was cool and quiet, the stars brilliant in the black sky above him as he drove over to Mo's apartment on Goethe Street. He was jittery as it was, but the traffic made things worse.

He parked the Lexus where he always did, in the parking garage next door to Mo's apartment building. In the outside foyer, he pushed the buzzer on her mailbox. He was glad she answered right away. At least that was encouraging.

"Yes?"

"It's me, Mo."

The inside door buzzed and he thought, so far, so good. After all, this was the closest he had been to Mo in weeks. He took the elevator up to the third floor and knocked on her door.

Mo was in her bare feet when she opened the door, dressed in jeans and a white blouse, tied in front. Her red hair cascaded down her back and she wore little makeup except for glossy pink lipstick.

God, she's beautiful. She knows I like that shade of lipstick, too. Is she wearing that on purpose?

Mo's features were delicate, her nose only a bud of cartilage, her face unlined by sun, age or worry.

His heart was running at a hard clip.

"Mo. You look great."

The hint of a smile showed on her lips. She tucked a wisp of hair behind her ear and nodded.

"Thanks. Come in."

Cleve took a seat on the couch. He ran his hands back and forth over the cushions.

"This must be new, huh?"

"Yeah. I got it a few weeks ago." She turned and headed for the kitchen. "Can I get you something to drink? I've got a few beers in the fridge."

"Since when do you drink beer?"

"I don't. You do." She looked at him over her shoulder. "They're from the last time you graced me with your presence." She came back and handed him a bottle of beer. She had a can of Diet Coke for herself.

Sitting two cushions away from him, Mo spread her arms along the back of the couch and gave him an impersonal smile. She sipped the Diet Coke and seemed lost for a moment in thoughts he had no access to.

There was a kind of tense silence between them.

She tightened her expression and shuffled in her seat, working to look even further in the opposite direction. She looked as though she wanted to jump out of her skin while she waited for him to speak.

Cleve murmured, "Are you still angry, baby? I don't blame you, if you are . . . but are you?"

"I have controlled the anger about what happened between us, Cleve, but it's still down there in my gut. It burns particularly hard when it comes to seeing men hurt women. I see it in my job all the time, you know."

"Yes, I imagine so."

Tears flooded her eyes before she looked away. He must have seen them. He read the panic in her face and quickly set his beer on the coffee table, then scooted over and wrapped his arms around her. She cried hard then, but there was nothing he could do except hold her. He ached for her while she trembled and shivered through it.

He rubbed her back in gentle, circular motions. "Shhhhh. It's going to be okay now. I love you, so much, Mo. I promise I'll make things right between us."

A few minutes passed before she dabbed at her tears with a Kleenex and looked up into his eyes. "It's not rocket science, Cleve. It's really not. It's the same thing I've always wanted, no more, no less. I need to know I am a part of something in your life, that I matter."

"Give me another chance, sweetheart. Honestly, I'll show you just how much you mean to me, Mo."

"Honesty is the root of all failure," she sighed.

"I'm sincere, Mo. I never wanted anything as much as I want you in my life."

She blew her nose, giggled and said, "You know, I can tell you're sincere by that smirk in your eyes."

With that he scooped her up in his arms and carried her into the bedroom. They stood beside the king-sized bed and undressed each other, fingers hurrying, fumbling at buttons.

The heat of the room pressed in on them. Skin went slick with the sweat of desire. Their bodies kissed, hot and wet, flesh to flesh, man to woman. His hands explored her, the soft fullness of a breast, the pink tip of a nipple, the moist lips of her femininity. She touched everything male about him, the hard-ridged muscles of his belly, the crisp dark hair that matted his chest, the rock-hard shaft of his erection, as smooth and hard as a column of marble.

They fell across the crisp sheets, a tangle of limbs, her red hair spilling across the pillow. She arched her body into the touch of his mouth as he kissed the beads of sweat from between her breasts and followed the trail down her belly to the point of her hip, the crease of her thigh, the back of her knee. He tongued the inside of her thigh and she opened herself to the touch of both his hands and his tongue.

"Ooooh, Cleve!" she moaned.

He gently sucked her clitoris between his lips and took her to the brink of fulfillment and then left her hanging there, aching with the need to join her body with his. She looked up at him, her eyes wide, her mouth swollen and cherry red from his kisses. She looked both wanton and hesitant.

He had never wanted a woman more, this sweet wonderful Maureen. Hands at her waist, he guided her astride him.

"Is this what you want?" he asked her.

She eased herself down, taking him deep, her fingertips biting into his shoulders.

"Oh, my God, Cleve!"

They moved together. He held her tight.

"Mmmmm, Mo," he murmured.

Their kisses tasted salty-sweet. Mo felt suspended in the rhythm of their movement, consumed by the intensity of the act. She fell back into the support of his arms and floated while he sucked at her breast. She circled her arms around his shoulders and held tight as the urgency built.

"Open your eyes, Mo," he commanded. "Open your eyes and look at me."

Her gaze locked on his as the end came for both of them. One, and then the other. Powerful. Intimate. More than sex.

He woke hours later, cradling Mo in his arms. The window straight ahead of him let in a butter-yellow morning light through a double layer of sheer white curtains that obscured the view to and from the road.

This is what I want.

He listened to Mo's soft, rhythmic breathing.

I never want to make this woman cry again.

CHAPTER EIGHTEEN

The light seeping in around Mo's bedroom curtains was the gray of predawn on a day that promised gloom and rain.

Cleve was aware of it, but didn't want to move for fear of waking Mo. She was sleeping so peacefully with her head on his chest. He thought about their lovemaking the night before and ached for more.

He felt more grounded than he had in months. He realized he had been given another chance and could not screw up again. Her earlier, scathing words had cut through him like a machete when they replayed in his head.

He promised himself he would never hurt her again.

Mo stirred and caressed his chest with her fingers.

"Mmmm. What time is it?" she murmured.

He glanced at the clock radio on the nightstand.

"Ten after eight, baby."

"Oh, no," she groaned. "I've got to get up, but I don't want to."

"So don't. Take a sick day. The office can get along fine without you, I'm sure."

Mo slithered away from him and sat up. Covering her breasts with the sheet, she continued to tease with her fingertips, but shook her head.

"No can do. We're shorthanded in the section as it is and I already used some sick days when I had the flu. I have to go in." She fell back, propped herself up on her elbows and searched his eyes.

"Last night was wonderful," she purred.

He stroked a few locks of her red hair. "Yes, it was." Cupping a breast, he said, "I've been thinking about an encore."

"It's awfully tempting, Detective Hawkins, but I have to get ready for work or I'll be late." She caressed his cheek. "I wouldn't want to rush our lovemaking like we did last night. Besides, if you really want that encore, I figure you'll be back tonight. What do you say? Deal?"

He kissed her. "Deal."

While she was in the shower Hawkins rolled out of bed and made a pot of coffee. While it was brewing, he walked over to look out the window. The gloomy overcast was not inviting.

Damned rain.

Rain poured down while chic, well-dressed women were picking their way past the rain puddles in their high heels, bending down under the little black umbrellas they all had, most of them holding their skirts down by pressing their left hand and forearm across their thighs as the wind pushed at them.

The aroma of the coffee was enticing and when it finished brewing, he poured himself a cup and put an empty cup in place on the table for Mo. He went to the front door to retrieve the paper.

He skimmed his way through the *Chicago Sun Times* until Mo slipped in from behind and draped her arms over his shoulders. A huge pink bath towel was wrapped around her, but he felt her nipples graze his back. She hadn't put her makeup on yet, and her face was shiny and vulnerable in its early morning innocence.

"You've got time for a cup of coffee, don't you?"

"Sure, but I'm running late, so if you'll pour it while I get dressed, I'd appreciate it."

"Bribery will get you everything, sweetheart." He held her hand and squeezed. As he shifted around in the chair, their eyes met.

"I'll miss you today," he said.

She kissed his forehead. "I always miss you, Cleve. I don't like to admit it, but I've been miserable without you, big man."

They kissed again.

"Let's make it work this time, okay, Cleve? I don't like being apart. It hurts too much, and I don't think I can take it again."

"I know, and I promise I'll be here for you from now on, Mo." He paused a moment and studied her eyes, then held up his right hand, as though swearing an oath. "I promise."

She kissed him again and then pranced off to the bedroom with the towel barely covering her beautiful, heart-shaped ass. A few minutes later, when he heard her coming back, he poured a cup for her.

She kissed him on the cheek and took a sip.

"Thanks. You know I'm not used to being spoiled this early in the morning. I could get to liking it...real fast."

She had put on some pink lipstick to leave a lasting impression with him for the day.

"Good God, Mo, I wish you could stay home today. You sure I can't change your mind?"

"Not a chance, gumshoe. Besides, I'm sure you have an important case to work on, don't you? I'd be surprised if you didn't."

"Yeah, I suppose I do," he sighed.

She gulped down the rest of her coffee and kissed him again. Tossing her cell phone into her purse, she asked, "So, when will I see you again?"

"I really want to come by tonight, and if all goes well with no hitches, I will. But please don't count on it. I'll call this afternoon when I see how things unfurl, okay?"

"Sounds good," she said, finding a smile for him.

"Now I may have to . . ." he added.

She quickly put a finger against his lips and shook her head.

"Just call me."

•   •   •

By the time Hawkins got to his office, thunder broke and an orange light could be seen bleeding out of the clouds in the east. The wind picked up and it was cold.

He parked his car, grumbled and got out, hunching his shoulders and flipping the collar of his jacket up in a vain effort to keep the cold rain off his neck.

He found Deckle huddled up against the door to his office. His hands were buried deep in his pockets, his baseball cap pulled down over his ears.

"Hey, Deck, where in the hell have you been, partner? You okay?"

The frail-looking man shrugged and wiped his running nose on the sleeve of his field jacket.

"I'm . . . I'm good. Jus . . . just hanging out with some fr . . . friends over on Kedzie."

"Oh, yeah?" Hawkins unlocked the front door and stepped inside. He looked at Deckle, who still stood in the same spot. "What are you doing, Deck? Come inside and warm up."

Deckle hustled inside and backed up to the radiator to warm his hands.

"I thought maybe...maybe you...you was ma . . . mad at me, Cleve."

Hawkins skirted around behind his desk and took a seat. He studied his little homeless friend.

"You and I have to talk, Deck." He paused. "We'll get to it after a while. You remember how to make coffee, don't you?"

Deckle cackled like a kid gargling broken glass and showed him a toothy grin. "Don't . . . don't tease . . . tee . . . tease me, Cleve. You know I would never forget how to make cof . . .cof . . . coffee." He cleared his throat, turned and eyed the empty pot. "I'll, I'll make some for you, right nah . . .now."

"Well, go ahead and get to it then. What's the holdup?"

Deckle grinned from ear to ear. "Fresh coff . . .coffee coming right up, Cleve."

"Yeah, it's not that I missed you so much...I just missed your coffee, partner. You've got that magic touch, ya' know?"

Deckle's grin widened even more. While his coffee was brewing, he went to the bathroom, washed his hands and splashed water on his face.

When he came out, Cleve said, "We're gonna have that talk, so slide that chair over here and sit."

Deckle grabbed the straight-backed chair and slid it up in front of the desk facing Cleve. He took the soiled White Sox cap off his head and shoved it in a hip pocket, exposing his rat's nest of greasy-looking brown hair.

"Buddy, you put me on the spot when you ran out of here. You realize that?"

The homeless man hung his head.

"Why did you do that?"

Deckle shrugged. He stared into his coffee cup as if he couldn't remember why it was empty.

"I jus . . . just didn't want to go to see no cops."

Cleve raised his hands as if he was surrendering and nodded.

"Alright, and I figured that might be it, Deck, but you left me in a lurch. Don't you understand, you have to report what you saw in that alley. You did see Glick stuffing a body into the dumpster, right?"

Deckle nodded.

"Well, then, we can't let that go. You understand, don't you?"

Deckle stayed silent.

"Dammit, I was worried about you, partner. I didn't know if you were dead or alive. I was about to check the friggin' morgue. You think it's fair to make somebody worry like that?" Cleve paused for a beat. "The cops won't hurt you. They don't want you for anything. In fact, they'll be glad you made out a report. You see what I mean?"

Deckle squirmed in his chair.

"What's wrong, Deck? Is there something else you want to tell me?"

Deckle started to speak, then stopped himself and frowned. He stared at Cleve and said, "I'm scared."

"Oh . . . scared of what, Deck?"

"Glick. That mis . . . mis . . .Mister Glick."

Hawkins pondered that for a moment. "Why, Deckle? Have you seen him?"

"Yeah . . . yes."

"Where?"

"In the hospital. He was in . . . in . . . the hallway, outside my roo . . . roo . . . room."

"You mean after I came to visit you that day?"

He nodded and searched Cleve's face.

"Yes, and I'm scared."

"Alright, just take it easy, Deck. Nobody's going to hurt you. I promise you that. Okay?"

Deckle hesitated, then nodded.

Hawkins stood and drained his coffee cup. "As I said, nobody is going to bother you, but you have to do exactly as I say from now on. Understand?"

"Okay."

"Good. Now, the first thing we've got to do is report what you saw to the police."

Deckle lurched, but Hawkins grabbed his arm.

"No, you don't, partner. I don't want to cuff you, but I will. There'll be no more running." He patted Deckle on the back. "Now, let's go and get this over with."

CHAPTER NINETEEN

Trish was in one of her shitty moods the day her husband chose to enlighten her about the bad news.

She felt she already had a lot on her plate with him not being able to migrate from Chicago to Springfield until the General Assembly sessions of the Illinois Legislature in November. That, and her latest issue of *Vanity Fair* had been crammed into her mailbox, soaking wet, thanks to the heavy rain and a careless mail carrier.

And to top it all off, she was horny.

Gerry hadn't taken care of business in...*what's it been?* She hesitated, then counted off on her fingers...*one, two, three. Yes!* She was right. It had been three long weeks of making herself cum.

She continued to ponder her problems while she rolled out of bed and fluffed her six pillows. Punching the last one, she thought, *Yes, I definitely need to get back home, and the sooner the better.* Even though she looked forward to the glamour and glitz of Chicago each year, especially the food and nightlife, she was anxious to get back to Southern Illinois and their spacious home in suburban, Bradfordton.

Located less than ten miles from the state capital, Bradfordton was a short drive for Gerry to get to work, but more importantly, for

Trish at least, most of her best friends lived close by in the adjacent suburbs. There were few real friends of theirs in Chicagoland. Of course, there were the Colliers, who were very special people, but other than that, there was nobody to connect with and embrace as a true friend outside of the political arena.

Trish had been scheming for two weeks or more and had been waiting patiently for the ideal time to lay her plans on husband Gerry. At the appropriate time, she would corner and brace him with the idea of turning her loose a month early so she could go home to Bradfordton.

I hate driving, but fuck it, I'll be glad to drive in this case, especially by myself. Then I'll be happy at home and hubby can do whatever floats his boat for a few weeks until early November when he joins me down there. Yay! Why not?

It was a Sunday morning, and Senator Albers, still in his pj's, had just polished off a heart attack breakfast he had prepared for himself while Trish languished in bed with the crossword puzzle from the *New York Times*.

Gerry's meal had consisted of six strips of bacon, limp, three eggs sunny side up, and a generous portion of home fries with onions cooked in ten heaping tablespoons of bacon grease. Three pieces of toast, slathered with butter, and three cups of black coffee later, he was ready to confront his wife.

He'd made up his mind that, pursuant to Hawkins' request—*more like a demand*—he would tell Trish all about the pornographic pictures of her that were floating around like pollen in the springtime. *God only knows who Concho and his buds have peddled those pictures to.*

It will actually feel good to unload this burden I've been carrying for six months or more, trying to hide our sex life involving other couples, including the Colliers. Damn! It was such a careless move to get wasted and involve those two. But, Jill is such a hot number . . . a real sexual animal...it was hard to resist, but I caved because Trish gave her okay . . . and let's face it, I was hot for Jill, too. That woman is breathtakingly beautiful. Those wide eyes are a radiant blue and give her a look of vulnerable innocence that makes a guy immediately feel protective. But now that sonofabitch Kent, has something to hold over my head.

Yes, it will feel good to tell Trish all about the blackmail and the money I've been swiping out of our savings account. Jesus! She's going to kill me about that, though. She shouldn't feel that way, but she will. I know her. She'll just rip my balls off, if I'm lucky.

"Gerry," Trish called from the bedroom.

"Yeah, honey."

He drifted up to the bedroom and found Trish lying on her back, naked, with her beautiful legs all akimbo exposing her well-groomed blonde pussy. She smiled with that familiar "come fuck me look" that Gerry always found so difficult to resist.

He sat on the edge of the bed and took in her beauty.

"Now?"

"Yes, now," she whispered, as if someone was watching. "What are you going to do, senator, play games and make me beg for it?" She giggled. "Okay, we've played this one before, Mr. Studly." She sat up and scooted in close, then blew her hot breath in his ear. "We can play it again, love." She reached into the opening of his PJ bottoms.

Gerry pondered her offer for a few seconds, then shook his head.

"Uuuh . . . not right now, honey, please." He pushed her hand away.

He had to confess and didn't want to have to build up his nerve all over again, even if it did mean forfeiting an anxious piece of ass.

"What?" Trish grabbed up the sheet to cover herself. "What is wrong with you, Gerry? Do you realize we haven't done anything for about a month? What in the hell? Are you going gay on me or something?"

"What? No! Stop that, now, Trish. I need to talk to you about something serious, and with that in mind, I hardly think now is a good time for sex, that's all."

"You've got to be kidding me. What could be so damned important, you don't want to fuck me? Just tell me, Gerry. What?"

"Okay, okay." He held up one hand as a stop sign. "I barely know where to begin, Trish, now that you are in a pissed-off mood. You have made it more difficult than it should have been."

"Okay, you win. My thoughts of giving you a blow job have melted away, Gerry." She scooted up on the bed and sat Indian style, with the sheet covering everything but her head. "There, you satisfied?" She grabbed a cigarette from her nightstand and lit up, then put an ashtray by her feet. "Go ahead, Geronimo. What's so friggin' important?"

Gerry got up and stood beside the bed. He saw the defiant expression on her face and began to pace.

"Okay, do you remember the last time we got together with the Colliers?"

"What do you mean, do I remember, Gerry? Of course I do. What a perfectly stupid thing to ask." She laughed. "I don't see how you could forget, either?"

"Okay, okay, I just wanted to choose a starting point here, honey. Don't make this harder than it is, okay?"

"Fine. Then don't be so secretive. Spit it out, will you?"

"Okay, after we all had sex that night, as a foursome, I bailed, but you and Kent and Jill kept going. Remember?"

"Yes, Gerry," she huffed. "Like I said, I didn't forget anything from that night. So?"

"Well, I was taking a video of all of you in the throes of ecstasy." He paused briefly. The silence in the room was palpable.

"There. You have it. I can only say that I'm sorry, Trish."

"Is that it? Is that all you have?" She tossed a pillow at his head.

"Well, none of you were aware, of course, when I did it. The lights were low and all of you were so involved you didn't notice." He couldn't help but grin. "To tell the truth, I don't think you would have cared *what* I was doing at that point, Trish."

Trish inhaled deeply, then exhaled a huge cloud of smoke. Smiling, she said, "I am not pissed, dear husband. I think it's a little kinky to tell the truth, but I would like to see the tape. Let me see it right now. Do you mind?"

"Well, that's the rough part, Trish." He cleared his throat and focused on her eyes. "The tape is gone, Trish, and I'm sorry, I don't know where it is?"

"What? No!"

She bounded out of bed. Her eyes were bright and moist with worry, and they brimmed with tears when she spoke.

"What in the hell, do you mean...'gone'?" Her face had lost its smile and her voice was excited. "Please, Gerry, don't mess with me."

"I'm not kidding. I wish I was, Trish."

She threw her hands up and covered her face.

"No! Gerry! This is terrible! What in the hell are you going to do about this?"

His voice dropped to a near whisper. "That's not the worst of it, I'm afraid."

"What?" Her shrieking was in sharp contrast to his own barely audible, words. "What in the hell could be any worse than this?"

"Somebody had still pictures made from the tape and I had to pay to get the pictures back or they were going to give them to the newspapers. I had to pay them off, you know, to prevent that from happening."

Again silence took the room.

"Christ, Gerry! This just keeps getting worse by the minute. What else is there? Give it all to me, Ger. Don't fuck around, please. What else?"

"I paid a quarter of a million dollars to get the pictures back. What else could I do? I've got them, but I'm so sorry, Trish. So sorry."

Trish sobbed, "Oh, my God, Gerry. You don't even know if you have all of the pictures, do you?" She thought for a moment. "And where is that fucking tape?" She shook her head back and forth. "Oh, my God! What are we going to do?"

"Well, I have hired a private detective to help me track down the tape and the bastards who are blackmailing us. It's not much, but it's a start. I'm trying to keep the cops out of it, you know? I'm open to any new ideas of course."

She used the sheet to wipe away her tears.

"Of course, Gerry. You are always open to suggestions, aren't you? And to think, I was going to have sex with you this morning. Good luck ever fucking me again, asshole."

The senator's voice could barely be heard.

"See? I told you it was all a bad idea, Trish."

CHAPTER TWENTY

When his old friend and partner on the force, Jeebers, called to invite Cleve to a poker party, Hawkins didn't give it a second thought. He turned his old drinking buddy down.

Even though Jeebers indicated that he was dry and hadn't touched a drop in two months, Cleve was wary and told his friend, "Maybe another time."

Every alcoholic knows what every other alcoholic is thinking. There's only one alcoholic personality. There are many manifestations of the disease, but the essential elements remain the same in every practicing drunk. Wino, ten dollar street whore, Catholic nun, college student, major-league baseball player, or three-hundred pound slob, the mindset never varies. That's why practicing alcoholics try to avoid the company of drunks who have sobered up. When a drunk tells you he doesn't have a problem anymore because he quit drinking, run away as fast as possible. Cleve knew that.

Hawkins brushed away those thoughts and called Lieutenant Ashbaugh before he left his office. He wanted to know if anything new had come up regarding the All Points Bulletin the cops had put out on Concho Martinez earlier in the week. He also hoped to have the lieutenant on hand when he brought Deckle into the station to file a report.

He found Ashbaugh's secretary was fielding his calls while he was appearing in court on a special case.

"Good morning. Lieutenant Ashbaugh's office. This is Janelle. May I help you?"

"Morning, Janelle. You must be fairly new, eh? I haven't heard your sweet voice before. This is Private Detective Cleve Hawkins. Where's your boss this morning?"

"Hi, Detective. Yes, I was transferred over from Vice. I've only been in this section a few weeks. The Lieutenant is in court all morning, and perhaps all afternoon too. He wasn't sure when we talked yesterday. Is there anything I can do for you?"

"Well, not really. Thank you though. Hmmmm. He'll probably be checking in with you sometime today though, right, Jan?"

"Yes. Around lunchtime, I suspect, at least that's what he told me yesterday. Are you sure there is nothing I can do to help, Detective?"

"Ahhhh, well, I don't think so, Jan. I wanted to set up an interview for a friend of mine. He witnessed some bad action over near Wells and Division."

"Well, that sure doesn't sound like something that should wait, am I correct?"

"I think you're right, Jan. Any suggestions?"

"Yes, I'll tell the lieutenant you called as soon as I hear from him. Meanwhile, how about letting his assistant, Detective Wellbourne, start interviewing your guy. At least you would have something on record for Lieutenant Ashbaugh to start with."

"Good idea. Who did you say that was?"

"Detective Dave Wellbourne. He was assigned to this section out of Robbery Homicide Division about three months ago. Dave's one sharp guy...if that's a concern."

"No, I'm good. There's no doubt Wellbourne is well-qualified if he's working for Harvey. We can start there and you'll bring Harvey up to speed when he calls in, right?"

"Yes, is that alright?"

"That's fine. We'll see you in about a half hour then."

"Right...and, hey, detective . . .?"

"Yeah?"

"I'm on a diet, so you don't need to bring any donuts with you, okay?"

"Yeah, I got it. See you soon."

. . .

Cleve found a place to park his Lexus in the "Officers On Duty" lot and went straight to Ashbaugh's section on the third floor. The nameplate on his secretary's desk read Janelle Harrison. He was struck by the way her physical appearance seemed to match up perfectly with the voice he'd heard on the phone.

She was a slender blonde woman wearing a lot of clothes. Her white skirt reached her ankles, nearly covering her black-laced high-heeled boots. Over the skirt she wore a longish ivory-colored tunic and a black leather belt with a huge buckle and a beige sleeveless sweater. With a beige scarf around her neck, she had ivory earrings that were carved in the shape of Japanese dolls. She also had rings on all of her fingers and a white bow in her hair. Her lipstick was pale pink.

Cleve noticed small laugh wrinkles around her eyes and thought she looked like fun, but all indications were this woman took her job seriously. After Hawkins walked in, Janelle sat stoically with both hands on the keys of her laptop and she hesitated only briefly before she looked up and smiled.

"You must be Detective Hawkins?"

"That would be right. Ms. Harrison, correct?"

She offered her hand and he shook it.

"Yes, but please...just Janelle is fine."

"Okay, Janelle it is. And this is Deckle."

The thin homeless man appeared to shrink into himself behind Hawkins.

Janelle nodded, then looked at Deckle.

"Deckle?"

"Yeh . . .yes, ,a . . . ma' am. I'm Deckle."

"Well, okay, gentlemen. Just follow me. I'll take you back to meet Detective Wellbourne."

Hawkins had known several of the eighteen detectives in Robbery-Homicide, particularly the major case squad, but had never met Wellbourne.

Janelle guided them back to where steel desks were grouped together and made islands across the expanse of the squad bay. Most of the desks were vacant. Hawkins recognized a few faces. The gazes that flicked his way were hooded, flat and cold. Cop eyes. The look was always the same, regardless of location. It was the look of people who trust no one and who suspect everyone of something.

They were guided to an interview room where Cleve took a seat indicated by Wellbourne as they entered. The detective smoothed a hand over his tie as he settled into his own chair, his eyes never leaving Hawkins' face until they switched to Deckle.

Wellbourne pointed to the other chair.

"You can pull that chair over and have a seat too, sir. Can I offer you a cup of coffee?"

Deckle nodded. Welbourne went over to the pot on the back counter and got a cup for him.

Usually, Cleve knew, the person being interviewed was seated with his back to the wall, put into that position—cramped behind a too-small table that was bolted to the wall on one end of the room—so they'd feel as if they were cornered. Wellbourne would have the option of increasing or decreasing the sense of pressure in the room by moving closer in his chair, which was on wheels, or sliding subtly back away from the suspect or, in this case, Deckle.

He powered up his laptop and took a long, slow breath.

"Okay, I'm Detective Wellbourne," he said as he typed. "I'll be taking your statement today." He continued to eye Deckle. "I am required to inform you that this entire session is being recorded on both video and audio. You understand, sir?"

Deckle was shaking like he had his hands on a jackhammer, but he acknowledged Wellbourne's question and nodded. Covering his face with both hands, he gently massaged his forehead with his fingertips and smiled, or what passed for a smile.

"Yeah . . . yes."

It wasn't one of Deckle's better days. He looked terrible, unshaven, his skin ashen and showed signs of sagging. Hair grew from his ears and nose and he had buttoned his shirt crookedly. He looked like he had gone through a long night of the soul. It took only a split second for his face to change from ecstasy to agony or vice versa each time he was asked a question.

"Your name, please?"

"Dec . . . Deckle." He looked at Hawkins, then looked away quickly, a small tic starting to pulse rapidly in his left cheek.

Welbourne scowled.

"Your full name, please?"

"That . . . That's all . . . Dec . . . Deckle."

Wellbourne rolled his eyes and looked at Cleve.

"Do you know this man's last name, Hawkins?"

"Beats me. I only know him as Deckle."

Wellbourne let out a heavy sigh and looked back at the homeless man.

"Alright, your address, please?"

Deckle looked at Cleve, then shrugged.

Hawkins stepped in. "He's homeless, detective. What you see is what you get, I'm afraid."

Wellbourne took his fingers away from his keyboard and laced them together in his lap.

"So tell me . . . why are we here today, Deckle?"

The little man looked to his friend once again. Cleve shifted in his chair and leaned in to speak to Wellbourne, somewhat secretly.

"Okay, here's the deal. I apologize, but I thought Ms. Harrison or someone had briefed you on the situation. Deckle is homeless, but he works for me at times, running errands and so forth. I allow him to stay overnight in my office from time to time, a night watchman, I guess you might say. Long story short, about four weeks ago, Deckle was walking down Wells Street at night, and saw a man carrying what looked like a body." Wellbourne started typing. "He watched this individual as he struggled to cram the body into a dumpster near Wells and Division. That person saw Deckle and chased him. In his haste to get away Deckle ran in front of a car on Clark street and ended up in St. Joseph's Hospital."

Wellbourne continued to type. "And this all happened about a month ago, you say?" He glanced at Deckle, then stopped. "Seems like you waited a long time to report this, my friend, I don't know if . . ."

"Whoa . . . hold on a minute, Wellbourne." Cleve scooted up in his chair. "Hear me out. This man hesitated all this time because he wanted to keep a low profile. He's been scared shitless., worried that the man carrying the body will catch him and harm him in some way. Pretty sound logic, really, when you consider everything. I mean, especially for a homeless guy, wouldn't you say? I had to all but hogtie him to get him to come in here today. To tell you the truth, he is spooked by the law. He thinks all cops are out to get him. See what I mean?"

Wellbourne leaned back in his chair and pondered the situation. He sipped his coffee and scrunched up his face.

"This shit is cold." He got up. "Let me get a fresh cup." He eyed Cleve. "Can I get you a cup, Hawkins?"

"No, I'm good."

Deckle watched both men as though he was seeing someone walking a wire high above a canyon.

Cleve stood and put a light hand on his shoulder.

CHAPTER TWENTY-ONE

Wellbourne got as much information as Deckle was able to provide, but Cleve was disappointed. The homeless man related everything he saw, or thought he saw, that night on Clark Street, but that wasn't much. However, he was able to give a fair description of the elusive Mr.Glick.

The police had no reason to hold Deckle. Mug shots were reviewed, but nothing was found, and it was determined that the mysterious Mr. Glick probably didn't have a criminal background. A written statement from Deckle was not going to be very helpful, even if he had been able to write one.

Pulling anything further from the man seemed impossible, or so Wellbourne reasoned. He thanked him for his time and cooperation, and Deckle left the station with Hawkins.

Cleve felt that perhaps he had wasted Deckle's time, and, in fact, he may have in some way put Deckle in more danger by bringing him in to the department. He was relieved, however, to learn that from Wellbourne that no bodies had been found in any dumpsters on the north side of Chicago in recent months.

He found himself wondering if Deckle was telling the truth...but then, why would he lie about seeing Glick on his floor in St. Josephs?

There was no shortage of relevant information to ponder when Cleve bedded down that night.

• • •

He thought he was dreaming when he was jarred awake by repeated banging on his door. It felt like he had just fallen asleep. Glancing at the clock radio on the nightstand, he rolled out and crawled into his jeans, wondering who in the hell would bother him at four in the morning. And for what?

I hope it's not Jeebers, all boozed up and wanting to cry on my shoulder.

He rubbed his eyes and raked his fingers through his hair as he stumbled to the door. After a precautionary look through the peephole, he became more alarmed.

Corky Hulce stood on the other side.

What in the hell does he want?

Cleve dropped the chain and swung the door open.

"What the fuck do you want, Hulce? Nothing could be so important you had to yank my ass out of the sack at this hour of the day – or, should I say, night?"

Corky's breathing was labored.

"Quit bitching, Hawkins. I'm here because I thought you should know as soon as possible. That's all." He choked on every word as he crowded his way inside. "Maclam is dead."

"What?" Cleve's eyes widened. "You're shitting me."

"Not hardly. I wish I was." He yanked the Bears skullcap off his head and stuffed it into a side coat pocket, then continued his uninvited march into Cleve's living room, the stub of an unlit cigar still in the corner of his mouth as he flopped down on the couch.

Shaking his head, he grumbled, "This is so crazy. I've been running like a fuckin' madman ever since I got the call." He paused for a beat. "You got anything to drink?"

Cleve shook his head. "I don't drink anymore. Don't keep it on hand either. It's pretty damned early for booze anyway, don't you think?" Waving a hand dismissively, he added, "I think there's a few beers in the fridge, though. Help yourself, but tell me, what's this shit about Maclam?"

Corky jumped up and headed for the kitchen.

At the same time, Hawkins sidled in behind him and slowly ran a hand back and forth along a top shelf above the pantry. He couldn't seem to find what he was looking for and muttered, "Damn it!"

He dragged a dinette chair over and stood on it in order to retrieve an open pack of Marlboro Reds he had stashed there two months earlier. He exhaled a sigh of relief as he plucked one from the pack and stepped down.

"That's the trouble with quitting. You can never find a fuckin' cigarette when you need one."

He lit up and rubbed a hand across his mouth like he was trying to shove his remark back down his throat.

"So, who told you Maclam was dead?"

With the cigar still stuck in the corner of his mouth, Corky closed the refrigerator door and popped open a can of Old Style. He removed the cigar and chugged half of the can, then plopped back on the couch.

"Here's the deal, Hawkins. It was about two-thirty when I got this anonymous phone call at the bar. I was in the middle of closing up. Everything was locked up and I had just finished doing the till when I heard the phone in my office. I wouldn't pay attention ordinarily, but it kept ringing off the hook, so I finally went back and picked it up."

"And?"

"And this guy on the other end says, 'If you want to collect your nosey whale friend, Maclam, you'll find him in a vacant lot on West 139th and School.' He laughed and said, 'No rush. It's too late for an ambulance.' Then he hung up."

"So, you called the cops, right?"

"Hell, no. Not yet. I didn't know what to do first. I panicked. You know how it is. Somebody tells you that shit, you ain't prepared. Besides, I figured you'd probably know exactly how to handle this, you being an ex-cop...and with Big Russ still on probation and all.

They're looking for him, you know. I'm sure of it. Last time I saw him, he told me he hadn't reported in over six weeks. He thought that was funny. Can you imagine?"

Cleve took a deep drag on his cigarette and shook his head.

"It's a wonder they didn't scoop his big ass up weeks ago." He glanced at the cigar stuck in Corky's mouth. "Do you plan on smoking that cigar or is it just for show?"

Corky ignored Hawkins. "Listen, I came here first because I figured you'd go with me to check this out and see if it's legit, ya know? Then we could call it in or do whatever you say."

"You've got huge balls, Corky. You know you shouldn't have waited for me or anybody else for that matter. You should have just called the police." Cleve shook his head. "I guess it's too late now. We might as well go with your lame idea. Come on. At least we'll find out if it's just bullshit."

•   •   •

Two blue and white Chicago Police cars were parked at the curb in front of the trash covered lot on School Street. Their blue lights pulsed repeatedly against the side of the adjacent buildings. A news van from WLS-TV had already staked out a spot on the opposite side of the street. Barricades were set up across the sidewalk to keep any other vultures at bay.

Hawkins parked near the corner of 139th and they walked.

"Looks like your caller was onto something, that's for sure. Somebody had to call these cops. Listen, I want you to stay back as much as possible. This is all police now. It's really none of our business." He glanced sideways at Hulce. "You should be damned glad somebody else called it in. You don't need to get involved."

They continued to walk to the scene now less than fifty yards away.

Hawkins said, "Somebody's dead alright. The medical examiner's vehicle is here and I think that's probably Floyd Ressler, the ME, crouched down over there. He doesn't come out unless there's a body."

"Damn!" Hulce broke stride and paused for a moment. He lifted his shoulders in a half-hearted shrug. "I can't believe this. I have no idea who would want Big Russ dead."

"It's not really a shock," Hawkins said. "He must have pissed off one of the low-life scum in his orbit somehow. That's all. I'm sure any of those assholes would snuff him for the price of a joint if they had the chance. Resentment comes with the territory. People who do bad things don't like to suffer the consequences of their actions, Corky. But you better believe they all do, eventually."

"Well, I sure as hell have no clue as to who it would be. Russ did tell me a lot of shit, but I hadn't seen him very much lately, so I don't know. Anything is possible with a guy like Maclam....with his background, I mean. I do know that he figured he would be one hell of a lot better off to give the appearance of being squeaky clean than ever to go back to Joliet. But then, why skip reporting in?"

•   •   •

Cleve knew the ME was always the first one to physically examine the victim at a death scene. No one touched the body before he did...not for any reason. It was his unpleasant task to take the temperature of the corpse to aid in figuring out the time of death. It was also his job to assess and make note of the visible wounds and a hundred other minute details.

Four uniforms on the scene were holding a few curious on-lookers back. The ME stood up from his crouched position when he glanced up and saw Hawkins approaching.

Corky swiped a hand across his face. He breathed in and out with purpose, trying to pull himself together, but stay in the background.

"Hey, Hawk! What in the hell are you doing out here? I could swear sometimes I think you guys can just smell blood in the air. I haven't seen you in ages. Is this your case?"

"Hi, Floyd. Nah, I'm not on the force anymore. I've got a private ticket, now. I was just passing by. Saw all the lights. Figured I'd stop and have a look. You know how that is."

"Yeah, now that you mention it, I did hear you'd retired. You've still got clothes on your back, so I assume business can't be bad. I've got my basics done on this one. I'm just waiting for the lucky detective who pulled the case to show."

After chatting with Ressler for a moment, Cleve followed him over to the body. It had not been bagged yet. Some of the blood on the ground had turned dark red.

Cleve held Corky back.

"You stay put. I'll see if it's Maclam and let you know."

Ressler stepped off to the side with Hawkins.

"My first observation, this guy was shot with two .20 caliber slugs, one behind the ear, and one dead center in the forehead." He pointed. "Those 20's don't exit, you know. They like to circle around and around in the brain pan. But that's not what killed this man. I think this was some sort of payback or revenge killing."

"Looks like the shots sure would have done it, Floyd."

"Nope. This guy was worked over real good before they shot him. See all these bruises on his face and neck? Both of his eyes are racooned and his nose has been crushed, the cartilage driven deep into his brain. His head looks like it has been smashed with a baseball bat or a pipe of some kind."

Hawkins noticed Maclam's broken teeth grinning up at them through a mass of pulpy flesh, bone and blood.

They stood up.

"No. This man actually died of blunt force injuries. Hit repeatedly with a piece of pipe, looks like. I don't think he even felt the shots, poor bastard."

In the background Hulce flicked his cigar and it landed with a hiss in a puddle. He covered his mouth and wandered away towards Hawkin's parked car.

When the medical examiner had finished talking to Cleve, they both looked down at Maclam's clothing, It had already been separated and bagged. His wallet was missing, and a watch and a ring were gone as well. They only knew about the ring because of the white band that was left around Maclam's third finger.

143

CHAPTER TWENTY-TWO

It was dawn by the time Hawkins had left the homicide scene on 139th Street and had dropped Hulce off at his car, parked on Surf Street.

His adrenaline was still spiked when he arrived at his office on Wells and checked his watch. It was going on six in the morning. He realized he'd never be able to get to sleep if he went back to the apartment.

I should check on Deckle, anyway.

He had brought a sleeping bag from his apartment earlier so the homeless man could sleep on a cot in his office. Cleve thought it would be a good way to keep the little guy safe for the time being, at least until he figured out what to do with him on a more permanent basis. Right now he knew there was probably a target painted on Deckle's back. The poor guy needed a friend.

The arrangement couldn't last forever, but Hawkins needed time to think. He found a place to park and then walked less then a block to his office. His thoughts were focused on the day ahead. He could never plan a week in advance or he damned sure would have. There were times when he even missed the scheduling he was afforded while he was on the police force.

Deckle lay face down on the cot, his arms dangling off to the side like a boxer getting a massage. It was a bit chilly in the room and he had removed his field jacket to cover his legs. Evidently the sleeping bag hadn't been enough to keep him warm. When he heard Cleve unlock the door, he rolled over too far and hit the floor with a bang.

He jumped to his feet before Cleve flicked the switch for the overhead lights.

Cleve crossed the room, rounded his desk, and turned on the desk lamp.

"Morning, Deck. How'd you sleep?"

Deckle rubbed his eyes. "I slept goo. . . .good, Cleve." He feigned a smile.

Cleve held up his empty coffee mug.

"I sure would like some coffee, partner. It's already been a busy morning. I need a cup in the worst way."

Deckle yawned. "Yeah . . . yeah. . . yes, sir. I'll ma . . .ma. . . make some right now, Cleve. Just be a min . . . minute."

He grabbed the pot and raced for the bathroom sink.

"I got you cov . . . covered, Cleve, just you . . .you watch."

"Whoa! Easy there, partner. No sense in breaking your neck."

The message light wasn't blinking on his landline phone, but Cleve had calls to make. It was Thursday, and he knew Mo had to work, so there was no sense in waking her up just to talk. He checked his watch again.

I have to touch base with Albers, though. I need to know if he really told his wife about the blackmail, or did he chicken out? Hawkins smiled for a second. *I'm betting our esteemed senator lost his nerve. I'll call him on his cell.*

It was just after nine when Hawkins called Albers. It only rang twice.

"Albers."

"Good morning, senator. Hawkins here. I trust you are wide awake?"

"Yes, Detective Hawkins, I am." He cleared his throat. "I guess I'm glad you called."

"What's that mean?"

"Well, your dandy idea of me telling Trish everything went over like an atheist at a Southern Baptist Jamboree. I'm still counting my lucky stars she didn't cut my nuts off."

"Take it easy, Albers. It had to be done and you know it." Cleve paused. "Are you allowed to go home?"

"Well, yes, but . . ."

"Good. Just chill out then. What, exactly, did you tell her?"

"Ha! Just like you told me, I told her everything. I even confessed that it was me who took the video while she was in the sack with Trent Collier that night."

"What?"

"I said, I told her that. . . "

"Yeah, I heard you, senator. So, you told your wife everything. Lahdee-do-dah-day. But once again, you left me out of the loop. Me...the only one who's trying to save your ass?"

"Well, I thought that . . . "

"No, you didn't think, Gerry! That's the biggest fucking problem I'm dealing with here." Hawkins stood and booted his chair sideways. "Goddammit! We're back to square one here. What happened to our deal where you were going tell me everything?"

Cleve caught himself from pacing when Deckle handed him a cup of coffee. "Thanks, Deck."

"You know what I think? I'm just going to tell you to shove this case right up your ass, senator. I don't need the grief. Are you hearing me?"

"Oh, no! Don't leave me in the lurch here, Hawkins. I need your help now more than ever, don't you see?"

"Yeah, I see alright. I see you're not giving a shit about playing straight with me. Here's what we're going to do, my friend. I want you to meet me this very morning before I go any further, because as of now I'm dropping your case."

"No, Hawkins. Please don't do that to me."

"You've done it to yourself, senator."

"Please . . . just give me another chance. I'm sorry for holding back. Just let me explain, and after that, if you still want you can dump me. Okay?"

After a long lull of silence, Cleve spoke.

"Meet me at The Sunny Side Up on Clark, near Division. It's a breakfast joint. You know where it is?"

"No, I don't. But I'll find it."

"Be there at eleven. If you're not, I'm history to you, for sure."

"Well, I have an eleven-thirty meeting scheduled in my office, but I'll call my secretary and tell her I'm going to be running late. Okay?"

"Whatever. Just be there, senator." Cleve hung up and gritted his teeth. He dropped into his chair and gulped some coffee.

How did this idiot ever manage to become a senator?

He sat brooding for a few minutes and drank his coffee while he pondered what he had on the Albers case so far.

"I'm going to toss this shit right back in his lap. I swear I will," he mumbled.

Deckle said, "Cleve . . . .can . . . can . . .I do . . . do any . . . anything . . . for you? You need me . . .to . . to go to. . . .the store? You need coffee filters and sug . . . sug . . .sugar, I know."

"I don't know, Deck." He cringed. "I mean, that stuff can wait, can't it? Just let me think for a minute, okay?"

He noted the time. It was almost nine-forty.

"Listen, Deck, I've got to meet a guy at eleven, and I'll probably be gone until about two, two thirty, this afternoon. Meanwhile, it's best that you lay low for a while. I want you to just stay put, understand?"

"Bu . . .but I have to eat, Cleve. I'm hungry. If I go see my friends, they always have stuff to eat. They'll give me. . . me something. I know. . know. . . know they will."

"I know you're hungry, Deck, but I don't think you should go anywhere by yourself right now. Just for a while. Okay? I'm going to run and get you something before I leave. You want eggs or is a couple of hamburgers and fries okay?"

"Cheesebur . . . burgers is okay, Cleve. A lot. . . lots of cats . . . catsup, too."

"Okay. Don't open the door for anybody. Do you think you can hold down the fort 'til I get back?"

"Yeah, sure . . . sure thi . . .thing, Cle . . . Cleve."

After Cleve had gone to the McDonald's three blocks away and returned with the food for Deckle, he was on his way back out the door to meet with Albers.

Suddenly he paused mid-step.

"Listen, Deckle, don't you worry about Mr. Glick. We'll find him and get to the bottom of that whole deal, I promise. Screw the cops. We'll do it ourselves. Okay?"

Deckle nodded and Cleve thought he saw the trace of a smile.

Traffic on Lakeshore was moderate to heavy with winking brake lights as far as the eye could see, and Hawkins found himself thinking about the cars he used to have as a cop in traffic jams. Each of the Special Forces Unit vehicles was equipped with what was called the Police Package and had flashing blue lights in the grille. Traffic would part like Moses and the Red Sea, he thought and wished he had one of those packages now to get through the ocean of slow moving cars in front of him.

He found himself being alert to the possibility he was being tailed after Maclam had brought that to his attention the week before he'd died. Taking Lakeshore allowed Hawkins to check more easily for a tail. Mid-morning traffic was not much better there, but he drove five miles below the speed limit and then took it up to fifteen above so he could easily check his mirrors for any vehicle following the same pattern.

He realized his Lexus could have been tagged with a GPS tracker while he was in the office with Deckle, or outside of his apartment— even while he was sleeping. Any time, for that matter. He would need to check for that as soon as possible, he thought.

He hadn't seen anything of note on the road behind him until he approached the North Avenue exit and then he noticed the frequent in and out manipulations of a late model, black SUV.

That could be a tail, for sure.

About twenty minutes later he was slammed with bumper to bumper madness. He mashed his horn and threw up his hands when he saw a Toyota, three cars ahead, stalled with the hood up.

He now sat at a dead stop while beyond the Toyota traffic was moving right along again at posted speeds. He flashed his brights— what you're supposed to do as a cop when you're in pursuit, but don't have a dashboard flasher.

Old habits were hard to break.

Just as he managed to pull around the stalled Toyota, he noticed the same black SUV still trailing four cars behind him. When he slowed in an attempt to let other cars pass, the SUV zoomed past him.

GYR54769. GYR54769. Cleve jotted it down on his brain's memory pad. *I have to remember that plate number.*

CHAPTER TWENTY-THREE

Before he went to meet Albers, Hawkins took his car to Jerry's Auto Repair on Sheffield. He paid his buddy to put the Lexus on a lift and helped him check for any tampering with it, including searching for a GPS tracking device.

At the same time, he jotted down the plate number of the black Chevy Equinox that had been shadowing him on Lakeshore Drive earlier. GYR54769. He would check it with the Department of Motor Vehicles as soon as possible.

There was no tracker on his car, as far as he or the wrench could see. Feeling a bit more confident, he left the garage to keep his appointment with Albers at the Sunny Side Up.

Senator Albers was not only on time, but actually had arrived about fifteen minutes early. Hawkins found him sitting in a booth near the wait staff station in the back. He was alone, perusing a copy of the *Chicago Tribune* and sipping his coffee when Cleve began to lower himself into the seat across from him.

"Ooops! Careful now. Don't sit on my hat over there," said Albers. "Here. Hand it to me. I just put it over there so I'd have more wiggle room, if you know what I mean." He was smiling at Hawkins.

"Yeah, sure." Hawkins scowled at him. "So, what's going on, Gerry?" Cleve ordered a cup of black coffee from a passing waitress, lowered his voice and leaned across the table. "Why did you lie to me again, sir? I thought I made myself crystal clear the last time we spoke. You said you told me everything...yet this new shit pops up. Do you realize my not knowing everything could affect the outcome of your case? I swear, if I don't like what I hear right now, I'll drop you like a bad habit. You could run out onto a packed Wrigley Field, bare assed naked, with a humongous tattoo of Hitler on your ass, and the fallout wouldn't be half as bad as the way you'll be ruined over this deal if the papers get it." He paused for effect. "So, let's have it . . . all of it this time."

The expression on Albers' face was pathetic. He held up a hand to cut Hawkins off, pressed his lips together and blinked. "Okay. Okay. I get it. I'm sorry if you think I deceived you in some way."

Seeing the anger start to work into Hawkins' face, he immediately regretted his choice of words. His voice jumped half an octave.

"I mean, I am sorry I lied, okay?"

The senator sipped his coffee, then stared off into space. His face was drained of color and he spoke in a quavering voice.

"Do you suppose this man who threatened me is really a gangster?"

Cleve breathed a heavy sigh and leaned in closer. "No, Gerry, he's an award-winning tango dancer. What in the fuck do you think he is? Listen, I'm gonna be out of here in twenty seconds flat, so you had better stop stalling and start talking."

"Okay, I hear you." He rolled his eyes and looked around as if to say "please don't talk so loud" before he whispered, "This all started last summer, right here in Chicago." He took another sip of coffee and cleared his throat. "There's always a slew of cocktail parties during the Senate's off-time and Trish and I attend quite a few while we're up here." He paused. "It's known in political circles as "sewing and bonding" time. We sow seeds for favors we need from each other and so on. Needless to say, there's a lot of drinking—not that I am using that as an excuse for what I'm about to tell you, mind you."

Hawkins nodded. "Yeah. Go on."

"So, at one of these parties, Trish and I hooked up with a congressional Rep and his wife. We found their tastes and interests paralleled ours, and as things progressed we became good friends." He lowered his voice until it was barely audible. "They turned out to be swingers."

The waitress stopped by to top off their coffee, breaking the silence that had started to build at that point, and Hawkins asked for an order of rye toast.

"So, were you and your wife ready for that action?"

"We have always experimented. We tend to think anything is okay when it comes to sex, as long it's consensual between the concerned parties." He shook his head. "I can't believe I'm telling you all of this. Anyway, that part was never a problem. We had several private parties and everything went just fine, with the four of us all included, until Trent approached me on the golf course one Saturday morning."

Albers glanced around from side to side, as if he suspected a spy was listening, and then continued.

"Trent said he had a proposition for me. He . . . uuuh. . . he wanted to have a threesome. He would leave his wife out of it and then, at some point during the evening, I was to figure a way to tape just he and my wife in action."

"Didn't that piss you off? Didn't you think that was a little off track—I mean compared to your usual deal?" Hawkins waved his hand dismissively. "Actually, never mind. What happened after that?"

"I told him that despite everything we'd already done, I didn't think Trish would go for such a scenario. He said she didn't have to know and I shouldn't tell her. At the right time, he would signal me and I would simply take a break, grab the phone, and while I was taping, he would keep the sex going until I had a good chunk of the action. Then I would join back in."

"Why did he want the tape?"

"He said I would be doing a big favor for him. He wanted it for his own personal collection. He swore nobody else would ever see it. He gave me his word."

Hawkins shook his head. "I think you're all a bunch of sickos, but be that as it may, it's not against the law." He paused and swallowed some coffee with a bite of toast. "What was he giving you in return for this tape? Four Wheaties box tops? It damn sure didn't come without any strings . . . did it?"

Albers cringed.

"So, just like that, you decided to do it for him?" Hawkins asked.

Albers lowered his eyes.

"No. Uuuuuh . . . we made a deal."

"A deal? What sort of a deal?"

The waitress approached. "You gentlemen ready to order?"

"Ah, I think I'm good," said Albers. "I'll take some more coffee, though."

Hawkins waved her off. "No, thanks, I'm good." She left the check in front of him and slipped away. When she was gone, Hawkins continued, "So, you were saying?"

"Yes, well. Trent knew I needed to have his vote for my looming Agriculture Spending Bill coming up in our fall session. He promised his support in exchange for that video. But somebody else must have made prints from it, too."

"Yeah. So, how did that tape get in the hands of the bad guys? That bed buddy of yours must have sold you out. What's this creep's name, anyway, Gerry?"

"What?" His brows arched in surprise. "Oh, no. I don't dare get him involved. He couldn't deal with it."

Hawkins gritted his teeth. "Don't you dare shut me out now, Gerry. What's this Romeo Rep's name? I need to talk to him."

"Oh, my God, no." Albers slid down in his seat and shook his head. "What have I gotten all of us into here?"

Hawkins leaned forward again.

"You need to relax, my friend, starting right this very minute. It's not going to do either you, your wife, or your friends any good if you back out. Got it?"

Albers sighed with a pained expression covering his face.

"Yes. I guess you're right, but this is all very unpleasant."

"So, what's his name?"

"Collier. Trent Collier."

"And his wife?"

Albers continued to shake his head in disgust.

"Jill."

Cleve removed a small notepad from his inside pocket. "Okay. Now, you can save us both some time if you give me their address."

"I'm not sure of the street number, but he lives on Rockhill Lane in Arlington Heights. For Pete's sake, go easy on him, will you? He's going to kill me for this."

Hawkins put the notepad away.

"That's all I need for now. I'll be in touch as soon as I have anything new. Just one more thing, Gerry."

"Oh, God. What's that?"

"You still have that driver or bodyguard, whatever, working for you, right? Cliff, I believe his name is?"

"Yes, of course. Cliff has been with me for years. Why?"

"Is he your only security?"

"Yes."

"Hold on," said Hawkins. He tossed a ten spot on the table by the check and stood up. "I've got the coffee . . . let's get out of here."

Once they were outside, Hawkins said, "Hire another security guy immediately. You'll need the best coverage possible, twenty-four-seven, until we nail these assholes who've been leaning on you. And tell Cliff he's going to be working more hours . . . and I want to screen anybody you're thinking of hiring before you take him on. Understood?"

"Yes, detective. Good idea."

"One more thing. You're pals with that bar owner, Corky Hulce, right?"

"We grew up together as kids. Same neighborhood."

"How much do you know about his friend, Big Russ?"

"You mean that big man?"

"That's the one."

"Not much, why?"

"He was the jailbird Hulce sent to hire me for your case. You know that, right?"

"Did you say 'was,' as in past tense?"

"He's dead, senator." Hawkins watched for reaction in the senator's eyes. "Somebody made confetti of his face, then shot him to death over on the West Side the other night. It's just a curious coincidence that you and Hulce were both connected to him somehow."

Albers took a step back.

"I'm sorry, but I don't understand what you're saying, detective."

Hawkins felt his cell vibrate in his pocket and he answered.

"Hawkins." Pause. "Yes." Pause. "Good work, Harve, great. That works for sure. Good work. Look, I'll come down as soon as I finish up what I'm doing. Probably about an hour, tops." Pause. "Yes . . . okay, see you then."

He clicked off and grinned at Albers.

"Looks like we caught a break, senator. That was a friend of mine at the police department, Lieutenant Ashbaugh. They just arrested Concho Martinez."

CHAPTER TWENTY-FOUR

Hawkins drove to the Chicago police department on Michigan Avenue to see Lieutenant Ashbaugh and check on the status of Concho Martinez, now in custody.

He found Ashbaugh with his feet up on his desk, a donut in one hand, a phone in the other.

Hawkins rapped a knuckle on the door casing. Ashbaugh grinned and continued with his call, but pointed to a chair in front of his desk. Leaning forward, he placed what was left of a donut on a napkin and held up a finger, signaling one minute.

Hawkins took a seat and checked out Ashbaugh's two ego walls, one on the left side of his desk, the other behind him. Both displayed commendations, certifications, diplomas and pictures—the remnants and mementos of a fifteen year career in law enforcement.

Hawkins sipped the coffee he'd picked up at a Seven-Eleven as Ashbaugh was finishing up.

"Okay, well, like I said, you should just tell Simpkins to get his people off their asses down there and the problem is bound to take care of itself." He paused. "Yep. You can tell him I said so, if you like. Yes. Okay. Sounds good. Later, Jim. Okay. Bye."

Ashbaugh hung up and shook his head in disgust. "Damned rooks. Between them and their superiors, they'll cause me to put in for early retirement one of these days."

He sipped his coffee, dusted the crumbs off his hands, and stood to shake Cleve's hand.

"Hey, Hawk. How's everything in your Mickey Spillane, Sammy Spade world?"

"I can't complain, LT. I manage to stay busy, that's about it. Same play, different script."

The Lieutenant nodded. "Well, as I told you on the phone, we've got your boy, down in holding right now. Since I knew you were on your way, I told Detective Andrews to hold off for a while on interviewing that snake. He's the cop who caught the case and he's been knotting Martinez up for over seven hours, filling out intake forms and all the other usual bullshit, plus some other shit he improvised. He had him fingerprinted and then sat his ass in front of a camera for an updated mug shot. This is not Martinez's first rodeo, that's for sure." He paused and grinned. "He's not a happy camper right now."

"Did you charge him with anything yet, Harve?"

Ashbaugh shook his head. "Nah. We told him the reason we snatched him up was for probation violations. There was a bench warrant out on him. He's none the wiser, at this point, because he knows that's an undeniable fact. Hell, he hasn't reported in over five months." Lowering his voice, he said, "The asshole really does have eyes like a fuckin' snake, Cleve. You ever seen this guy?"

"No, but I did see his mug shot the day my client picked him out of the books. I appreciate that, by the way, and thanks for giving me the heads up on this guy, too. I realize you didn't have to do all that. I owe you."

"Fuggetaboudit, Hawk. No problem. The way I look at it is we got one less scumbag on the street to worry about. We'd love to nail the asshole for something, though, so we can keep him locked up."

Hawkins fumbled around in his coat pocket.

"Before I forget, I need another favor from you." He handed him a slip of paper. "I need to get a BOLO for this plate. That tag was on a late model black Tahoe that was following me on Lakeshore earlier today. I'd like to know who it was. Sooner, the better, of course."

Ashbaugh eyed the paper for a moment and took the last bite of his donut.

"GY54769? Is this all you need?"

"That's it. That plate was on the Tahoe, but you know how it goes. It might be on a blue Volkswagen by now."

Ashbaugh swung around in his chair.

"Gotcha. I'll have the info for you before you leave if you want. No big deal." He picked up a rubber band and played with it as he leaned back in his chair.

"That would be great, Harve."

"No sweat, as I said. But, maybe you can do something for me, Cleve."

"Yeah, what's that?"

"An easy one." He pulled out the center drawer of his desk and removed some five by seven black and white pictures, held together with a huge paper clip.

"Tell me what you know about this man."

He plunked them down, flipped them around so Hawkins could see. Pausing a moment, he said, "I heard through the grapevine you showed up at that crime scene the other night when that guy was found, tits up, over on 139th Street."

Hawkins was taken aback for a split second, then sat back when he saw who was in the pictures.

"Yeah, sure. That's Big Russ Maclam."

"Right you are, Hawk. We got that off his prints. Now, tell me everything you know about him." He leaned back, studying his fingernails for nicks and anticipating an answer.

Cleve stared into his coffee cup and heaved a sigh.

"It's a long story, LT, but suffice to say, I was introduced to Maclam by a tavern owner who knows one of my clients. On the night Maclam was killed, that same tavern owner got a call telling him where Maclam was. Then that caller hung up."

"Hung up?"

Hawkins nodded. "So the tavern owner came to my place in the wee hours of the morning and asked me to accompany him to the location. I did. My cop curiosity more than anything else, Harve. Neither of us knew for sure at the time that Maclam was dead. That was it, as far as I was concerned. I took him to his car and went home."

"Now all I have to do is find the guy or guys who wasted Maclam. Did you see what they did to that poor bastard's face before they killed him?"

"Yeah, somebody was pissed off, for sure, when they did that deed. Death wasn't going to be good enough for them." Ashbaugh shook his head.

"Is that all you needed?"

"Yeah. I'll let you know if we need anything else on that tavern owner and so on. Detective Simpkins has the case. He might be calling you."

Ashbaugh took a last swig of coffee and stood up.

"If you're ready, I'll take you down to see your friend Martinez then."

Just outside the security door leading to the interview rooms, three handcuffed prisoners were chained to a long steel bench, all big, bulky, black men with corn-rowed hair, drop-crotch jeans, and wife-beater shirts.

A slim white man, wide-eyed and frightened, with volcanic acne and ratty-looking hair sat next to them.

Concho Martinez had had nothing to say. Nothing at all. He hadn't waived his rights nor invoked his right to a lawyer.

Across the table from Detective Sergeant Andrews, Concho now sat in the box, his back to the wall, his mysterious dark eyes sat back in deep sockets. Ashbaugh had been right, Cleve thought. They were snake eyes and had a tendency to dart from side to side, from Andrews and then back to Ashbaugh and Hawkins.

His mouth turned downward by nature, a lipless horseshoe centered on a heavy five o clock shadow. Martinez wore his long dark hair in a rubber-banded ponytail like a biker.

Ashbaugh and Hawkins remained standing at first. Detective Andrews acknowledged them with a nod and took the lead.

"You do know why you're here, right, Concho?"

He remained silent and Hawkins could see the muscles working in the man's jaw.

"You were found lingering around the outside of the Pussy R Us tittie bar out by O'hare Field." Andrews marched on. "What the fuck were you doing out there? That's off limits per your probation. You know that, right?"

Still, no answer. Ashbaugh winked at Hawkins and left the room.

Martinez raked his fingers through his hair, a sign of agitation. He folded his arms over his chest, watched Ashbaugh leave, and said, "Wanna make something of it."

He smirked, with a warmish curl of his upper lip like a sneer of condescension or, worse, a parody of Elvis appearing and disappearing.

Andrews was silent for a moment and reached for his coffee.

"What's a used rubber like you doing around there, anyway, Martinez?"

Concho looked gut-punched. He wrapped his arms around his own midsection. His dark eyes met the detective's and for just a fleeting moment were bright like a man with a fever, but opaque still and hiding secrets. His face was tight with anger. He gave Andrews a hard look.

"Fuck you."

"No. Fuck you," Hawkins said. "Looks like you'll be going back to the honeymoon suite at Statesville, asshole. You won't talk to us, you'll be on your way."

Concho glared.

"You haven't contacted your probation officer in over five months, and you know that puts you in deep shit, let alone the rest of the charges we've got on you. Pretty fucking stupid if you ask me," said Andrews.

Concho stared straight ahead. "Nobody asked you."

Hawkins pulled out a chair and sat beside Martinez with his arms extended, hands clasped together.

"How about telling us what you did with the fifty-thousand dollars you conned from a state senator six weeks ago?"

Martinez turned in his seat. He looked surprised at first, but then just shook his head and continued to stare straight ahead.

"I don't know what you're talking about."

Andrews reached out and pinched the collar of Concho's jacket between his thumb and forefinger.

"Pretty expensive leather you've got there, Martinez. Who'd you assault to get it?"

Martinez slapped his hand away. "Keep your shit hooks off, pig."

Andrews stood and booted Concho's chair out from under him. He flew backwards and went sprawling on the floor.

"Ooops. Sorry, shithead. How clumsy of me." He picked up the chair and shoved it back to Martinez, who was already back on his feet.

Andrews smirked. "Sorry. I guess I'll have to be a little more careful, eh?"

"We've got a guy who identified you as a blackmailer, Martinez. Extortion, too. You 're going to be going away for a long, long time. You can bet on that, amigo. So, how about it? Help yourself out here, and we'll talk to the judge. Who knows, we may be able to get the charges knocked down to just breaking probation, if you cooperate."

Concho sat up straight.

"I don't know what you're talking about." He shook his head. "You're wasting your time when you could be out on the street doing something useful, like peddling parking tickets." He looked at one, then the other man, and his eyes rested on Hawkins. "You've got the wrong guy, and you assholes know it." He waved a hand, as if he was shooing a fly away. "I'll take my chances in front of the judge. Fuck both of you. I want my lawyer."

●　　●　　●

Hawkins was leaving when Lieutenant Ashbaugh came back and handed him a note.

"There you go, Hawk. That tag came back showing it's registered to this guy. Does that name ring any bells? Jacob Caldwell, 4116 Harbor Way, Montgomery, Illinois."

"Not offhand, no. I'll track him down though. Thanks, Lieutenant."

CHAPTER TWENTY-FIVE

It was another rainy day in Chicagoland, driven by a wind that cut to the bone, but bad weather was never a big deal for Hawkins. When he left the police department, he turned up his collar, got in the Lexus and headed towards his office on Wells.

His favorite radio station, Kiss-FM, was playing "Enter Sandman" by Metallica. He listened to part of it, but, deciding he needed some quiet time to think, he turned it off.

For a while there was no sound except the slapping wipers and the wind and rain splattering against the windows like handfuls of fine gravel. It was typical early November in Chicago with the possibility of snow arriving any day.

Hawkins was aware of the possibility of being followed again and used all his mirrors and experienced eye to spot possible tails.

He thought about Concho, who probably knew a lot, but just wasn't willing to give anything up. Maybe he would change his mind and flip, but Cleve doubted that. He knew the police would have to have some strong proof in order to get the thug to turn on whoever was behind everything, possibly even the murder of Russ Maclam, Cleve thought.

Hawkins had said more than once that even the smartest criminals do stupid things, so perhaps those two crimes were connected somehow.

He found himself ruminating about the Albers case. How twisted could people be? The senator's sex life was not the norm, that was for sure, but Cleve suspected that kind of action occurred all the time in Washington. Illicit sex, adultery, swinging . . . all of that and more. But maybe in Chicago, not so much. Nobody wanted to talk about it because too many powerful people were involved. Politicians, staff, lobbyists.

The fact is, half of the newsies are most likely sleeping with somebody they shouldn't be sleeping with so forbidden sex doesn't get reported. It's no big deal. If word got out—in the papers—to the public, it might get a little embarrassing at cocktail parties with all the senators' wives from Podunk Idaho or Little Creek, Minnesota and such, but that would be about it.

Cleve also needed to check on his homeless friend, Deckle, who was currently camped in his office and most likely getting anxious for his return.

•   •   •

He found Deckle sitting behind his desk with his feet up, head down, and his unshaved chin buried in his chest. He was wearing his cheap sunglasses over a White Sox ball cap and must have been watching television when he nodded off. Reruns of *The Andy Griffith Show* were showing on the small portable TV Cleve had brought in to keep the homeless man company.

From the top of the filing cabinet where the TV sat, Cleve heard Gomer saying, as if on cue, "Well, Gawleeeeeeeee!"

When Cleve slammed the door, Deckle jumped.

"Wha . . . wha . . . what hap . . . happened?"

His feet dropped to the floor with a resounding thud and his bleary eyes attempted to focus on Cleve, standing in the doorway, grinning.

Deckle scurried around the desk and rushed to put away his sleeping bag and cot.

"Hi, Deck. Hey, that's alright. Slow down. How about brewing us a cup of Joe, my friend?"

"Yeah . . . yes, sir. Jus . . . jus . . . just one minute, Cle . . . Cleve.

He dropped his sleeping bag and scrambled over to the coffee urn while Cleve hung up his coat and took a seat behind his desk. He noticed the answering machine was blinking as he rolled up his sleeves.

"Anything happen while I was gone that I should know about, Deck?"

Deckle wandered back from the bathroom with a full pot of water. His hand trembled as he poured it into the Mr. Coffee.

"No. Like . . .like wha . . . what, Cleve?"

"Well, you know, partner. Anything at all. Anybody come by?" He glanced through the mail while he waited for an answer.

"Nuh . . . no. Ooh . . . ooh . . . yeah." He pointed to the blinking red light on the answering machine. "The . . . there."

"Yeah, I see that. Who is it? Do you remember?"

Deckle paused a moment and then a light seemed to snap on behind his eyes. A smile came across his lips.

"One . . . one was . . . Miss Mo . . . Mo . . . Mo . . . "

"Maureen? Are you trying to say Maureen?"

"Yes, sir. Miss . . . Maur . . . Moreen called."

"Okay, Deck, thanks. Who's the other call from?"

Deckle shrugged and rolled his eyes.

Cleve waved a hand dismissively. "That's okay. I'll check it."

He punched the first flashing button and listened to the message.

"Hi. Is this the office of Fearless Fosdick? Hope I've got the right number." There was a long pause before Maureen continued: "It's just me. Call me back when you get in, big guy." She paused. "You haven't been answering your cell either, by the way. I hope everything is okay." A long pause followed. "Okay, call me."

Cleve shook his head. "Damn!"

He punched the second button. "Hey, Hawkins. This is Detective Wellbourne, at the PD. I've got some information for you. Call me ASAP."

It was Wellbourne alright. *Mister Hardass.*

Deckle finished putting his bedding away and sat on his stool, with both hands wrapped around his coffee cup. He stared at the floor, as was his norm.

After a moment or two, Cleve made a sour-looking face.

"Damn, partner! Sorry, but this is some bad-tasting stuff. It tastes like the kind of coffee you get free with an oil change. I wonder if you're losing your magic touch, Deck."

Deckle started to get up, but Cleve held up his hand like a traffic cop.

"No, no. Just relax. It'll be okay, Deckle. We'll drink it. By the way, you're probably starving about now, aren't you? I think you'll feel better once you have something to eat. Maybe you'll be up to your usual good game then, okay?"

Deckle had begun to nibble at a hangnail and now curled in on himself, turning into a human comma on the other side of the desk. He forced another smile and let out a measured sigh between his teeth.

"Oh... okay, ...sure thing, Cle ... Cleve."

"Just let me get a few things out of the way here and we'll get some chow. I've got to make a couple of calls."

With that, he punched Mo's number in on the landline.

She picked up after three rings.

"Vice. Maureen speaking."

"Hi, Mo."

"Oh, hi!"

"Sorry I missed your call. I just got in. I've been thinking about calling you, anyway." He paused. "Two minds thinking the same thing...or something like that, eh?"

"Yeah. I've missed you, Sherlock." She said it with that cutesy little smart-alecky thing in her voice that drove him nuts. He wondered who might be listening on her end as he smiled as he watched Deckle sweeping the floor.

"I've just been real busy, baby."

"Well, that's a good thing, isn't it?"

"In some ways, yes. In some ways, no. Most of the time I feel like I'm just wandering around in the dark with this Albers case."

"I heard you were at the scene of a homicide on the west side, too. He was a friend of yours, right?"

"What? No. Who told you that? It's the farthest thing from the truth, Mo. I didn't even know the guy that well. In fact, I only talked to him two or three times. You might not remember, but I told you once, he was a bird dog for my blackmail case. Actually he hired me."

"Well, one of the girls in Homicide mentioned it to me in the break room. That was one of the reasons I called. I wanted to see if you were alright."

"Sometimes that office grapevine might produce sour grapes, my dear." He paused for a beat. "No, I've got my hands full with the senator's case. Maclam was just on the periphery, actually, and no help at all. Maybe a coincidence. I'm not sure."

"Sounds like you have one of those complicated cases on your hands again."

"You may be right, Mo."

"When were you planning on seeing me again? Not a whole week from now, I hope."

"No. Of course not. Like I said, I miss you, Mo. I'll be working on the case tonight. How about dinner tomorrow night?"

"Well, I'll have to see. My calendar has been pretty full lately."

A long pause followed.

"Cleve? Are you still there?"

"Yeah, I'm here."

Mo giggled. "Just kidding, you big galoot. Of course I'd love to have dinner tomorrow night." She sighed. "You didn't think I was serious, did you?"

"No way. Hell, I knew you were jerking my leg. Let's plan on me picking you up around seven. Okay?"

"Sure, sounds good. Bye."

"Bye, baby."

After he had hung up, he told Deckle, "Put that broom away, Deck. We're going to the diner. I'm hungry. You're hungry too, right?"

Deckle's grin widened, his need for dental work painfully obvious. "I sure . . . sure am . . . hungry, baw . . . boss."

With one foot out the door, Cleve felt his cell vibrate on his hip and he paused mid-step to answer.

"Hawkins."

"Hawkins? Sergeant Wellbourne here from homicide."

"Yes, detective. Sorry I missed your call. What's up?"

"I figured I should get a hold of you. Are you still interested in what your homeless friend saw in the alley over on Division?"

"Yeah, sure. What have you got, Wellbourne?"

"Well. I just learned a body washed up on the bank of the Chicago River at Dearborn. No ID on the unsub, but the prints came back. His name is Bentley Raymond Glick. No record that we can find. I think you told us a man with that handle was the one your pal was spooked by. Anyway, I thought you should know."

"Roger that. Thanks, detective. Thanks a lot.

CHAPTER TWENTY-SIX

Cleve was right on time for his date with Mo the next night. He pushed the buzzer for her apartment number and she let him into the foyer and waited for him by her apartment door.

It seemed as though Mo looked more beautiful each time he saw her. Her infectious smile made Cleve realize how fortunate he really was. To his way of thinking, the best way to describe her would be to say she was voluptuous, with a saucy hint of devilry lurking in the sparkling of her eyes and the impertinent cast of her mouth. The little makeup she did use was applied expertly.

She wore a modest green dress with a small floral print and long sleeves which went perfectly with her green eyes and flaming red hair. A small gold locket gleamed on a thin chain against her chest where the neckline of the dress formed a V.

He swept her into his arms and their kiss lasted for what seemed to him a lifetime. His hot lips stirred her to moan.

When it was over, Mo whispered, "I've missed you, big guy."

Cleve caressed her cheek with his fingertips.

"Not as much as I missed you, baby."

She took his hand and guided him into the apartment.

"I'm impressed. You're right on time tonight."

"I'm trying to reform." He swept her into his arms again.

"Where are we going for dinner?"

"Oh, I was thinking some hot dogs and fries would be good for a change. What do you say to that?"

"I'd say you're a cheapskate, sir." She smiled. "But anyplace is fine as long as I'm with you, Cleve. You must know that by now."

They kissed again.

"I'm thinking since we both like Italian," Cleve said, "how about Trattoria Ten over on Dearborn? We haven't been there in a while, have we?"

"Not that I remember. Let's do it."

Three hours later, after cocktails and an Italian meal of calamari, lasagna and all the extras, the couple went to Cleve's apartment for a nightcap.

On the way there, Mo said, "No shop talk tonight. Right, honey?"

"You've got it." He crossed himself and said, "I promise. No detective stuff shall pass my lips."

At his apartment, they got comfortable with a drink. Cleve grinned and said, "Well, babe, we have a couple of choices to round out this great evening. We can watch a classic like *Gone With the Wind*, which I have recorded on the DVR . . . or . . .we can meet in the bedroom and discuss absolutely nothing."

"Hmmmm. Interesting choices, Hawkins. No shop talk, though, right?"

"That's correct. So, which will it be? Personally, I'm sort of leaning more towards the bedroom option, myself." He kissed her on the forehead and winked. "Just sayin'."

"Actually, big guy, I would like to take a shower before I do anything."

"A shower?"

"Uh-huh. You go get in bed, I'll come along in a few minutes."

"A shower?"

"Go on," she said. "I won't be long."

Cleve headed back toward the bedroom. When he heard the shower running, he peeled off his clothes. After a few minutes, when the shower was still running, he went to the bathroom door, turned the handle and opened it.

The room was steamy. Mo's clothes were in a small pile under the sink. The steam billowed up over the drawn shower curtain. Cleve nudged it back and looked in. Mo had her eyes closed and her head arched back while the water ran down over her body. Her white buttocks were in sharp contrast to the rest of her slightly tanned body. She was humming an old Billy Joel tune when he got in behind her and wrapped his arms around her.

"Oh, my God," she cried. "What are you doing?"

"Cleanliness is next to Godliness," he said. "Want me to wash your back?"

She giggled and handed him the soap. He took his time lathering her back. When he was finished, she turned to face him and rinse off. Her breasts were the same startling white as her buttocks had been.

"Want me to wash your front?" he asked.

She laughed and slipped her arms around him. Her body was slick and wet when he kissed her.

With the shower still running they went, towel-less, to the bed.

They stood admiring each other for a few special moments. She looked at the lines both time and pain had etched into her lover's face. He looked at her and saw the longing and regret in her eyes and realized more than ever before that he could not lose her.

He knew she deserved more in life than he had given her.

Cleve lowered her to the bed and dragged his mouth down her beautiful neck to her breasts. Mo arched beneath him, inviting him, begging him to take the tight bud of her nipple between his lips, crying out as he suckled strongly on the tender point.

He swept a hand down her side, over her hip, pulling her leg around him, bringing the moist heat of her womanhood up against the quivering muscles of his belly.

A deep animal groan rumbled at the base of his throat as she reached down and took his erection into her hands. He closed his hand over hers and tightened her grip, and at the same time bent his head down and caught her earlobe between his teeth.

"That's how tight you are when I'm inside you," he whispered, sending more arousal singing through her.

Cleve watched her face as he entered her. He thrust into her fully, deeply, and the tight white heat of her gripped him, squeezing all other thoughts from his mind. They moved together, straining together toward a fulfillment that obliterated the bounds between the physical, the emotional and the spiritual.

They reached it, one, then the other. Breathless, shaking, holding tight.

I love you.

The words were on her lips but she held them back.

I love you.

He held that thought within his heart, still afraid to give it away.

• • •

Near the outskirts of Elk Grove, Big Jake Caldwell stood on his deck and looked toward town. He took in the field across the road where ash-blond cornstalks stood un-harvested, row upon row, in testament to the wet fall and an early winter.

His dislike of Chicago's cold, snowy weather was hard on him. He would be heading for Clearwater, Florida, as soon as some loose ends were tied. All of his business enterprises in the Chicago area were running smoothly, except one.

He was still pondering his problems with the blackmailing of Senator Gerald Albers. What a clusterfuck that had turned out to be, he thought. He wasn't used to having incapable people working for him. When one was discovered, no matter how long their tenure had been, Jake simply got rid of the jerk.

He puffed on his Cuban cigar and sipped a Jack and Coke while he tried to plan a way around the mess that had been created by his number one enforcer, Truck Stebbins, and his so-called "reliable" pal, Carlos "Concho" Martinez.

He leaned on his silver-handled cane and called out to his main squeeze, Gwen, who was in the den, manicuring her nails and watching *General Hospital* on the 85 inch Samsung television.

From somewhere in Jake's throat came a rumbling, burping noise.

"Hey, Gwennie, get out here."

Gwen heard him, but took her time responding. Her soap was at a crucial juncture and she didn't want to miss one single line of dialogue. The calm air in the room was fragrant with peppermint and reefer.

"Okay, honey," Gwen shouted. She frowned thoughtfully and wedged her hands on her hips. "Be there in just a minute."

"Goddammit! Now, Gwen!"

She heaved a heavy sigh, paused her show and hustled through the sliding glass doors and out onto the deck.

"Sorry, honey. My nails are still wet." She was swinging her hands to and fro in the air and blowing on her fingertips. "But they're almost dry," she announced.

"Listen, I've got more important shit to worry about than your fuckin' nails, sweetheart. Get on the phone and find Truck. And don't bother to ask me, cuz I haven't a clue where he is. He's not answering his private number is all I know. I already tried. Tell that no-good sonofabitch I want him and his pal Concho on my doorstep no later than four this afternoon. No excuses either. Got it?"

"Okay, honey. I'll try."

"Bullshit on the trying, Gwen! You heard what I said? Find his fat ass and give him the message. I want him here now, not tomorrow."

Gwen didn't blink.

"Okay, honey. Sure thing. I'm on it."

Her wet nails no longer mattered. Gwen left the television on pause and started making calls.

Exactly seventy-five minutes later, Truck Stebbins was parked on the hassock in Big Jake's den, smoking a cigarette, nursing the bottle of Coors Gwen had served him.

By the time Truck arrived, Jake was totally beside himself. While waiting for his man's arrival, there had been more time for him to stew and dwell on the mounting problems with regard to the blackmail of the senator. His back was turned toward the man as he gazed out the window. The rage seethed inside him and hissed like steam in a pressure cooker.

"Sorry I kept you waiting, boss," Truck said as he mustered a brittle smile.

Jake turned to face him.

"Why do you have a fucking I-phone if you can't be reached on it? The only response out of that thing is a recording telling me your mailbox is full. How is that any good to me?"

Truck shrugged. "Damned if I know. There's nothing wrong with the phone as far as I can tell. Are you sure you dialed the right number?"

"Fuck you! I know how to use a phone, dammit. Where is that Mexican dude you bragged on so much . . . Concho Martinez? I said I wanted you both here."

"The cops nabbed him a few days ago, boss. He's in Cook County jail as we speak."

"Oh, great! They arrested him? What for?" He laughed. "This is real good. I thought you told me, he was clean?

"And he is. It's bullshit. They've got nothing big on him. It seems he just hasn't been reporting to his probation officer for some time now. There was a bench warrant out for him. I didn't have any idea, Jake. None of us did."

"That's just fucking ducky. Well, now, hear this. I've got big plans and I want to get out of here and head south. But now I have to worry about some small time con blabbing to the cops?"

"Nah, you know Concho . . . boss, he wouldn't say shit if he had a mouthful. Besides, he has too much to lose."

"Yeah, you bet he does...like his fuckin' life. Say, wasn't he the one you picked to handle Maclam?"

"Yeah. Him and a couple of the other boys worked that guy over pretty hard. Trouble is they got a little carried away, just like I told you." He shrugged. "So they had to pull his plug."

"And am I wrong in assuming he also took care of Glick?"

"No. That wasn't Concho's job. He was nowhere near the Glick deal." Truck hesitated. "Listen, Jake, I swear, Concho won't talk. Right now, I'm more concerned about that private eye, Hawkins."

"Who? Oh yeah. You mean that small-time snoop you guys mentioned when you were out here before?"

"Yeah. One and the same. He is on to Concho somehow, and now one of our snitches in Cook County says his cop friends have been letting him sit in on Concho's time in the box, along with that Detective Andrews. Hawkins is still asking a lot of questions. He's a real pain in the ass."

Jake shook his head. "What's this guy's fucking problem? Why is he so interested? Who's paying the asshole, anyway? He's gotta' be getting paid."

"Yeah, I know. Before his unexpected demise, Maclam was the one who hired this Hawkins to track down Albers' blackmailers. I guess he was doing a solid for his friend Hulce. He didn't want to touch it himself because of his bad sheet."

"And who is Hulce?"

"He's the owner of the Last Resort Bar over on Belmont."

Big Jake clucked his tongue.

"See? So many fuckin' people are too close to my business. That's a big problem . . . you know that, right?"

Truck shrugged and swigged some more beer. "You're absolutely right, but we didn't have anything to do with that deal, Jake."

Big Jake glared at him.

"Buck passing ain't getting it anymore, Truck. I've had it. Seems to me the loose thread in all this is our friend , the private eye. A fuckin' nobody snoop. It's a damned shame you can't take care of my light work without a screw-up, Truck. Where does this Hawkins lay his head at night?"

"We've had him tailed, but we're not exactly sure where he lives. We're still working on that part. We do know where his office is over on Wells, though. And, get this, we recently found out his girlfriend works at police headquarters."

CHAPTER TWENTY-SEVEN

State Representative Trent Collier was thin and fit. He had white hair that curled down over his collar, too-white veneered teeth, and rimless, made-for-television glasses over pale blue eyes.

Hawkins had only been slightly surprised when Albers had named him as the man who had participated in sex trysts with him and his wife, Trish. After all, Cleve thought, he was a politician. Of course he would want to keep a steamy video of his last sexual encounter with Albers' wife.

When Hawkins called on him, Collier held out his right hand, but the detective eyed it as if it were a steaming cow pie and declined.

"Good heavens, sir," Collier sputtered, "you have me at a disadvantage, rapping on my door at seven in the morning. This is a gated community. How in the world did you gain access?"

Collier slowly eased his way back from the front door and into a breakfast nook located just off to the left. He was obviously rattled.

"I've yet to have my first damned cup of coffee, my friend. Who are you and why are you here? Are you a salesman or a vendor of some kind?"

Hawkins nudged the door closed.

"Neither, Mr. Collier."

"Well . . . well, my wife is away visiting her mother in Wilmette, so if you need to see her, you're out of luck."

"My name is Hawkins, sir, and I'm here to see you, not your wife."

Collier tightened the sash on his robe and raked his fingers through his silvery-white hair and then, pouring a cup of coffee, said, "Well, please be aware, generally speaking, you need to schedule an appointment with my secretary in order to see me, Mr. Hawkins. Her name is Sally Law and you can go through her at my office, downtown, during normal business hours. Hold on, I'll give you my card."

He paused briefly and cracked a smile.

"Say, you look like one of my security people. Are you the police or something?"

"Sort of."

"And what, pray tell, does "sort of" a police officer mean?"

"I'm a private investigator."

"Oh, I see. Well, then, I'll just give you my office number and you can work with Ms. Law on a date and time we can get together. How's that?"

Collier had the tense look of a man who lived with excessive stress. Hawkins noticed his fingernails were bitten down to the quick.

"Well, we're skipping all of the usual formalities today, Mr. Collier. While political protocol may be your call under ordinary circumstances, I think once you've heard what I have to say, you'll agree with your friend, Senator Albers. Our meeting had to be as soon as possible . . . no matter which way we sliced it."

Collier's eyes widened. He was jarred at hearing Albers' name coming from a stranger . . . and a private detective at that.

"The senator gave me your address here in Oak Park. He also gave me your phone number and told me how to bypass that useless contraption you call a gate."

"I'm sorry. Are we talking about Senator Gerry Albers?"

"Bingo! That's the guy."

Collier suddenly looked as pale as a sheet of computer paper.

"Well, why on earth would Gerry tell you, or anybody else, where I live and what . . . "

"Shhhh! Calm down, sir. This is no big deal. The senator simply hired me to pick up that naughty sex video and any other pictures you may have of you and his wife, Trish, in bed together."

"What? Oh, my God!"

"Yeah. I didn't stutter, Mr. Collier. Close that gaping jaw. He wants the video he filmed for you—sweet guy that he is—sharing his wife and all. Look, I haven't got time for a song and dance about how you don't know what I'm talking about, and I personally don't care about what you may or may not be doing with the stuff, but Gerry does. So, hand them over."

Collier, who had been slouching against the wall, now found his way to an overstuffed chintz sofa and dropped like a sack of wet laundry.

"I don't understand. Why? If Gerry wanted the video that bad, he could have asked me."

"He asked me to do it. By the way, what did you want with it, Mr. Collier? I'm just curious."

Collier continued to shake his head back and forth.

"You wouldn't understand, of course, but quite simply, I enjoy viewing the tape long after such get-togethers have taken place, Mr. Hawkins. Let's just say it brings back fond memories."

"Yeah. I can pretty well imagine you enjoying such trash, just you and five-fingered Mary."

Collier was on his feet. "I resent that remark, sir. Who do you think you are anyway? Barging into my home and talking to a state representative like that. Have you no respect?"

"Just go get that tape and I'll be out of here. The sooner, the better. I need to hurry home and take a shower."

"Well, I no longer have that tape, as a matter of fact. I gave it to some friends who wanted to see it."

"That's just great, Collier. Speaking of respect, you've been passing a private sex tape around like a recipe for your wife's homemade lasagna?"

"Well, no. That's not true."

"Oh, bullshit. When can you get it back—or do I have to involve a shitload of other people?"

"No! No! I'll get it back right away. I promise." He raised his right hand as if he were taking an oath. "Just leave me alone for a day or so and allow me to make some phone calls."

"No."

"No? No what, Mr. Hawkins?"

Cleve perched on the edge of a matching chintz armchair.

"No, I'm not leaving without the tape and any pictures you've copied from it."

"My God, man. Why can't you give me a little time on this thing?"

"I am. I'm giving you five minutes to go in the bedroom—or wherever you have stashed that tape—and hand it over to me. I'm not playing games here, Collier."

"No...I can see you're not giving an inch, Mr. Hawkins." He got up and paced the floor for a moment.

"I've seen men like you before...while I was in the Army. Real hard asses. Bullies, every stinking one of them. I always had to laugh when somebody just a bit tougher came along and put them in line."

"Get that fucking tape, Collier. I'm losing my patience. Should I call a friend of mine at police headquarters and have him come out here with a search warrant in his fist?"

Collier held up both hands in a pushing back gesture.

"Okay, okay. I'll get it right now."

He hurried from the room and Hawkins heard a door open and close somewhere in the back. When the door opened a second time, Collier hustled back down the hallway with a ten by thirteen manila envelope in his hand. A thick, red rubber band was wrapped around it.

He was within three feet of Hawkins when he tossed it to him.

"There you go. Now, please leave."

"Whoa. Not so fast, my man. How can I be sure this is the tape we are talking about? I understand there could be more than one."

"Oh, for Pete's sake. Why would I give you a bogus tape, Hawkins? No, that's all there is. And, when you leave here, I don't ever want to see you again. Understood?"

"If it's the real deal, you probably won't ever see me again, but if it is the wrong item—in any way—I will be back, Collier. You can bet your soiled boxers on it."

"Damn you!" Collier began to move toward the door to show Hawkins out, but he mumbled back over his shoulder, "By the way, just in case it should come up. I actually *did* lend that video out to a friend, about a month or so ago."

Hawkins stopped. "Oh? And who was that?"

"A collector friend of mine, who I would trust with my life. So, no problem. I'm just saying. Why do you need to know that, anyway?"

"You had best tell me right now if you don't want any of this coming out in the papers."

"Okay, but it's probably just going to cause more trouble. I just know it will. His name is Glick, Bentley Glick."

•   •   •

Hawkins found that parking spaces on Wells Street were scarce that morning, but he spotted one about two hundred yards from his office. He parked and headed in to check on Deckle and to make some phone calls.

He was less than fifty feet away from the entrance when a maroon Chevy Tahoe slid up along the curb beside him. The doors, front and back, opened on the sidewalk side and one man got out of each of them. The one who came from the front wore a gray suit and black shirt open at the neck with the collar points spread out over the lapels of his jacket. He was taller than Hawkins and had his slick black hair combed straight back in waves.

The guy from the back seat wore designer jeans, cowboy boots and a brown bomber jacket with a short mandarin collar. His hair was a rat's nest of curls, and he sported a neatly-trimmed brown beard.

The Suit said, "Get in the car. We want to talk to you."

His partner with the curly hair stood to Hawkins' left.

The Suit said, "Mm hm," and jerked his head at the open back door of the Tahoe. "Now get in."

"And just what do you want to talk about?" Hawkins asked.

"We want to talk to you about fucking around where you got no business fucking around, asshole."

"Oh, you want to talk to me about that, eh?"

"Come on, come on," the Suit said and flashed his jacket open to show Hawkins the holstered gun on his belt.

"Let me see that again," Cleve said.

When he opened the coat again, Hawkins hit him with a powerful left hand just under his ribs where his sternum ended. It paralyzed his diaphragm and he gasped, doubled over and pitched forward on the sidewalk.

Hawkins saw his partner's hand go inside his jacket toward his left armpit just as the driver of the Tahoe threw open the door on his side and came out of the car and rushed around toward Hawkins.

Hawkins looped his right fist to the man's jaw, gave a left to the stomach, followed by a punch to his nose.

Blood gushed out at once and he dropped to the pavement, out cold.

Curly now had his gun half out of the holster, his hand still under the jacket. Hawkins grabbed his wrist with his left hand and held Curly's gun hand against his chest, the gun caught under the jacket. Hawkins hit him two more times with his right, straight to the nose and jaw.

Curly sagged and Hawkins shoved him away.

Well, I guess the fun is about to begin, he thought, as he stumbled to his office door.

Deckle waited just inside the door.

"Dial 911, Deck. We need to report an assault."

Cleve went to his desk and pulled out his .357 Magnum and moved over to the front window, tapped open a small section of the blinds and checked outside.

Curly appeared to be the last one scrambling to get back inside the Chevy before it sped away.

CHAPTER TWENTY-EIGHT

Two uniformed cops showed up in response to Deckle's 911 call about the assault on Hawkins. They took the report with Cleve's description of the two thugs who had assaulted him. Neither Cleve nor Deckle could provide them with a plate number for the Tahoe.

In retrospect, Hawkins felt the reporting was a waste of time, but at least it was on file now.

The sky had darkened and it began to snow. The flakes danced like thick swarms of fireflies beneath the streetlights, lit early, on Wells. Only five days into November, yet there was snow in Chicagoland. That was no surprise to Hawkins and other natives of the Midwest. Everyone knew after October 15th anything was possible weather-wise.

After the police had gone, Cleve settled in behind his desk, shuffled through the mail and drank a cup of Deckle's coffee. The homeless man straddled a hard-backed chair and smoked a cigarette butt he'd discovered in his field jacket. For the few minutes that followed, the room was as quiet as a mausoleum.

"Cleve, I . . .I sure would like to go see my friends now. I thank . . .thank . . . you for every . . . every . . . thing, but I fee . . . fee . . .feel like

I'm . . .I'm in jail now." He snickered. "It's jus . . just been so . . . so . . .long."

Cleve studied the little man's face and realized he was right. Now that Glick had been found dead, perhaps Deckle would be okay on the street. On the other hand, he might not be safe because a killer was still on the loose. It was a quandary, but Hawkins wasn't going to wrestle with it any longer. If Deckle wanted to leave, he'd let him go.

"Okay, Deck. You're right, you should be on your way, I guess. Glick was found, as I told you, my friend, but that means his killer is on the loose. You realize that, right? I mean, you know the potential danger?"

Deckle nodded and smiled. "I understand . . .Cle . . .Cleve. I . . .I'll be care . . . careful. I prom . . .prom . . . promise. Can . . . can I go?"

"Well, I can't keep you. Since you won't let me drop you off at the shelter, I'd appreciate it if you would check in with me every other day or so for a while, though. Okay? Just so I can see you are still alright. Know what I mean?"

He patted him on the shoulder. Deckle nodded and smiled.

"Okay, Cle . . . Cleve. Sure."

With that, he turned and headed toward the door, but then he stopped and turned to face Hawkins.

"Uuuh, Cle . . . Cleve?"

"Yeah, Deck?" *Let me guess.*

"Could . . . . could . . . You . . you . . . you . . . lend me a cup . . . cup . . . couple of bucks?"

"Oh, yeah. You'll need to eat, won't you?" Cleve stood up and dug into his pocket. "Here's ten bucks, my friend. Promise me you'll get something decent to eat before you do another thing. Okay? And listen, you be sure you get to the mission in time to get a sack for the night, okay?"

Deckle showed Cleve his toothy grin.

"Sure thing, Cle . . . Cleve."

Then he was gone.

Cleve looked out the window and watched him as he ambled down Wells Street, heading south. He kept staring until his friend was merely a speck in the distance.

I hope to hell I've done the right thing. He breathed a heavy sigh. *I did the best I could, my friend. Now you're on your own again, dammit.*

He moved back behind the desk and listened to the messages on the answering machine. There were three. The first was a telemarketer attempting to sell him a lower interest rate on his credit card. Ignoring that, he listened to the second one.

"Hello, Hawkins. This is Detective Andrews at headquarters. I thought you should know somebody paid the twenty grand and sprung your boy Martinez early this morning."

There was a long pause followed by, "Call me, okay?"

"Shit!"

That's just great. My one solid lead is out. Free as a bird.

The last message was from Senator Albers. "Mister Hawkins, this is Gerald Albers. I need to know what is going on, sir. Please call me as soon as possible, okay?"

Hawkins dialed police headquarters and asked for Andrews. The detective answered after three rings.

"Andrews."

"Hello, sergeant. This is Hawkins returning your call. So, Concho Martinez was cut loose, is that right?"

"Yeah. Real early this morning, before eight o'clock, as a matter of fact."

"Who paid his bail? Do you know?"

"Yes, as a matter of fact. Hold on Hawkins. I've got it right here. Just give me a second."

Hawkins heard the rustling of papers.

"Here ya go...you still there?"

"Yeah. Go ahead, Sarge."

"Yes, well, according to our night shift super—who oversees things right up until nine in the morning—a woman paid his bail and he was released into her custody at seven-forty-six this morning. She waited for him to finish all the paperwork for release, then walked out the door with him."

"A woman, huh? You got a name?"

"Yeah. I got it right here. Her name was Gwendolyn Cosgrill. That name mean anything to you?"

"No, not really. Thanks for the heads up, though, Andrews. Much appreciated."

"Yeah, no problem. Hey, sorry we had to let the scumbag go, but the good news is Martinez has to report to his probation officer within twenty-four hours, or else another bench warrant brings him right back in here. If I had to guess, I'd say he is in the wind now, though. You know how it goes."

"Thanks, Sarge." Hawkins hung up.

Yeah, my friend. I know how it goes, alright. You can believe I'm going to find his ass, though.

Cleve poured himself another cup of coffee and dialed Senator Albers' cell.

Albers answered after the first ring as if he'd pounced on his phone. "Hello."

"Senator, this is Hawkins. I'm returning your call."

"Yes, Hawkins. I wanted you to bring me up to date on your progress. I was thinking we should get together someplace for lunch, or dinner, if you can find a way. I'll buy, of course."

"We'll see, but let me ask you one thing. Has anyone contacted you regarding payment of more money?"

"No. absolutely not. Everything has been quiet. I'm glad, quite frankly. Why do you ask?"

"Well, that's their usual deal in these extortion cases. I can tell you this, senator. I still have a ways to go to complete the investigation. I do have some new information, though, and I figure it's just a matter of time before we nail these guys. Takes time, but I've learned that if I squeeze enough pimples, one of them is bound to burst. Meanwhile I must caution you to be alert at all times, sir."

"You still think they might contact me?"

"Probably. I'm sure of this much, though. The people we suspect are armed and very dangerous. They know we're on to them and they would have absolutely no qualms about hurting you or your wife."

"Oh, my God! Should I take Trish away somewhere until this blows over?"

"No. Do not leave town, sir. Just go on with your life as usual. But be on your toes at all times. Did you hire more security, as I suggested?"

Albers cleared his throat. "No. Not yet. I was waiting to see what you had to say before I went that far."

"Senator. You'd better start listening to what I say. I can't stress that too strongly. You must have adequate protection until this situation is rectified and the bad guys are put away. Do you understand?"

"Yes, yes . . . okay."

"I hope for both of your sakes that you do. Now, I spoke with your pal Trent Collier yesterday. He's a real piece of work, isn't he?"

"Trent is okay. He's just spoiled. He's used to everybody catering to his every wish. He can be obnoxious. Is that what you mean?"

"No. I just meant he's an asshole."

"Oh."

"I don't know how or why you see fit to hang out with a jerk like that, but that's not my concern. What I am concerned with is his floating that sex video around. You know, the one you recorded."

"Oh, no!"

"Yeah, but don't get your panties in a knot, senator. I'm on it. We'll discuss all of this later. Meanwhile, I intend to call on your wife and ask her a few questions."

Albers' voice dropped a whole octave. "You really have to do that, Hawkins?"

"Yes. I'm afraid so. Don't worry. I won't tell her anything she doesn't already know. I've got to run, senator. Remember what I told you. Get that extra security on board."

"Yes, okay."

After Hawkins had hung up, he locked the door and walked over to Division street to pick up a foot-long grilled chicken sandwich from Subway. There was a biting wind and the snow was beginning to stick. He took the sandwich back to his office to have with a cup of black coffee. He started making a fresh pot.

Where's Deckle when you need him, he laughed to himself.

As he scooped the coffee grounds into the filtering basket, he thought about Deckle and wondered how he was doing. In fact, he wondered if he would ever see him again.

•   •   •

Hawkins punched in the security code Gerry Albers had given him for his parking garage and and drove down the first row of cars until he spotted Trish's Audi A8 parked right next to a beige tarped, twenty foot cabin cruiser parked in the adjacent space. Hawkins pulled into the slot next to it.

He walked over to the residents' elevator, punched in that code, and took it up to Albers' floor.

The senator's wife appeared to have no qualms about opening her door to a stranger after Hawkins rang the bell.

"Hello, Mrs. Albers. My name is Cleve Hawkins. I work for your husband, Gerald, and I need to ask you a few questions, if I may."

"Well, now is not really a good time. I'm a little busy. Is this something serious or can it wait till another time...perhaps tomorrow?"

" Well, no. As a matter of fact it is kind of important. I'd like to get this out of the way as soon as possible."

"I see. Very well, then."

She stepped aside and guided Hawkins to the parlor. A full bar, complete with beer dispensers and a well-stocked liquor shelf was situated to the right. Trish immediately went about making herself a drink.

"Have a seat, Mr. Hawkins. Can I get you something to drink? A beer, coffee, or perhaps something stronger?"

"No, thank you. You go right ahead, though."

Cleve took a seat on one end of the sofa and quickly surveyed the room. The furnishings looked expensive, even exorbitant . There were lots of oils on canvas, tastefully dim lights, antiques and Oriental rugs.

"Nice place you have. May I ask how long have you folks lived here?"

Trish continued to stand behind the bar as she added crushed ice to her drink. She paused for a moment and studied him.

"What did you say you were doing for my husband? Are you a cop or something?"

"I'm a private investigator."

"Oh, then. That's why you're asking questions."

Trish sashayed over to the sofa with her drink in hand, a ruby-colored liquid in a martini glass. She took a sip, then grabbed a pack of Salems and curled up in the corner of the sofa at the opposite end from Hawkins. She lit her cigarette with a silver lighter from the coffee table.

"Why in the world does my Gerry need a private eye?"

"It's confidential. I'd say that's for him to tell you, Mrs. Albers."

"I see. Tough guy, huh?"

She smiled and stared into space, smoking and drumming a worried little rhythm with the tips of her fingers on the side of her glass. She nibbled at the corner of her lip and everything about her body language told Hawkins she was alarmed.

"Okay," she finally said. "We've had this apartment too long, to be honest. I prefer the quieter life down south, Mr. Hawkins. But to answer your question, we've had this leased for . . . let me see..." She gazed out the windows facing Lake Michigan. "...sorry, I have to think about that." She giggled. "Isn't that crazy? Yes . . . we've had this place for three years this coming April. Why is that important?"

Hawkins shrugged. "Just curious. I'm assuming you don't like living here then?"

She sighed and exhaled a big cloud of smoke that left a halo dangling above her.

"Oh, it's okay. But I'm always glad to get back to the Springfield area when the damned congressional session is over. We can relax for a while, you know? I get so terribly bored when I'm away from home for long periods of time. Of course, the restaurants in Chicago are marvelous. So there is that."

She sat with perfect posture, staring into the middle distance. Cleve surmised she was dealing with images and arguments tumbling through her mind. Pandora's box had opened wide for her, and all her memories were spilling out, one running into the next without her permission.

Her eyes were blue and appeared to be far from innocent. Her lips had a puffy, bruised look about them. She had a long narrow face, graced by high cheekbones and her full, wide mouth suggested a woman who'd once been beautiful. She also had a shapely figure with ample breasts that Hawkins hadn't failed to notice.

After a while he began to feel like she was looking him over, as if he were a T-Bone steak on sale in the butcher shop.

"What else did you want to ask me, Mr. Hawkins?"

"I have to be honest with you. My other questions are of a personal nature. I feel a bit awkward asking, Mrs. Albers."

She smiled, warmly now, and inhaled again.

"Please . . . call me Trish . . . and go right ahead. Ask away."

"Well, I understand that you and your husband have participated in sexual foursomes with other couples, like Trent Collier and his wife. Is that true?"

Without hesitation Trish said, "Yes, that's true. Now, what was your question, Mr. Hawkins? Did you want to know if I enjoyed it?" She giggled and leaned in a bit toward him. "The answer is an unequivocal yes. What else did you need to ask, Mr. Hawkins?"

CHAPTER TWENTY-NINE

Hawkins wasn't the least bit jarred by Trish's brazen response to his question. It was as if any sense of pride had become a thing of the past for her. Her answer even seemed to Hawkins to dare him to dig deeper into the subject of her sex life.

"I appreciate your honesty, Mrs. Albers. Perhaps it will be a plus in helping me with your husband's case."

"Really?"

Trish's eyes widened and her lips parted. She raised a hand toward her neck. Hawkins heard her take a breath as though somehow going on living was unbearable.

"Well, I am happy that I can help. What is it exactly that you are investigating for Gerry, anyway? Obviously, it must have something to do with our personal lives or you wouldn't have the balls to ask me about our foursomes, now would you?"

She stood up. Hawkins watched as she wrapped her arms around herself and stood quietly for several moments. Wiping her eyes with a corner of her sleeve, she took several deep breaths, and sat back down.

"Sorry. I'm not sure I'm really feeling that well at the moment. What else can I do for you?"

Hawkins hesitated briefly, thrown off by her anger now, and then said, "Mrs. Albers, are you having an affair with Trent Collier?"

Trish gave him a long-suffering look.

"Ha! You really don't believe in beating around the bush do you, detective? What makes you think I would be having an affair with anyone? I happen to love my Gerry. I want you to understand that. I would not do anything to hurt him." She paused. "Besides, if I were to do anything like that, I certainly would not pick Trent to fool around with." She smirked and slid her pinky between her wet lips. "His wife, Jill, is more my taste."

Cleve eyed her and forged on.

"You are forthright, Mrs. Albers. I'll give you that."

"Trish. Please call me Trish. Mrs. Albers sounds so . . . oh, I don't know . . . old fashioned, I guess. No, in the great scheme of things, Trent is as important to me as a low fart in a high wind. Know what I mean?" She sat back down and leaned toward him until their shoulders touched. "I don't believe I could ever be unfaithful to my husband."

Cleve shook his head and pulled back.

"Are you aware that Collier has a tape of you and he having sex?"

Trish nodded and hung her head. She lifted her eyebrows but not her eyes, as if she suddenly preferred to avoid direct contact.

"Oh, yes. I'm very aware of that. Gerry told me. That was different, you see . . . I had his permission. There doesn't seem to be much I can do about that tape, though, Mr. Hawkins. I wasn't aware that my husband was filming us at the time."

"What was your reaction when your husband told you about the tape?"

"I was pissed off. I was too overwhelmed to make any sense of it at first. I felt betrayed, to tell you the truth. I was furious. Gerry knew it, too. I wanted to kill him."

Cleve could see the tears rising in her eyes, welling up and until they suddenly spilled over and streaked down her cheeks.

"I've got that tape, Mrs. Albers."

"What?' Oh my God! How did you manage that? You haven't looked at it, have you?"

Hawkins handed her the tape.

"No. I haven't watched it and in answer to your other question, let's just say, Collier was quite happy to surrender the tape. By the time we finished our conversation, he agreed it would be best."

"Good, and I appreciate you not looking at it." She hesitated a moment. "I guess you are a gentleman after all, Hawkins. Thank you for that." She lit another cigarette, sat back, and blew smoke at the ceiling.

"I've thought it over and I've decided to give the tape to you, Mrs. Albers. That's another reason I stopped by. I wanted to be sure you got it. But I think it would be a good idea if you destroyed it. As long as it exists, there could be more trouble. I'm sure you can understand."

Trish wiped her eyes and nodded.

"You're right. I'll take care of it, I can assure you, Hawkins."

"Good. Just a couple more questions then, if you don't mind?"

"No. I suppose not. Does Gerry know you were coming here, by the way?"

"Yes. We spoke just this morning as a matter of fact."

"That figures. You would think he could have given me a heads up, you know? Anyway, go ahead."

"Do you have any enemies or old friends who might be holding a grudge of some kind against you, personally? Maybe even someone from your past who your husband may not know about?"

She shook her head. "No, not that I can think of. You know, this is beginning to sound more serious than I thought, Mr. Hawkins. Exactly what is going on?"

"As I said, you'll have to ask your husband. I'm really not at liberty to tell you everything. One more question and I'll be gone. Do you know a man named Martinez?"

"No. I don't believe I do. Why? Who is he?"

Cleve stood and cleared his throat.

"Just a person of interest in the case, then. Relax, Mrs. Albers. I think your husband will tell you everything you need to know, but I should be going. Sit tight. I'll see myself out. Good day, ma'am."

"Ha! So now it's got to be 'ma'am'?" Trish shook her head. "Goodbye, Mr. Hawkins."

• • •

After his release that morning,, Concho sat across from Big Jake Caldwell for the first time. Gwen had delivered him as instructed. Martinez knew who Caldwell was, but had never met him, even though he worked for him, indirectly, through Jake's henchman, Truck.

Three other people were in the den with them. Gwen was curled up at one end of the sofa, painting her nails. She had changed clothes and wore a frilly white blouse with a cameo choker. Her skirt was hot pink and fit tightly, with a slit up the side. It was obvious she felt she had to keep Jake's interest percolating.

Truck was also at the glass-topped table along with Big Jake and Concho. Another thug named Toke stood by the door, with a tall can of Budweiser in his hand. A cigarette dangled from his lips.

Jake was talking to Concho. "So, of course you clammed up while they hit you with their usual shitload of questions . . .right?"

"Of course, Jake. They did a lot of asking, but I gave them nothing."

"Who was in the box while they pressed you...besides the cop?"

"What do you mean?"

"Just what I said. Who was in the room? Was there more than one cop?"

"There was just that detective, name of Andrews, and one other asshole, who might have been a cop."

"Yeah, I know who Andrews is. Who was the other flake?"

"Like I said, this other guy might have been a cop. He smelled like a cop, you know, except he wasn't wearing a suit and tie. Andrews called him Clave or Cleve or some shit like that."

"Cleve?" Jake looked around the table. "What kind of a fucking name is that?"

"All I know is he was asking me shit, too."

"Oh, yeah. Like what?"

"He wanted to know about the money the senator gave me. He asked me what I did with it."

Jake's tone hardened and chilled. "I'll bet it was that fuckin' private eye again. That's who it was asking you the questions?"

Jake glared at Truck. "How in the fuck does a private eye get to be in the box asking questions? I thought you told me that you and some of the boys were going to crack his fuckin' head and tell him to back off."

Truck cleared his throat. "Yeah, Jake, uuh, we grabbed his ass on the street and tried to jam him into the car, but he got away. We never got a chance to tell him shit. I personally think we need to take him off the board first chance we get."

Jake's dark eyes stayed locked on Truck.

"Oh, yeah? And who's going to handle that? You?" He shook his head. "I swear, you'd fuck up a wet dream if you had the chance." He turned to Concho. "What're you grinning at, Martinez?"

"I was just thinking how I'd like a shot at that private eye. I'll guarantee he won't get away."

Jake studied his face for a moment.

"Somehow, I believe you, Mex. You handled that asshole Glick for me, didn't you?"

Concho nodded.

"Anybody tell you why he had to go? I'm just curious."

The other man shook his head no.

"I figure that's none of my business, Jake. I just do what has to be done. I don't ask questions."

"Good. But just so you know, you eliminated a big-assed problem for us by taking care of Bentley Glick. He was a rat bastard who used to do your line of work, but he started getting mouthy and talked too much. Know what I mean? I couldn't trust him no more."

Concho nodded. "Like I said, it ain't none of my business, boss."

Jake continued to study Concho's face.

"Trouble is, we got a problem with putting you to work for a while. Just getting out of jail, you're too hot...or I'd be having you handle this private eye. He's been getting too close to me and my business."

"I like a challenge, Mr. Caldwell."

"Yeah, but this sneaky bastard has seen your face, my friend. That's no good. You have to lay low for a while. I want to put the squeeze on that senator one more time before I go south. But that private eye has got to go first. Understand?"

Concho lit his cigar and nodded. "Just say when, boss."

"We can't have any fuck ups...like some other assholes have pulled around here, lately." He shook his head and eyed Truck.

"He won't see my face, boss," Concho said, taking a second to admire his cigar. "In fact, he won't see me coming at all."

CHAPTER THIRTY

Hawkins felt the absolute emptiness of his office when he arrived the following morning. It was only a Tuesday, and he had a full week ahead of him without Deckle's company. Maybe longer. There was really no way to tell when the little guy would show up at his door again.

He couldn't help but wonder how his homeless friend was faring. Was he still visiting his pals on the South Side's bowery? Had some harm come to him?

While he made a pot of coffee, his thoughts regarding Deckle persisted, but, realizing he had to let his concern go regarding his friend, Cleve began to concentrate on his next move with the Albers case. He knew he had to locate Concho Martinez.

But where to start?

He also thought about calling Mo, but let that idea go for a time when he would be in a better frame of mind.

After pouring a cup of coffee, he skirted around his desk, sat in his chair and glanced at the blinking message light that now nagged him into listening.

"Hello. This is Edward Hilldebrand and I think we can all agree that life is too short. Have you considered the cost of your final expenses? None of us want to burden our loved ones with those expenses after we pass on, do we? That's why Glory Be has devised an affordable assistance plan for you and so many just like you. We are confident you will find . . . "

Hawkins shut it down before it got more depressing and listened to the second message.

"Hello, this is your final chance to take advantage of lower interest rates on your Visa and Master Card accounts. Please call this 800 number immediately to take advantage of this onetime offer of . . ."

Cleve shook his head in disgust.

There ought to be laws to shut those assholes down.

He sipped his coffee and pulled his check ledger from the bottom drawer. He realized it was time to pay some bills before he did anything else, including making phone calls.

An hour later he took out his phone and scrolled down to Senator Albers' number. The senator answered him on the second ring.

"Good morning, Hawkins."

"Good morning, senator. I'm just checking in. I suppose your wife told you I stopped by."

"Yes, of course she did. She was quite upset, I might add. You do realize you managed to frighten her out of her wits. Why was that necessary, Hawkins? I knew your stopping by to see her would be a bad idea and, unfortunately, you proved me right."

"I assure you, sir, I did my level best to do the opposite. My intention was not to alarm your wife in any way. Did she tell you I gave her the Collier tape?"

"Yes, she did. I appreciate that, by the way. God only knows what Trent would have done with it. I have never trusted that leftist weasel and if it weren't for his Wheat Bill, I would have severed our relationship a long time ago."

"That brings to mind other things I need to discuss with you, senator. Let's get together for that lunch you mentioned the other day. I really don't want to discuss our business over the phone. The sooner we meet, the better."

"I agree. When have you got in mind?"

"Today? Can you make yourself available this afternoon for a late lunch?"

"What time?"

"Well, I've got a few other things to catch up on, so I'm looking at one-thirty or two o'clock."

"Right. I'll have to check, but I think I can do that. Where are we meeting?"

"I don't know. Your choice."

"Let's see. I'd like to keep it close, if you don't mind. I can think of several places. Have you ever been to Acanto's on Michigan? They have great food and a fabulous beer selection."

"That'll work," said Hawkins. "I've been there before. It'll be fine."

"Good. I'll see you there at two then?"

"Right. Goodbye, senator."

•   •   •

The two men met as planned and were given seating in the booth near the back requested by Albers at the door.

"I must admit, it's good to see you again, Hawkins."

"Yeah, well, we needed to get together. I feel I'm losing the thread somehow with your case. Too many people involved, to be honest. The more people who know about any, or all, of this, the worse it will be for you and your wife. You do realize that, right?"

Albers suddenly looked sullen and muttered, "Oh, I know."

He was spared any further comment when the waitress approached. Her name tag read "Ginger."

She filled their water glasses.

"Welcome to Acanto, gentlemen. Can I bring you something from the bar?"

Albers said, "I'll have a Jack and Coke, thank you. A slice of lime, too, please."

Hawkins waved her off. "I'm fine with water right now. Thanks."

When she was out of sight, Albers opened up.

"I wish I had never gotten involved with Trent and his wife. In fact—I'm not trying to shift blame here—but it was Trish's idea to become intimate with them in the first place." He sighed. "She was attracted to Collier's wife, Jill."

"So I understand. You both may regret that relationship now, but you still have to work with him on that Wheat Bill business, right?"

Albers lowered his voice and surveyed the dining area around them. He always seemed to think someone was listening.

"Well, yes, but just remember, it's those pictures that are the threat in the blackmail scheme. Trent had nothing to do with the pictures...as far as I know."

Hawkins eyed him. "You are too jittery, my friend. For the sake of privacy, and to put your mind at ease, I'll be addressing you by your first name from now on, Gerry. Understand?"

"Yes, I do, but I cannot help being on edge. After all, whoever this is knows they have me over a barrel. And I've come to realize it has to be somebody higher up the food chain. That really frightens me for a lot of reasons." He shook his head. "This is all about politics, Hawkins."

"Somebody had to get the pictures after they became familiar with your sex life, and that appears to come damned close to being Collier and his wife, I believe."

Albers shook his head no.

"It has to be someone else," he said. "As I told you before, Collier's Wheat Bill is tied to subsidies that I've been trying to wangle through the House in Springfield for some time. It's a damned good bill and will benefit our Illinois farmers for years to come. Trent is not a bad guy. He'll take all the credit and I don't mind. I don't think he would willingly release information that jeopardized both him and his wife, as well as Trish and me. It doesn't add up."

Ginger came back with Albers' drink and set it down in front of him.

"Are you gentlemen ready to order, or would you like a little more time?"

"Give us a few more minutes," said Albers.

Hawkins took out a small notepad and pen before he continued.

"So, Collier's not your problem here, is what you're saying? Any other ideas as to who might be behind this?"

"No, I wish I did." Albers looked around. "But, you have to realize how important all of this is, Hawkins. It's not the money they want. It never was. Not really. But, if they can get me to vote thumbs down on the bill, it would give their own interests an opening to win the gubernatorial election next year. The way I see it, the money is simply gravy for whomever is enforcing the scheme for the political higher ups. We need to know who that is. Who is being paid to control me."

"I was clear on that, Gerry, but that was before this tape came into play. So, I'm going to run some names by you. You let me know whether you know them or not. Okay?"

"Sure. Go ahead."

"Concho Martinez."

Albers shook his head. "Never heard of him."

"Bentley Glick?"

"Uuuuh . . . Glick is an acquaintance, yes."

"Okay, we'll come back to him in a minute. How about a woman named Gwendolyn Cosgrill?"

"Same there. Gwen is a friend of my wife's."

"Okay. How long have they been friends?"

"What do you mean, how long?"

"Just what I said, Gerry. I mean have they been friends for years, months, what?"

"Years, no. Trish met Gwen about a year ago, I'd say. She was at a big cocktail party we attended out in Oak Brook as I recall. Trish talks to her once in a while. Beyond that, I don't know. Why?"

"Let it go for now. So, how about Bentley Glick? You said you know him?"

"Well, actually, I don't know him that well. He's a friend of Trent's. I only met him a couple of times. He's a dirty animal. I would never allow him anywhere near Trish, that's for sure."

Hawkins checked his notes and then said, "Okay, let's order something to eat. Then I want to know more about this Cosgrill woman."

CHAPTER THIRTY-ONE

Hawkins couldn't sleep that night. He was anxious to pursue the solid lead that might take him directly to Concho Martinez and, through him, ultimately to Albers' blackmailers.

He realized that if he tracked down Gwen Cosgrill, he would have a good chance to gain some ground and perhaps his stalled investigation would get kick-started.

Evidently, Trish Albers knew this Cosgrill woman. He would pay her another visit.

He slipped out of bed and padded across the carpeted floor towards the window to peek through the blinds. The moon had yet to be overrun by the clouds, and the night was cast in a silver glow. Lightning spread across the sky in the distance like spider web cracks across dark glass. It cracked like a whip and thunder rolled after it, booming like distant cannon fire.

What was left of the moon was shining intermittently across the clouds as they scuttled past in advance of the threatening storm. Hawkins sighed.

Good old Chicago. One day snow, the next, thunder, lightning and rain.

Fatigue hung on him like dead weight and he fell back onto the bed. Within a few minutes he was sound asleep.

When he woke around ten in the morning, he was still sprawled across the bed and he realized he had missed his nine o'clock appointment with Harvey Ashbaugh. He had lined it up two days prior, figuring perhaps the lieutenant would have more information on Concho Martinez.

He also wanted to get a look at the Gwendolyn Cosgrill woman. Perhaps the cops working down in booking had something on video showing her, either coming or going, when she'd bailed out Martinez. A decent image of her face was all he would need.

He sat up, stumbled to the bathroom, finished his business there, then shuffled back to bedside and grabbed his cell. He called Ashbaugh who answered after the second ring.

"Good morning, lieutenant . . . this is Hawkins. Sorry I missed our get-together this morning. I didn't forget, I'm just running behind."

"It's okay, Hawk, but don't tell me you had a late night at the bar?"

"What? Hell, no. I just slept in, is all."

"How in the hell could you sleep with all that thunder and lightning banging around all night?"

"It was easy . . . on my back, of course. Hey, I'm on my way out the door right now. Are you still at the coffee shop?"

"Yeah, I'm at Stan's Donut joint. You'll be happy to know they still have the best donuts in town."

"Yeah, I'll bet. Well, can you hold on until I get there...or have you got to get going?"

"No, Hawk. I'm good. It just so happens I've got plenty of company with the jelly donuts here and I'm only about five pages into this morning's *Sun Times*. How long will you be?"

"Twenty minutes, max."

"Okay, I'll be here. Don't get lost."

"I'm on my way. Stay put."

Hawkins didn't bother to shave, but jumped in the shower, brushed his teeth and slid into a pair of jeans. He put on a white shirt, grabbed his raincoat and was out the door. He started to go back for his gun, but remembered his Glock was still in the glove box of the Lexus.

It had stopped raining, but an after-scent of the storm still lingered.

After he found a spot on the fourth level of the parking garage, Hawkins took the elevator down and walked back two blocks to Stan's Donuts place on Dearborn. Ashbaugh spotted him when he came through the door. He checked his watch and waved his friend over.

"You're good, you. You told me twenty minutes and it's only been nineteen. Pull up a chair."

Hawkins took a seat and looked for the waitress. She drifted over to their table as soon as he was situated.

"Coffee, sir?"

"You don't have to call me 'sir,' Judi. I was only an enlisted man."

Judi Francis had been at Stan's for over ten years. All the cops knew her and she knew most of them by name. She was an attractive redhead who wore glasses, but always seemed to have them dangling on a lanyard rather than on her nose. She had the reputation for treating cops with a particular kindness. She always gave them their deserved respect.

Hawkins put Judi in her mid to late thirties at most, and she wore the years well.

She smiled, turned his cup over, and poured the steaming coffee.

"What's your choice in donuts this morning, Hawk?" She playfully poked him in the shoulder with her finger. "See, I did remember your name...even if you haven't been around here since Daley was mayor."

They shared a chuckle that died quickly.

"Ahhhh, just give me a couple plain, Judes. Thanks."

After she walked away, Ashbaugh put his paper down. "You didn't really think she remembered your name, did you?"

Hawkins stirred sugar into his coffee.

"Yeah, sure. Why wouldn't she?"

Ashbaugh laughed. "Oh, no reason, except I told her I was expecting you any minute."

"Figures."

"So what's happening with that shakedown case you were working on? Did you do any good?"

"Nah. I'm still slugging away. As a matter of fact, I wanted to ask you if you had anymore dope on that asshole, Martinez. I know he's involved, but I've about reached a dead end with him since he made bail."

Judi brought Hawkins his donuts and freshened up the coffee for both men.

"Will there be anything else for you two?"

"No, Judi. I think we're good," Ashbaugh said with a wink.

He leaned in with both elbows on the table.

"Okay, Martinez. Well, your boy has got a rap sheet as long as an elephant's dick. There's a little bit of everything on it, drugs, assault, B-and-E. He's a regular walking encyclopedia of fuck-ups. I had a chance to speak to his parole officer. He said Concho moved back to Chicago about eight months ago. Before that he lived in Fond Du Lac, Wisconsin, for a couple of years."

"Wisconsin. Really?"

"Yeah, and according to his PO, other than not hooking up with his probation officer as ordered, Martinez had been keeping his nose out of trouble—as hard as that is to imagine."

"I wonder why he came back to Chicago? He's sure as hell not the nostalgic type is he?"

"Who knows? We do know he's been blowing off one menial job after another. He's been a regular fast food, Burger King and McDonalds nomad."

"He's got to have another source of income, Harve. Know what I mean?"

"But where's he getting it? Maybe he's fallen back on his old standby of peddling drugs."

"Can we keep more eyes on him, somehow?"

"I don't know. Hell, we're practically sleeping with the guy as it is. How long do you want us to keep it tight?"

"At least a couple of weeks would sure help...and day and night until we zero in on what he's up to."

"Well, we do have some informants. But I can't do you any good this morning. Our snitches are all under their rocks this time of day, as you know."

"Just do the best you can do, Harve. I'd sure appreciate it. Maybe one of your informants will have something sooner or later."

"Yeah, but I've got my hands full with another case right now, too. You probably heard about it."

"What's that?"

"We're trying to nail a serial rapist who is just evolving—according to the profile—into a murderer, and to make matters worse, people are out there using the situation to settle scores and fuck over their enemies."

"Oh, great. It sounds like you really do have your hands full, alright. Making any headway?"

"Ahhhh, a couple of good leads, but it all takes time. We've got a shitload of the usual phony tips. You know how that goes. Is there anything else I can do for you, Hawk?"

"Well, I'm not sure, but I got a good tip the other day. I'm told that woman who bailed Martinez out is an acquaintance of the senator's wife. What does that tell you?"

"Beats me."

"Well, I'm thinking maybe that's how the extortion scumbags got their information on the private lives of the senator and his wife. If that's true, I might be able to sail the rest of the way and nail whoever is pulling the strings."

"Sounds plausible. Let me check with my people down in booking about the Cosgrill woman. I'll see if they have anything on their video. Give me a little time. We'll have to review the tape. See if there's a good shot of her face and go from there. I should have something later today, if you want to check back."

"Sounds good, lieutenant. I'll call before I come. Thanks."

Ashbaugh tossed ten bucks on the table and stood up. As he slipped into his overcoat he said, "I've got to shove off, but you know how to get a hold of me. Take it slow, Cleve."

"Thanks. You do the same. Later."

Hawkins gave Judi another ten, swallowed the last of his coffee and stood up.

"Nice seeing you again, Judi. I've got to get going. I'll be dropping in again soon, though."

"Thanks, Hawk. Yeah, don't be such a stranger. Stop by anytime and don't wait a year either. Bye now."

Hawkins put on his coat and left. He walked the two blocks back to the parking garage, headed to the elevator and rode it up to the fourth level where his Lexus was parked. As he passed the stairwell, a man wearing a black beret stepped out in front of him. His partner, a heavy set bald man, edged in from behind and jabbed Hawkins in the ribs with what felt like a gun.

The one with the beret said, "Okay, Jeff. You figure this is our guy?"

Jeff was shorter and wider than Hawkins, with a round bowling ball head and a thick fleshy body that made him look like an overgrown Pillsbury dough boy. He wore a blue Navy pea coat, open over layers of flannel shirts. All the shirttails were hanging out.

"Yeah, this is the one. Looks like that snoop from the north side who doesn't belong here. Come with us, asshole. We're going for a ride."

Cleve glanced over his shoulder. "I don't think so, fat ass."

"Hear that, Mike? Maybe this asshole needs a little help to find his way home."

Jeff looked to be in his late twenties. His breath stunk and his face was plagued with pock marks, a serious case of runaway acne.

Mike made a snickering sound that whistled out his nose.

"Fuckin A. Let's get him on his way."

Hawkins stood his ground.

"Are you guys for real or is this being taped for America's Funniest Home Videos?"

Mike took out a piece of pipe that looked about ten inches long and his chunky buddy took a half-step forward and waved a .45 caliber in Hawk's face and jabbed it into his nose.

"Your fun time is up, snoopy. We're gonna run your ass out of Chicago, and you're never coming back."

Hawkins just sighed.

"Can't do it, boys. Tell me, did Mikey Corleone put you up to this shit?"

Mike jabbed the pipe into Hawkins' gut.

"You don't get to ask questions, smartass. You just do what we say, got it? Now, get moving. You're going with us." He was breathing hard and his nose whistle seemed louder.

Hawkins still stood firm.

"That's some nose whistle, pal. Is it natural or did you have to shove something up there?"

Jeff growled and said, "This fuck thinks we're kidding, Mike."

Mike swung the pipe and Hawkins stepped inside and slammed him in the forehead with his forearm.

He said, "Uuuh," and dropped the pipe, then fell backward over a low cement wall.

Jeff waddled forward, tucked the .45 in his belt and started throwing a flurry of overhand rights and lefts without much in the way of control, trying to do it the way he'd probably gotten away with for years.

Hawkins sidestepped and punched him twice in the face and once in the neck. He drove a straight kick into his groin. The man stopped swinging, coughed and fell to his knees.

Then something hard hit Hawkins behind his right ear and he went down. He kicked up at the man, but it was too difficult to see through the starbursts.

Mike kicked him again and again in the ribs and the back of the head.

"Motherfucker!"

He was slow and he was stupid, but he was also strong.

Meanwhile, Jeff had recovered enough to wave the pistol at Hawkins' head.

"Let me just finish this fucker right here, Mike."

Mike waved him off.

"No. Too fuckin' messy. Jake told us 'clean.' He wouldn't go for this asshole's brains being splattered here."

He grabbed a handful of Hawkins' hair and yanked his head back.

"You get another chance, smart guy. Get out of town and keep your fuckin' mouth shut or we'll finish this job once and for all. You got that?"

He bounced Hawkins' face up and down on the cement.

"You got that, shithead?"

Hawkins made an attempt to claw at his eyes, but he missed.

"Jesus Christ, Jeff," Mike said. "Come on. I gotta get to the hospital."

Jeff kicked Hawkins again, this time in the head. Then there were footsteps walking away and what seemed like a long time later, Hawkins heard an engine fire to life and then fade away.

Hawkins lay face down on the cement. No one came and no one saw.

CHAPTER THIRTY-TWO

Hawkins woke up in St. Joseph's Hospital on Lake Shore Drive. Dread pressed down on him like a giant hand. He was hooked up to an IV and a patient monitor beeped as it kept track of his vital signs. His face was swollen and discolored in splotches and the scent of rubbing alcohol hung in the air.

The head of his bed was slightly raised and the door to his room was wide open. Lights in the hallway were down low, giving the polished floor a pearly glow.

An attractive nurse was busy posting notes to his chart. She was a petite, sinewy woman whose auburn hair was striped with gray and gathered into a loose pile on top of her head. Her name plate read L. Ravencraft and she appeared to be all business.

"Mr. Hawkins, do you have some next of kin you would like us to notify about your being here?"

"No."

"No one at all?"

"I'll take care of it. Thanks, anyway."

"Very well. Thank you, sir. If there's anything we can do to make you more comfortable, please push the buzzer and someone at the nurses' station will answer. Doctor Lescay will be coming by to see you shortly."

She turned and left.

Cleve ached. He felt as though he had gone ten rounds with a kickboxing champion. His memory began to function and remembering how things had gone down, he wanted to jump out of the bed and leave. He felt both hot and cold as well as sick and angry. His pulse roared in his ears and he wanted to hit someone, smash something and yell.

He tried to sit up. The consistent beeping of the patient monitor sounded louder and the frequency of the beeps soon made it sound like something was revving up for a lift-off.

Mo eased into the room and stood over him. She gently pressed him down onto the bed.

"Hey, big guy, take it easy." She smiled at him. "You're not going anywhere." She leaned over and kissed him on the forehead. "I'm glad you're awake, though. You had me worried."

It all started to come back to Cleve, but it remained a fuzzy picture. He remembered getting ambushed and kicked, but after that...nothing. His mouth was dry, and he didn't trust himself to speak in a normal tone of voice.

"Where am I, Mo?" he croaked.

"You're in St. Joseph's on Lake Shore Drive, babe."

"How did I . . . "

"Shhhh." She squeezed his hand. "An alert secretary from the Rowan and Campbell law offices was driving out of the parking garage when she spotted you on the ground and called 911. Thank God she did."

"Yeah, I guess so." He reached up and felt the bandages wrapped around his head.

Mo's tentative smile faded into a look of concern. "You're wrapped up pretty good, Cleve. They had to do a lot of preliminary checks, including a CT scan, because you were in a real bad way when the EMT people brought you in."

"Are they done with the tests?"

"No. They have to do another scan of your head and get more x-rays of your ribs and so on. I think they have been waiting for you to wake up." She caressed his cheek. "Kind of a silly question, but how do you feel, Cleve? I mean, is there some injury maybe they can't see?"

"I feel like a semi hit me and kept right on going. Damn! I ache all over, baby." He squeezed her hand. "What does my face look like?"

"Well, like I said, they've got your head wrapped up pretty good, but from what I can see, your cheek is bruised up pretty bad and it looks like you'll be sporting a couple of raccoon eyes for a while. That one eye is almost shut." She kissed him again. "Sorry, Cleve."

"Ah, it all goes with the territory. We know that by now. It's not the first time I've had my ass kicked."

"Who did it? Did you see who it was?"

He shook his head. "There were two of them. I never seen them before, but one of them was packing a gun. I guess I'm lucky to be alive, huh?"

"Oh, God, Cleve. You've got to get out of this business before it's too late." Tears filled her eyes and she looked away for a moment. "This isn't what I wanted," she whispered. She kissed him again, this time on the lips. "You're right, though, you know. You've just been mighty lucky so far. But that luck could change. Any day. We both know that." A tear rolled down her cheek and she whispered in his ear. "I can't lose you."

He patted her hand.

"We'll talk about it later, baby, okay? How did you find out about this?"

"Your cop friend, Lieutenant Ashbaugh, called me at work. He's supposed to be coming by as soon as he can. He called the nurse's station about a half hour ago. They told him you were sedated, and you are." She grinned. "So you might as well kick back and enjoy the buzz, buddy boy. You're not going anywhere and neither am I."

Mo continued to sit by his bed and although he had dozed off, Cleve was awake when Doctor Lescay came by nearly an hour later.

He was a lean, hard stick of a man with a serious expression, and a frown curved his mouth inside the framework of his neatly trimmed mustache and goatee. He thumbed through the papers on Cleve's chart, then tapped his index finger on his chin and smiled broadly.

"Mr. Hawkins, I'm Doctor Lescay. How are we feeling, sir?"

"I've felt better."

"Yes. I'm quite sure you have. Well, you've got a lot of bruises and abrasions, possibly some bad contusions, but early X-rays are negative for fractures. Your left eye is nearly shut. Looks like you took some pretty nasty punches from someone, sir. I understand you are a retired police officer. Do you feel this attack was job related?"

"No. I believe it was random."

"Oh, is that right?" He used his stethoscope. "Let me have a look, if you don't mind." He nodded at Mo. "Are you his wife?"

"No. Just a close friend, doctor."

"Would you mind stepping out for a moment, ma'am?"

Mo started to leave, but Cleve said, "Yes, she does mind. And if she doesn't mind, I do. She's fine doc. Okay? Go ahead. Do what you have to do."

Mo turned red with embarrassment.

"I'll just be out in the hall, Cleve. You'll be fine."

The doctor nodded at her. "Thank you, ma'am."

Lescay went about checking Cleve's lungs. After he used his bright light to check his eyes and ears, he pulled back the gown covering Cleve's torso and performed finger-presses on his ribs and stomach. When he examined his left side, Cleve yelped.

"Damn! That's a little tender right there, doc."

With that the doctor backtracked and pressed the area again.

"Right there, eh?"

"Damn! Yeah!"

"Well, I cannot be absolutely sure, of course, but I think the chances are you do have a cracked rib. Other than that possibility, I don't suspect there's anything too serious. Not that you haven't been hurt...and I'm sure you are feeling it. There is serious bruising here and there, but it may only be superficial. I think that's what you just felt when I pressed on that area. There's no question you have some internal bruising. The X-rays should give us something more definitive."

"You think I could have a cracked rib?"

"Hard to tell. Like I said, we're going to run a couple of tests and do some X-rays, then we'll know for sure. Meanwhile, I'm going to prescribe some Norco for pain because your injuries will be uncomfortable for a while. I'm going to keep you here for a few days for observation in any event. Okay?"

"I guess I haven't got much choice, do I?"

"Well, no. Not really."

Lieutenant Ashbaugh craned his neck around the door casing.

"Hi, is this the Hawkins residence?"

Doctor Lescay moved off to the side and said, "I was just leaving, sir. Come in. Mr. Hawkins is awake. I'll send your lady friend back in, too."

"Thanks, doc."

Cleve shifted forward as far as he could go.

"Hey, Harve. Thanks for coming. Would you mind cranking the head of this thing up a little?"

Ashbaugh looked over the buttons, pushed one. The motor hummed and the head of the bed raised up.

"That's better. Thanks."

Mo slipped in behind Ashbaugh, then stepped in front of him and kissed Cleve on the cheek.

"I'm staying, but I'm going down to the cafeteria for coffee. Can I bring back anything for you two?"

"Thanks, Mo, but I'm good," Ashbaugh said.

"Nothing for me right now, Mo. Thanks," Cleve said,

After she left, Ashbaugh said, "Sorry I couldn't get here sooner, Hawk. It seemed like everybody waited until I was on my way out the door before they asked me all kinds of shit. Never fails. Anyway, what in the hell happened? Did you know these guys?"

"No. And I just want to go home."

"Yeah, that'll happen." Ashbaugh scoffed. "You don't look so good, my friend. You'd better let the doctors do their thing to help you." He paused and took a seat next to the bed. "So, you have no idea who was behind it?"

"No, but I know there were two of them. Two punks carrying a piece of pipe and a gun."

"Where did they get you besides there, behind that ear?" He pointed to the right side of Cleve's head.

"All over, I think. One asshole jabbed me in the ribs with a piece of lead pipe. I can still feel that. And his fat buddy kicked me repeatedly after I was down. I remember seeing that bastard's shoe coming at my head over and over before they finally took off."

"Did they run away or drive off in a vehicle?"

"No, they didn't run. They drove off in a car, I think." He shook his head. "I know what you're thinking, but just leave them to me, Harve. I'll take care of it."

"You have to stay away from this, Cleve. Let us take care of finding these assholes. Are you thinking these guys have something to do with that extortion case of yours?"

"Yes. I think it's all connected. Like I said, I'll catch the bastards. That's just it. I'm closing in on them now and they know it."

"That reminds me," said Ashbaugh. "I've got something for you." He pulled out a white envelope with a picture inside. He slid the picture out and held it up.

"There's your Gwendolyn Cosgrill. Ever seen her before?"

Cleve studied the picture, "No. I can't say as I have. But you can be sure of one thing. I'll be seeing her real soon."

CHAPTER THIRTY-THREE

Big Jake Caldwell was pissed off. When his men had reported back after their failed attempt to kill Hawkins, they had no good answers for the boss, and they knew it.

"All you had to do was shoot the son-of-a-bitch and get out. I can't believe you two managed to blow an easy job like that. What do you mean, you left him on the garage floor, Jeff? What are you, nuts? You should've finished him right there and then. Why didn't you? Now he can ID both of you clowns."

Mike finally spoke. "Well, boss, you said you wanted it finished real clean. You said that more than once too. So, we planned on hauling his ass down to the gravel pit in Thornton. We thought we had the asshole right where we wanted him, but then we couldn't get him inside the car."

"Why not?"

"Well, he just managed to fight us off. He was just lucky on that score. Anyway, by the time we were ready to load him up, he had caused so much commotion, we thought it best to just haul ass and get out of there...before any witnesses stumbled on the scene."

"Such bullshit. What a lame fuckin' excuse."

Jake shook his head and heaved an ashtray at them. It smashed against the rocks around the fireplace and shards of glass scattered every which way.

"I guess I'll have to handle this shit myself since I can't depend on any of you." He waved his hand dismissively. "Get the fuck outta my sight."

Jeff and Mike left, and Concho grinned as he stepped into the den after their departure.

"My offer still stands, boss. I'll handle that snoop for you. Just give me the okay."

·   ·   ·

Cleve finished staring at his face in the bathroom mirror of his hospital room. It bothered him that he had taken such a beating. His bruises were in full, colorful bloom now, and the swelling around his left eye and cheekbone stretched the skin to the point it looked shiny and tight, the color of a ripe plum.

Mo sat at his bedside. She had taken time off from her job in order to help him in his recovery. Cleve had signed all of the required HIPPA papers, and that gave her permission to be privy to his hospital stay and treatment even though she was not his spouse.

He shuffled back in from the bathroom and sat on the edge of the bed.

Mo yawned. "I haven't gotten any decent sleep the last couple of nights." She rubbed her hands over her face. Her makeup was long gone. Tucking wisps of her red hair back behind her ears, she said, "Listen, I'm going down to get a cup of coffee. Can I bring back anything for you?"

"No thanks. But I've got to get out of this place, Mo. I swear, I'll go nuts if I have to spend another night in this bed."

"You've only been here a couple of days, baby." She gently stroked her fingers up and down his arm. "Just imagine, you could have been kept here for a couple of weeks."

"I know, but still . . . "

Doctor Lescay came in. He smiled and said, "Good morning, Mr. Hawkins." Nodding at Mo, he said, "Morning, ma'am."

"Good morning, doctor."

"You're looking much better today, Mr. Hawkins. Hospital food must agree with you."

"That's not one bit funny, doc. I want to go home. So, what's the story on my tests? What do the X-rays look like?"

"My, we are anxious, aren't we?" the doctor muttered as he shuffled through the papers on the patient clipboard. "Well, I see your X-rays showed contusions of four ribs—no surprise there, it's just as we suspected—but the good news is the CT scan was negative for any irregularities. You are a fortunate man, indeed, Mr. Hawkins."

"Good. Then I can go home, right?"

"Yes, but you'll have to take things slow for a while, give those ribs time to mend. Lay back here and let me have another look." He took out his light and looked in Cleve's eyes. "You still look like you were on the losing end of a boxing match, but I see nothing significant in your eyes that would indicate more serious problems other than the obvious bruising." After checking his ears, he said, "I would still like to keep you here for a couple more days. I understand you live by yourself, so it would be just as a precaution." He rubbed Hawkins ribs to check for sensitivity, then continued, "We want to be sure you are strong enough to take care of yourself."

"Are you kidding? I'll be fine, doc. Rest assured. I would tell you if I was feeling something I shouldn't." He nodded toward Mo. "Maureen will keep close tabs on me, that's for sure. I'll have to wear sunglasses for a while, but I feel great. I'm good to go."

"You have a strong nature. Tell me something, Mr. Hawkins. The violent beating you were victim to is very unusual in this part of town, is it not? Usually the victims we see are from the south side or from over on the west side of town. Your encounter seems like it was a random event. Just curious, what's your opinion on that?"

"Doc, decent people, like yourself, are always shocked to learn bad things could happen within the boundaries of their quiet lives. They figure violence is something that happens to other people—those who live on the south side of town, people who tempt fate. Violence is because of a petty drug deal gone bad, a thug beating up his girlfriend, or a brawl at the bar on Cicero Avenue where troublemakers hang out to practice their expertise."

Lescay lifted his shoulders in a half-hearted shrug. "Yes, that sounds about right. So, your attack must have been rare?"

"No. far from it, doctor. Believe me, my mugging was nothing unusual. In fact, I can honestly say such attacks occur every day and the perpetrators are not selective as to where, nor when. And, rarely are they caught."

The doctor shook his head. "It's a shame. Why we can't do more to prevent these incidents."

"We simply can't give up," said Cleve.

"Well, sir, not to change the subject, but I'm going to sign your discharge papers. It will be noted, however, that I want you to follow up with your family doctor within the next four days. Again . . . just as a precautionary measure."

"Will do, doctor. Thanks."

• • •

Hawkins was glad that Lescay didn't pursue the follow any further because in truth he had no family doctor. The general practitioner he'd seen for twenty years, Doctor Edison, had passed away eight years prior, and Cleve had not sought a replacement.

Once in her car, Mo said, "I'm going to take you to my apartment, Cleve. You need to get your strength back. I'll cook to make sure you eat right, and I'll be able to keep an eye on you."

"No need to do that, Mo. I'll be fine. Just take me to the parking garage on North Dearborn. I need to pick up my Lexus."

Mo slammed her palms on the steering wheel.

"Dammit! You make me so mad, Hawkins. You're so bullheaded. Why can't you allow me this chance to look after you?"

"Hey! Don't get mad, Mo. I'll be fine. You heard the doc say I'm okay."

"He also said you were to take it easy. I know you. You'll have to be tied down."

He reached over and caressed her cheek.

"I've got things to do. You don't have to take off work to play nurse to me, Angel. I'll be fine."

Silence prevailed. Neither of them spoke for the rest of the trip, but Mo was fuming. Finally she spoke.

"You cannot be stumbling around with those painkillers in your system. You know that, right, Mr. Smart Guy?"

"What painkillers? You mean that Norco crap he gave me?" He snickered. "I haven't taken any since that first day. I've got the prescription in my bag. Why don't you take it with you and pick it up for me. That way, you'll have something on hand, in case you ever need it."

Mo pulled in to the parking garage on Dearborn and drove up to the fourth level.

"Okay. Where did you park up here?"

"Right over there," He pointed to a spot on the other side of the stairwell and they saw his car sitting by itself, like a forgotten orphan.

"Okay, this is good, baby. Listen, please don't be pissed at me, okay? I'll be alright, I promise. Let me check the car before you leave, though. Just my luck, those punks saw where I parked and messed with it, somehow."

He got out and strolled over to his car. Mo watched as he circled around it, then kneeled down and inspected underneath. Finding nothing suspicious, he got up, unlocked it and sat behind the wheel. He fired it up and grinned.

Seems like they left it alone. Thank God for small favors.

He got out and walked back to Mo's car. Leaning in the window, he kissed her. "No problem, as far as I can see. I'll come by your place later on, as soon as I'm done with a few things, okay?"

"What choice do I have, you stubborn galoot? You had better not be lifting anything and just promise me you'll go slow." She reached up and rubbed his lips with her fingertips. "Promise?

I did just see you crawling around on the ground over there. Is that what you call, taking it easy, Cleve?"

He kissed her fingers. "You've got my word, angel. Bye."

After she drove off, he opened his car door and got in. His ribs were complaining...*for some reason. It's because of the way I've been moving. They aren't used to my regular moves yet. Yeah, that's it.*

It seemed as though he had been away for a month or more. He checked the glove box for his gun. *It's still here. Good.* He punched in KISS-FM on the radio and caught the tail end of "Highway to Hell" by AC DC.

As he drove out, he glanced at the stairwell adjacent to where he had taken the beating. "It'll be the last time you fuckers get to put a hurt on me," he murmured.

Driving toward his office on Wells, he stayed alert for any tails, but he also thought about things he'd left behind a couple of days ago, like locating Gwendolyn Cosgrill. The other big thing on his mind was Deckle.

Where is he? I wonder if he tried to get me at the office. And Albers . . . I need to call him asap.

Finding a place to park, almost two blocks away from his office, he pulled out his cell phone and called the senator.

It rang six times before Albers answered. "Hello. This is Gerry."

"Senator, this is Hawkins. Listen very carefully. A new wrinkle has surfaced. I need to meet with you as soon as possible."

"Hawkins? I'm glad you called. I've got some questions for you, too."

"Me first, Gerry. When can you come by my office?"

"Uuuh . . . . you mean over on Wells? That's probably not a good idea, sir. Can we meet somewhere else, say on neutral ground?"

"Sure. I guess so, but it has to be right away."

"Why? Have you got some good news for me, I hope?"

"Yeah. I think you'll be happy with what I have for you, senator. Are you familiar with The Redhead Piano Bar?"

"Hmmm. I've never been there, but I've heard of it. Is that the place over on Ontario?"

"That's the one. Can you be there between four and five today?"

"I don't know. It's such short notice."

"Listen up, Ger. I just got out of the hospital. I was in there for injuries sustained in an ass-kicking from people who want me off of your case. In fact, I think they wanted to take me off the board permanently. So, don't give me any shit, my friend. I'm not in the mood. Now . . . will you be at the Redhead on time?"

Albers cleared his throat. "Uhhhh, sorry. Yeah, sure. I'll see you there." He paused. "I hope you'll be in a better mood by then, Hawkins."

CHAPTER THIRTY-FOUR

Hawkins grew up knowing you cared for the ones who had fallen and couldn't get up. He had also learned, you ate no shit. Once you started eating shit, it had a way of becoming your regular diet. He would find the two thugs who had jumped him and make them pay.

The morning he was released from the hospital was graced with a clear, electric-blue sky. There was no bright sunshine yet, but he wore sunglasses anyway and frequently shoved them on top of his head and rubbed a hand hard across his eyes.

After Mo dropped him off in the parking garage, he drove to his apartment and performed a thorough check of his place to be sure no breaking and entering had occurred. He was confident that whoever was shadowing him would continue to do so...and probably go to any lengths now to kill him as soon as the opportunity presented itself.

He went through the apartment, room by room. After finding everything seemed to be just as he had left it two days earlier, he relaxed a bit.

The stubble on his face had grown thick because he hadn't shaved in a couple of days. He decided to take care of that before the day progressed any further. He shaved and showered, then changed clothes and holstered his .25 Cal. Berreta. He strapped it on his ankle and gave it a quick slap with his palm.

He drove to his office on Wells.

When he opened the office door, the air inside fronted him with the distinct smell of empty and unused. It was silent as a mausoleum. The sunlight that fell through the window was brittle and swam with motes of dust.

After a thorough check, he felt convinced that his office had not been invaded either.

So far so good.

When he started to make a pot of coffee, he found bits of mold floating around inside the pot. He realized it had been days since Deckle had been there to make any coffee for them. He rinsed out the carafe and made a fresh pot.

Deckle, where are you, my little friend? Just let me know you are still alive, will you?

He waved his concern off and suddenly stood straighter after folding up his feelings and putting them away. Every cop he'd ever known could do that when he or she had to.

Taking a seat behind the desk, he noticed one light blinking on the landline. When he checked, he found no message had been left. Whoever it was had hung up rather than bother to leave one.

Hawkins was sure he must have forgotten to touch base with someone in the past couple of days, but who? As he thought through things, he tapped a finger absently on the desk. It sounded much like the steady drip, drip, drip of a faucet in an otherwise quiet room.

A few minutes later he got up and poured himself a cup before settling in to sort through the information he'd have for the Senator later that afternoon. He stared into his coffee, heaved a sigh, and then took out the envelope and lay Gwendolyn Cosgrill's picture on the blotter.

Where in the hell are you, lady? I need to find you before you skip town . . . if you haven't left already. I think I know where we'll look. I'll pay a visit to your friend, Trish Albers, for starters.

To break the silence surrounding him he turned on the small television for some background noise. He noticed *Matlock* still hadn't changed his seersucker suit.

Hawkins nursed his coffee and sorted through the stack of accumulated mail. Around noon, not wanting to venture out into the public looking the way he did anymore than necessary, he phoned in an order for a supreme pizza from Lou Malnati's and ate his lunch at his desk.

He completed his past-due paperwork and brought his files up to date while he deliberately stayed away from The Redhead's Lounge until three-thirty that afternoon. He still didn't quite trust himself. He knew he could go in early, sit at their bar and tip a few while he waited for Albers, but that habit had been broken many weeks before and he had no intention of tempting the beast again.

At around three he locked up the office and, since it was close by, he arrived at The Redhead by three-fifteen.

Hawkins was all too familiar with the layout. Booths lined both walls and the bar was in the back. A handful of customers were there when he walked in, a few huddled in booths, some at the bar near the piano.

Hawkins got a tonic and water and chatted with his friend, Harold Pitkins, the afternoon bartender, until the senator showed up at exactly four o'clock with one of his new bodyguards, who he left outside.

Standing just inside the door for a moment, Albers held his gray Fedora with his fingertips. He was obviously letting his eyes adjust to the darkness of the interior. He slowly cased the place until he spotted Hawkins, then marched back to join him in a booth. Pitkins left and went back behind the bar.

"Mr. Hawkins."

Hawkins laid his sunglasses on the table and shook his hand.

"Gerry."

"Any problem finding this place?"

"No, but . . . good God, man! You look terrible."

Cleve kept his voice low. "No shit, Sherlock. What gave you the clue? Is it my bloused eyes or my fouled up complexion?"

"No . . . no, I mean, no, I'm sorry. I . . . I just didn't realize . . . I mean . . . I didn't think it would be that bad."

"Could have been worse." He pointed to the seat opposite him. "Have a seat."

Albers' eyes kept widening as he sat down.

"What do you mean, could have been worse?"

He was noticeably shaken. He fished around in his coat pocket and pulled out a pack of Pall Mall Lights. Hawkins watched as he started to flick his lighter.

"You can't smoke that in here, ace."

"Oh, yeah. Yeah, you're right." He looked around, then stuck both his unlit cigarette and his lighter into a coat pocket. "Damn. Sorry about that. What was I thinking?"

Hawkins studied the man.

"You need to relax. This place used to be one of my favorite watering holes when I was a drinker. They've got good music and the food is exceptional for a lounge."

Albers took in his surroundings.

"Hmmmm. It sure looks nice. I should bring the wife. She likes piano music. In fact, she plays a little herself."

Hawkins gave him a half-assed smile. "Is that right?"

There was an awkward pause before either of them spoke again.

"Okay. I had given you some names to think about, Gerry."

Albers thought for a second then said, "Oh, yeah. Sure, I remember that. Why?"

Hawkins slid an envelope out of his inside pocket and laid the picture of Gwendolyn Cosgrill on the table just as a burr-headed waiter stopped at the table.

Hawkins cautiously flipped the five by eight picture face down.

"Gentlemen. I'm Felix." He put menus in front of each of them and checked his watch. "I'll be your waiter for the next hour or so. What can I get for you?"

"Thank you, Felix. I think I'll have a double Jack on the rocks, water on the side, please," Albers said.

"Just give me another tonic with a twist of lemon, if you don't mind," Cleve said.

"Alright. If that will be all for now, I should tell you our appetizers are half off for the next hour or so, if you're interested. I'll be right back with your drinks."

"Bring us a basket of pretzels or something too, will you, Felix?"

" Yes, sir. Pretzels. Will do."

After he had gone, Hawkins flipped the picture over and turned it so it was facing Albers.

"Ever seen this woman before?"

Without hesitation Albers said, "Sure. What is this, a game, Hawkins? I already told you, that's Gwen. She's one of my wife's friends."

"No, Gerry. I didn't have the picture when I gave you her name. I just wanted to be sure we're both on the same page, my friend. Now I have to speak to your wife again, and I need to do that as soon as possible."

Albers slumped back in his seat. His face suddenly took on a white pallor.

"Yes . . . if you need to, of course."

"When, Gerry?" He paused as he noticed the senator's demeanor had suddenly changed. "What's wrong, pal? You look like you're gonna puke. You feel alright?"

"When you called, I had something to share with you, but we never got around to it. We were busy talking about your attack in the garage."

"Yeah. Sorry. So, go ahead. What've you got?"

"I got a phone call two days ago. I don't know who the man was, but he obviously knew me. Anyway, he threatened me."

Felix came back and delivered the drinks. "Anything else, gentlemen?"

Hawkins waved him off. "We're good, Felix." He leaned forward. "What did this guy say, Gerry?"

Albers looked around. He was obviously choosing his words with the care of a man walking across a minefield. Concern creased his forehead as his brows pulled together.

"Is it okay to discuss so much of this here?"

"Keep it down, but let's have it."

"Well, he told me to have the detective drop the case. He said if you didn't leave it alone immediately, they would make sure Trish never walked again and you would be a dead man. He sounded like he meant it, believe me." He exhaled before he continued. "Of course, this was a couple of days ago, before I knew about you being hospitalized. I tried to call you at your office, but it went to the answering machine, so I hung up. Sorry. I didn't leave a message."

Hawkins nibbled on his lemon rind. "Did he say anything else?"

"Nothing. The line went dead after that. I can't believe any of this is happening," he murmured, looking toward the front door. He turned back and stared at Hawkins, as if frantically weighing his options.

"Don't lose any sleep over the call, Gerry. These guys are just running scared. They know I'm getting close to their number one guy." He tapped the picture that lay before them. "That's why it's so important for me to talk to your wife about this Gwendolyn Cosgrill. So, when can we do that?"

"How about as soon as we leave here? I'll call Trish and tell her we're on the way."

CHAPTER THIRTY-FIVE

Trish Albers made a habit of displaying style and class wherever she happened to be, even at home. It was mainly for the purpose of showing off her status as the wife of Illinois Senator and regional statesman Gerald Albers.

An independent and proud woman, she didn't like her life shuffled every which way just to accommodate the notions of lower class citizens. She always dressed to impress, though, no matter who showed up at her door.

However, she still hated unwanted surprises, so when her husband phoned to say he was bringing Detective Hawkins home with him, she was pissed off. She needed prep time and explained that to Gerry...in so many words.

"Why would you want to bring him here, Gerry? Haven't we had enough of that detective and his infernal questions? He already knows everything about us...from the brand of toothpaste we use, right down to who we sleep with...and when."

"Please, Trish. Just stop talking and listen. This is very important. Do you honestly think I would bring an investigator to our place—or anyone else—if it wasn't vitally important?" He paused for a moment.

"For God's sake, wait until you see this poor guy. Those animals beat the living shit out of him."

"Oh, my goodness. Why did they do that?"

"Well, I guess it was because he persisted in investigating our case. That's why."

"Oh, so it's our fault now? Bullshit! It sounds to me like you'd better tell your detective friend to stop nosing around. He should buzz off and forget about the whole thing. Maybe then they won't bother him...or us either, for that matter. Did you think about that?"

"Come on, I can't do that now. It's too late."

"It's never too late to put a stop to things...if you really want to. My God, Gerry, what sort of people have you got yourself mixed up with, anyway?"

"Trish, let's just discuss all of this later on, if you don't mind. For now, I just want you to be hospitable and accommodating for Hawkins. You are good at that sort of thing, and we need him. Don't you see that?"

"I suppose. But you sure are rushing me, and you know how I hate to be rushed."

"Okay, then, let me go. We're leaving now and should be there within a half hour, probably twenty minutes if traffic isn't too bad."

"Oh, alright. I have no choice anyway, do I?"

Albers expelled a loud gush of exasperated air. "Bye, dear. See you in a few."

Trish spent the next fifteen minutes sitting at her vanity, primping with her makeup. She stopped for a moment, staring in the mirror, and muttered, "I swear sometimes, my life is a misery carnival with shit for prizes."

•   •   •

Hawkins' impatience was humming like an electrical field around him. He was anxious to speak to Trish Albers and get the show on the road.

This method of interviewing wasn't his normal modus operandi. People were easier to read when they were caught off guard. To him, an interview was like a psychological chess match, and he was usually three moves ahead of his opponent, manipulating them into corners, tricking them into giving up information. He had no patience for nervous talkers.

He wanted answers to specific questions and they had to be the truth. He knew people were more apt to trip up if their inclination was a lie.

He waited in his Lexus while the senator wrapped things up on his cell phone. When Albers was done, he waved, pulled out of the parking lot and headed north to his Lake Shore Drive apartment. Hawkins followed. He was relieved to be on the move again.

Trish greeted Hawkins and her husband at the door, effortlessly, elegant in a figure-slimming beige skirt and a crisp, white cotton blouse.

"So, we meet again, Mr. Hawkins. Come in, come in. Gerry, you can take care of the drinks while I see to it that Mr. Hawkins is comfortable in the other room."

She caught herself staring at his damaged face.

"What in the world happened to you, detective? You look as though you got the bad end of an argument." She held up a hand. "Don't tell me. I know. I should see the other guy, right?"

"It's a long story, ma'am."

Trish threw her hands in the air. "Oh, for Christ sake, please? I am not a ma'am." She gave him a phony smile. "Don't address me as such, okay, detective? Call me Trish, or Mrs. Albers, if you like. Anything besides ma'am. Makes me feel like I'm seventy years old." She winked at him as she led the way back to their spacious living room.

"I understand," said Hawkins.

He lowered himself on the couch and sat leaning forward, elbows braced on his thighs. He took out a notepad.

"I didn't mean to insult you."

"It's okay. No big deal." She edged closer. "But my goodness, that eye really does look bad. Have you tried putting ice on it?"

The senator entered the room with two drinks.

"Hawkins, can I get anything for you?" He glanced at his wife. "The detective doesn't drink. Can I get you something else? How about some coffee?"

Hawkins waved him off. "No, thanks, Senator. Let's get this business out of the way, shall we?"

Trish's eyes widened. Her gaze cut from Hawkin's battered face to Gerry and her lips parted. She placed a hand on her neck.

"What does he mean, Gerry? What in the hell is he talking about? Don't just stand there with your mouth open. Tell me what's going on here."

She crossed her arms and hugged herself as she glanced at Hawkins. Gerry lit a cigarette and strolled over to the bar for an ashtray.

"Everything's alright, honey. He just wants to ask us a few questions. Just take it easy." He took a drag on his cigarette and shook his head. "We just got here, for Christ sake."

He looked at Hawkins.

"Go ahead, Hawk. Take over, would you please?" He said it over a long stream of exhaled smoke and then took another deep drag and exhaled again through his nostrils.

"Have you received any threatening phone calls, Mrs. Albers?" Hawkins asked,

She shook her head and touched her throat again.

"God, no. Why would you ask such a thing, Mr. Hawkins?" She glared at her husband. "Am I supposed to expect weird calls now? Is that it?"

Hawkins pulled the envelope containing the picture out of his inside pocket and handed it to her.

"Just checking. I had to ask. It's just procedure. On a different subject, Mrs. Albers, would you take a look at this picture and tell me if you know this woman?"

She looked at it and gave him a weak smile as she handed it back.

"Yes, of course I know her. She's a friend of mine. Gwen Cosgrill. Why?" She glanced at her husband. "What has she got to do with anything?"

"When was the last time you saw her, Mrs. Albers?"

Trish took a big swallow of her drink and set it down on the coffee table.

"Oh, I'm not sure. Let me think."

Hawkins said, "Gerry, give me one of your cigarettes, will you?"

"Sure thing." He handed the pack of Pall Malls over. "Help yourself."

"I remember now," Trish said. "I saw Gwen about a month ago. We met for coffee after our appointments at the Shears Delight hair salon. A lot of us girls do that. We schedule our appointments for the same day and have lunch or coffee afterwards. Why?"

Hawkins scribbled down his notes. "That was about a month ago, you say?"

"Yes. That would be about right. Would you mind answering my question now?" She waited. "How is my friend involved in any of this?" She gave him another weak smile. Her hands were trembling slightly and she swept back some of her loose black hair and tucked it behind her ears. "I mean, really?"

Hawkins looked up. "I'm not entirely sure myself, as of right now, ma'am." He took a deep drag on the cigarette and leaned over to share the ashtray with Gerry.

Trish glared as she stood up. "Damn! There you go again with that 'ma'am' crap."

"Sorry. I'll be able to explain better in a moment. Just bear with me, please, Mrs. Albers."

"Gerry?" She took a step back, gripping his forearms hard as she sucked in a lungful of air and visibly worked to compose herself. "I don't like this one bit, Gerry."

"It will be fine, Trish. Just answer his questions, please."

"Now . . . this is very important," Hawkins said. "Did you ever discuss your sex life with your friend?"

He saw Trish hesitating and thought she actually blushed, but couldn't be sure.

"It's nothing new, Mrs. Albers. Women compare notes all the time, I'm sure."

Gerry rubbed her shoulders.

"Go ahead. Tell him, honey."

"Be quiet, Gerry," she snapped. "Yes, Mr. Hawkins. As a matter of fact, we did discuss it a few times, as I recall." She shook her head. "Why in the world do you need to know that?"

Hawkins ignored her question.

"Is she married?"

"No, she's not. She goes with a guy pretty steady, although it's nothing serious from what she says."

"I know this may make you a bit uncomfortable, Mrs. Albers, but I also need to know if you and Gwen ever had sex with each other?"

"What? Heavens no! I'm not attracted to her in that way, detective." She fanned her face with her hand. "Gerry, is it warm in here or is it just me?"

Hawkins cleared his throat. "We're almost done here, folks."

"For God's sake, I hope so," said Gerry.

"I should tell you," said Trish. "Gwen and I have not known each other that long. I don't know that much about her. She's just a social butterfly I met at a party and she's fun to talk to."

She borrowed her husband's cigarette and took a drag, before handing it back to him.

"So, what's really this about?" she asked Hawkins.

"The man's name Gwen goes with? Is it Concho, by any chance?"

"No, she never mentioned a name like that. I think I would remember that, for sure. No. She told me one time his name was Jake."

"Jake? Jake who? Did she mention his last name?"

"No. She just called him Jake."

"Last question, Mrs. Albers. Do you know where Gwen is right now? Do you know where she's living?"

"No, Gwen was actually pretty secretive about some things in her personal life. She didn't like answering a lot of questions about herself. But, it seems to me, she told me one time she was living out in Oak Park."

Hawkins thought about the name Jake. He realized he had heard that name mentioned somewhere else recently.

CHAPTER THIRTY-SIX

When Hawkins got to his office the next morning, Deckle was sitting in a crumpled heap at the front door. There was a deep cut on his forehead, starting above his swollen left eye. The flesh around it was already starting to bruise. His nose was bloodied.

By the way he was curled and holding his stomach, Hawkins could tell at the very least, his ribs were bruised, if not broken.

"What the fuck!" He patted the homeless man gently on his shoulder. "Deck! Deckle, can you hear me? Dammit to hell, answer me, Deck!"

Deckle tried to rise, but needed the support of Cleve's strong hands to help in getting him upright.

"Hang on, partner. We're going to get you some help, pronto. Don't move."

Hawkins spent the next three hours at St. Joseph's Hospital on Lake Shore Drive while Deckle was examined and doctored by the medical staff on duty in the emergency room. Some X-rays were needed, of course, and Hawkins wasn't allowed to talk to his friend until the primary examination was completed. A nurse eventually came out and told him he could go back and see his friend.

"How you feeling, partner?"

"O . . . okay."

"You feel like telling me what happened?"

"I don't re . . . re . . . remember, Cle . . .Cleve."

"You mean, you can't remember who attacked you?"

"No. There was two big . . . big men, that . . . that . . .that's all I know. It . . .it . . .was so dar . . .dark."

"Where were you when they jumped you?"

"Not . . . not . . . too far . . . away from you . . .you . . .your pla . . .place."

"And, you didn't recognize them?"

Deckle shook his head. "Nuh . . . no . . . no, I don't know."

Cleve pondered what little he had just been told.

"Okay, Deck," he said finally. "We'll find these guys. You just take it easy and cooperate with these doctors and nurses, okay? Remember, they're trying to help you. You know that, right?"

Deckle nodded.

Cleve tapped his shoulder. "I don't think they are going to keep you this time, Deck. So, I'll be back later when they release you and take you with me. Okay?"

Deckle nodded again.

Hawkins stopped by the cafeteria on the way out to buy a coffee. He used his cell to phone Lieutenant Ashbaugh.

A secretary put him through right away.

"Lieutenant Ashbaugh."

"Harve, it's me, Hawkins."

"Hey, Hawk. You're calling again. That must mean it's time to ask me for another favor." He chuckled. "How you doing with those injuries, buddy? I hope you're looking better than the last time I saw you."

"Getting better each day. You're right, though. I still need some help."

"That's nothing new. Our relationship continues to be give and take, my friend. I give. You take. Actually, the score in that department is ten for Hawkins, zero for me." He chuckled. "So, what's up, partner?"

"Airplanes and hard dicks, but what I need is some more intel on that Cosgrill woman. She's the one who bailed out that sleazeball, Concho Martinez."

"How could I forget? We had him in the box, couldn't get him to say shit if he had a mouthful. And, it seems to me, we gave you everything we had on that Cosgrill woman, last time you asked."

"Yeah, I know, but there has to be more, Harve. Something – anything—a driver's license number, last known address, anything that might help me locate her. Believe me, she is key. It's damned important, and I want to seal this one up. I'm getting sick of all the foreplay."

"I'm sure you are or else you wouldn't be asking."

"Right." Hawkins heard his friend's heavy sigh.

"Okay. Just give me twenty-four hours, I'll see what I can come up with. How's that?"

"I couldn't ask for more, LT. Thanks."

"Okay. I'll call you on your cell as soon as I can. Meanwhile, my advice to you is stay away from parking garages, detective." He snickered. "Bye."

. . .

Just before noon Hawkins got a call from Ashbaugh.

"Hawk, I still couldn't find much. I've got good news and bad news, though. The bad news is on the paperwork your girl had to fill out when she bailed Martinez. Where it asks for address, she put 2950 Sheffield Avenue...which turns out is a vacant lot. Cute, eh?"

"Shit."

"Right. But the good news is she listed her occupation as waitress and place of employment as the Gaslight Bar and Grill on South Kedzie."

"Okay, it isn't much, but like you said, it's a start. I'll yank on that thread and see where it leads me. Thanks, Harve. I owe you."

"No shit? Again? Jesus! I'd hate to hang by my balls since you last told me that." He laughed. "Good luck, Hawk. Catch you later."

•   •   •

Hawkins continued to wait for Deckle to get discharged and when the doctors finally released him, Cleve drove over and picked him up. He stopped to pick up a sack of burgers along with two Cokes from White Castle. From there, he drove to his office on Wells.

"Listen, Deckle, I want you to lay low for a few days. Here in my office is as good as anywhere. I'll try to move you up to my place after a while, but we'll have to wait until dark because I'm being watched. You understand?"

"Ye . . . yes, Cleve."

"You should be safe here for a while. How are you feeling?"

"Bet . . . better."

Cleve pointed at his torso. "So, they taped up those ribs, huh? I know how that feels, partner. Take a deep breath and they hurt. Are you in a lot of pain, right now?"

"They would . . . wouldn't give me . . . any . . . pain . . . pain pills to take with me." He scrunched up his face, showing his disappointment.

"Yeah, they can be real stingy with those pills nowadays, Deck."

He reached into a side drawer of his desk.

"Here." He tossed him a bottle of Bayer. "Take a couple of those now, and again after four hours, when it gets real bad. Okay?"

"Okay. Thanks, Cleve."

"Pull up your stool now. Let's chow down on some of these sliders." He handed him a couple of burgers and one of the cokes. "Mmmm. Nice and greasy...just the way I like them."

Deckle stuffed a whole burger into his mouth.

When they'd finished eating, Cleve said, "I have to go out on some business for a while. But, I don't want you leaving here. Got it?"

Deckle nodded.

"I mean it, Deck. I'll be gone awhile, but I don't want you to answer the door under any circumstances, and do not answer the phone unless you hear me on there, telling you to pick it up. Understand?"

"Okay . . . Cle . . . Cleve. When . . . when will you . . . you . . . be back?"

"I figure I should be back before dark, partner. You'll be alright. Just calm down and try to get some rest."

At the door, Cleve turned and said, "Remember what I said, Deck."

"Okay."

Once on the road, Hawkins headed for Kedzie Boulevard. He thought about Mo and considered calling her, but decided to put it off until later in the afternoon.

•   •   •

The Gaslight Bar was an oasis of life in an afternoon canceled due to overcast skies, and its amber lights and Coors signs reflected a glowing welcome out the windows. Cleve parked the Lexus and walked a block back to the front door. Country music could be heard from the sidewalk with George Jones belting out a tune about a lost love on the jukebox.

Inside, Hawkins scanned the length of the bar looking for a good place to sit. It was still early afternoon and not busy. A couple of guys were in the back shooting pool at a coin-op table, and the strong smell of beer, cigarettes and cheap perfume were all part of the Gaslight's charm.

He stood for a moment and drank in the atmosphere before easing over to the bar and taking an empty stool. He scanned the neon-lit beer signs in their oval windows and saw a couple taps filled with the latest flavors of Sam Adams.

The Sox were playing baseball on a TV that was crammed up on a shelf behind the bar. Ceiling fans spun overhead. There were more Budweiser beer signs and mirrors behind the bar and framed jerseys for the Blackhawks, White Sox and Bears on the wall.

The bartender was a plump, pretty brunette in her early forties, who favored a broad swath of mauve shadow above each of her eyes. She was busy washing glasses in the bar tubs.

A grizzled man sat at the end of the bar. He was rawboned, with a belly that advertised his love of rich food. Glancing sideways at Hawkins, he did a quick study and offered the tiniest of smiles, then yelled, "Hey, Marge, You got a new one...and while yer at it, give me another set up, will ya'?"

He took another pull on his beer and quickly wiped his lips with the back of his hand.

"Give me a sec, Charley. Can't you see, I'm up to my ass in soapy water back here, my man."

She looked at Cleve and gave a smile that would make Mona Lisa look as if she were in the midst of a laugh riot. She finished the last glass and wiped her hands and arms on a bar towel.

"What can I get for you, friend?"

"Ah, I'm easy. Give me straight ginger ale with a twist."

Her grin tightened and soured. She lifted her shoulders in a half-hearted shrug and raised an eyebrow.

"That's it?"

"Yeah. Better go ahead and take care of Charley first. I'm in no hurry," said Hawkins.

She breathed a sigh. "Right. I'll get your ginger ale in just a sec."

With that she went about pouring two fingers of Jack Daniels and a glass of draught and delivered them to Charley. That done, she shook her head and filled a beer glass with ginger ale, fumbled around and found a twist of lime and dropped it in the ginger ale.

"There ya' go, friend. Anything else?"

"Yes, a little information if you don't mind, Marge. How long have you been tending bar here?"

"Oh, ha! Too damned long. But actually, about eight years. Why?"

Cleve pulled out the picture of Gwen Cosgrill.

"Maybe you know this woman then?"

She barely took time to look at the picture.

"Yeah, sure. I know her. That's Gwen."

"Oh. Did she work here?"

"Who, Gwen? No way. That gal wouldn't put her hands in dishwater. Are you kidding?"

"Well, how do you know her then?"

"She was a regular customer for a hell of a long time, that's how. But I haven't seen her much... lately. She'd always just hang out and let the guys buy her drinks." She lowered her voice. "A regular barfly, that one. Gwen is a knockout. Has a body that would turn any unsuspecting straight man with a pulse into a drooling idiot." She laughed. "Why are you looking for her, anyway? Did she steal something from you?"

"Nope. Just wanted to talk to her about a friend of hers I've been trying to locate. I figured she might know how to find her."

"Who's the friend? Maybe I know."

"Her first name is Trish."

"Nope. Never heard of nobody named Trish. I would remember that name for sure. Say, what are you a cop or something?"

"Hell, no. I stay clear of the law as much as possible." He paused. "So, when's the last time you saw Gwen?"

"Ahhhh, maybe a month or so ago. She was in here with that Mexican boyfriend of hers. Concho. Now, there's a scary one. I guess they're playing house now." She glanced over his head. "Hold on a minute. I got customers just came in. Regulars. You know how that goes."

"Yeah, That's okay. I have to be moving on anyway, Marge. Just one more thing, if you don't mind. Do you know where Gwen is living now?"

"Yeah, they live in a trailer park in Oak Park. That's all I know."

"Thanks, Marge. Nice to meet you, and thanks for your help. You can bet I'll be stopping back."

CHAPTER THIRTY-SEVEN

It was still sprinkling when Lynie Sue slipped on a windbreaker and drove her golf cart through the mobile home park. Hawkins followed in his car.

He stayed alert as she led him up and down several small streets and then pulled over to the shoulder of one. He started to open his door when he saw her wave and point to a two-tone green mobile home on Lynch Street. Then she drove away.

It was obvious that Lynie Sue didn't want to get involved with anything that might occur at Gwen's trailer.

I guess this is it, thought Hawkins. His eyes scanned the immediate area. A few stubborn autumn leaves shook loose in the strong breeze and spiraled to the ground while two mongrel dogs sniffed around garbage cans adjacent to the trailers.

Hawkins got out and approached the place she'd pointed out on the opposite side of the street. He had his ID out and ready as he took the three small steps up to the front door.

When it opened, a television was blaring *The Price Is Right* from a room behind the attractive, fortyish woman standing in front of him. Her hair was blond-streaked and uncombed and she looked concerned, but not surprised at having a visitor. She was wearing a black cashmere sweater, loose over her jeans, and silver, low-heeled shoes with laces.

Her gaze was hard on Hawkins, as if she was afraid to look away.

"Yes, sir. Can I help you?" She held the door ajar.

Hawkins showed her his ID.

"Are you Gwendolyn Cosgrill?"

"It's Gwen. Yes."

"My name is Cleve Hawkins. I'm a private investigator. I'd like to ask you a few questions. Can I come in?"

Gwen didn't answer, but she stepped back to allow him in.

Hawkins walked in, turning slightly sideways as he passed her so he wouldn't lose direct sight of her eyes. He spotted a pair of men's cowboy boots sitting by the door.

Gwen reached over to close the door after Hawkins had entered, but he stopped her. He wasn't sure who else might be in the trailer.

"Do you mind leaving the door open? I'm a bit claustrophobic."

She hesitated. "No. I guess not. What is it you want to ask me, detective?" She smirked. "I knew you were on your way. Lynie Sue's a good friend of mine."

Hawkins smiled at her. "Good friends are hard to find, aren't they?"

"You bet."

"Well, I won't take too much of your time. Tell me, ma'am—speaking of friends—do you have a friend named Concho?"

Hawkins saw the "tell" in her eyes when she hesitated to answer and the blood drained from her face.

"Who did you say?"

"Concho. Concho Martinez."

She turned her back on him and took a seat on the settee. Digging a cigarette out of her purse, she lit up and took a long, considered drag as she studied him. Her hands appeared to Hawkins to be trembling.

"No. No, I don't know anyone by that name." She shook her head. "Odd name though, isn't it?"

"Nevertheless, that is the man's name."

"Oh, really?" she asked, eyebrows arched, radar suddenly on high alert. "No, I really don't know anyone named Concho."

Hawkins raised a finger and shook his head.

"Please don't lie to me, Gwen. I'm not the drug police. Nobody is going to bust you for having a few Xanax tablets in your purse. I am not your enemy. I just want answers. I want the truth. So, please do not bullshit me. It won't work."

Tears sprang into her eyes and she jumped up.

"No, no, I would never," she said, making a wide-armed gesture like an umpire calling a runner safe at home plate. "I'm not lying. I do not lie, sir."

Holding her ground, she caught a breath in her throat as she lifted a hand to pull one long streak of blond hair out of her eyes. She stared at him and at the same time, Hawkins saw something like great pain peeked through her attempt at a calm composure.

"I'd like you to go, Mr. Hawkins. Leave right now," she huffed.

"I'll be happy to do that, Ms. Cosgrill, as soon as you give me a truthful answer. You see, I know you bailed Concho Martinez out of jail in December. Are you accustomed to helping felons get out of jail, even though you don't know them?" He seated himself on the couch, and squared an ankle over a knee. "Really? I'll give you the benefit of the doubt, Gwen. Perhaps you just forgot. Is that possible?" He continued to stare as she shook her head. "I don't think that's possible. Bail is very expensive, isn't it?"

Gwen took another drag on her cigarette and paced the living room.

"I really don't need any of this, detective. What right have you got to question me about anything? You're not even a cop."

"No, I'm not a cop. Never said I was. And I am sure you don't need the stress, Gwen. So let's start telling the truth, shall we?"

Gwen walked back toward the settee and Hawkins gave her a moment to regain some sort of composure before he leaned forward and continued.

"Listen, I'm working for a client who's being blackmailed for a lot of money. We want to find out who's doing it and put them away. But if I am to find out who is behind their scheme, I need the truth."

He waited for her to look up, looked in her eyes and said, "I need the truth in order to get at the truth, Gwen. You understand?"

She took a deep drag on her cigarette and sat back down. "He doesn't stay here all the time."

"Who?"

"Concho. Who else are we talking about?"

"So, this Martinez just spends the night once in a while? Is that right?" He shook his head. "Your friend, Lynie Sue, thinks you two are married, you know. So, he must come here often. Right?"

She shrugged, let out a long, carefully measured breath and said, "He comes and goes. Isn't that what all you guys do?"

"Probably not all of us, but I get it. When was the last time Concho was here?"

"Two nights ago. He brought me those flowers." She nodded toward a vase of pink roses sitting on top of the television. "He's good to me. He can be a nice guy when he wants to. You don't know him."

"Yeah. Real nice guy, alright. He's on parole and hasn't kept an appointment with his parole officer in four months. Were you aware of that situation?"

She shook her head no. "Concho doesn't say much. He keeps his personal business to himself, know what I mean?"

"I suppose. So you're saying he doesn't tell you anything about how he makes a living, who his friends are . . . nothing like that?"

"Right. What do you want with him anyway? He's not the blackmailing type, if that's what you think."

"What makes you say that?"

She shrugged again. "I don't know. He just seems like too nice of a guy, I guess you'd say."

"Why did you bail him out of jail? What was he in there for? Do you even know?"

"It wasn't my idea. A guy friend of mine asked me to go and bail out his friend Concho. He was busy, so he gave me the money and asked me to do it."

"Who's the friend?"

"I'm sorry. I'd rather not say. Why don't you be smart, detective. Let sleeping dogs lie."

"I thought we'd covered this ground already, Gwen. Remember that part where I told you to quit bullshitting me and tell the truth?"

"Yes, but I don't want to get any more people involved if I don't have to, ya know what I mean?" She took another big drag on the cigarette and took her time crushing it out in the ashtray on the coffee table. "I already feel like I've said too much."

She studied his face for answers and suddenly realized the terrible position she was in. Tears rolled down her cheeks.

"I don't have anyone else," she whimpered. "You'll have to protect me, somehow. They'll hurt me."

"Nobody is going to hurt you, Gwen. You have my word on that."

"But you don't know these people. I think they killed one man, and I really believe they are capable of killing another." She sat back down and buried her face in her hands. "Oh, my God."

"What is your friend's name?"

She looked at him through teary eyes. "How do I know I can trust you?"

"You'll just have to take my word, Miss Cosgrill. I've got the reputation of being a standup guy, if that will help."

"I don't know why I should believe you . . . but I guess I do."

She took time out to blow her nose on the Kleenex she pulled from her sleeve and looked up at him. In a weak voice she said, "His name is Caldwell. Jake Caldwell. But you had better be real careful if you plan to go near his house. He has a gang of vicious friends."

"Okay. Where does this Caldwell live?"

She rolled her eyes and cleared her throat.

"On Ridgeland Avenue . . . I really don't know the exact address. It's a very big place, hard to miss."

"Good. One more question, Gwen. Where is Concho living right now?"

She stood up, adamant now. "I don't know where he lives, okay? I really don't." She began to pace again. "I have wanted to break it off with Concho. I'm just afraid Jake will find out about us and then we'll both be dead."

"How do you know when he's coming by? Does he call?"

"Yes. He calls just to make sure I'll be home."

"Do you have his number?"

"No. He won't give it to me."

Hawkins handed her his card.

"Call me the next time you hear from him. Understand?"

"Okay. I'll try."

"No. Don't just try . . . you do it, Miss Cosgrill. I'm counting on it."

CHAPTER THIRTY-EIGHT

Hawkins knew he would need back-up for his visit to the home of Jake Caldwell. His gut told him Caldwell was, in fact, the ringleader who had been behind extorting money from Senator Albers.

With that in mind, on Friday morning Hawkins called Lieutenant Ashbaugh. He was put through immediately, and after five rings Ashbaugh picked up.

"Ashbaugh."

"Good morning, Lieutenant. Hawkins here."

"Well, lookee here. What's up, Hawk? And please don't tell me about friggin' airplanes again."

"Nah. But I really do need your help this time, lieutenant."

"You must want something pretty bad, since you're calling me lieutenant instead of Harve. Why the formality? I sense you're kissing my ass again. Could I be right?"

Hawkins whistled into the phone and said, "Damn! You are in rare form this morning, aren't you, lieutenant? Maybe I should just stop by, huh?"

"Nah. I'm okay. I'm just shaking off one hellacious week, that's all. How can I help you, Cleve?"

"Do you remember that extortion case I've been working on?"

"How could I forget?"

"Right, well, I've got a hunch it's time for a showdown. I've managed to get the name of ringleader of that blackmailing group. It's Jacob Caldwell. What's more, I know where he's hanging his hat."

"Do tell. And I assume you have the proof it will take for us to cuff him, right? You want me to waltz out there, read him his rights and make the arrest? Is that about right?"

"Well, no. Not exactly, but . . ."

"Proof, Charlie Brown. Proof. Do you have it? You need proof . . . evidence, you know? So, what have you got that will legally allow me toss this guy's ass in the slammer—even if it's just for a little while—or at least hold him until he gets his mouthpiece involved?"

"Okay, how about this? There's Concho. Remember that guy? Concho Martinez is a wanted man for breaking the rules of his parole, is he not?"

"What? Martinez? Oh, yeah. I'm sure we've got a BOLO on him alright. But what has that scumbag got to do with this Caldwell character?"

"Plenty. I have it on good authority that Martinez hangs out at Caldwell's place, practically lives there, I'm told. He works for Big Jake. So, I figure if your people were to stake the place out until they see Martinez go in Caldwell's house, you can show up with an arrest warrant in one hand and a search warrant in the other. You know, using good old probable cause? Harboring a fugitive, at the very least. You'll end up having a damned field day, Harve. You can show up, make your presence known, and see what shakes out after you cuff Concho."

"Hmmmm. I don't know, Hawk, I . . ."

"Furthermore, I have reason to believe those two thugs who jumped me in the parking garage on Dearborn work for Big Jake. They should be camped nearby, too. I'll tag along, of course, and I can sure as hell ID those two. And who knows what else you'll discover while you're out there?"

"Whoa . . . you *did* say the leader's name is Caldwell, right?"

"Yeah. Jacob Caldwell. Big Jake, to his crowd. I failed to tell you, but one of those punks in the parking garage let Jake's name slip during the commotion."

"You mean they said Caldwell's name? You're shitting me."

"No. Not 'Caldwell.' He just said the name "Jake"."

"Oh...but that could be a coincidence, don't you think?"

"Come on, Harve. Neither of us believes in coincidences. You know that. And here's something else for you to consider. I've always wondered how Big Russ Maclam was involved in my case. You may remember he was found with his throat cut a while back, out on the West Side."

"So, what about it?"

"Well, for a number of reasons, I've always thought Martinez was involved in that killing, somehow, someway. At the time, you told me you had some latent prints from that case . . . didn't you?"

"Hell, I don't remember Hawk. If you say so, yeah. That's a stretch, though, don't you think? I mean that homicide occurred several weeks ago, if I'm not mistaken. I'd have to bring myself up to speed on that too. Shit! You realize I haven't even had my morning donut and second cup of coffee yet, and you're already aggravating me..and my friggin' ulcer?"

"Sorry, Harve."

"Yeah, sure. I mean this thing of yours just keeps getting deeper and deeper. Keep it up and I'm going to need Midol. I sure as hell hope you are right with your hunches, this time, Detective Hawkins."

"Me too, my friend. Me too. Listen, my source says Big Jake's living in Oak Park on Ridgeland Drive."

"Ahhhh, yes. I understand that's where a lot of those fat cats are living now. You keep saying a reliable source filled you in. Who in the hell is that? Who tipped you off on all of this shit?"

"Would you believe it was Caldwell's girlfriend?"

"His girlfriend? No! Come on. How in the hell? Never mind. I'll check, but I'm sure Jacob Caldwell is on our radar for God knows what. I'd love nothing better than to bust his ass. It would be a nice feather in my cap—what with me wanting captain's bars on my shirt."

"Yeah, well, here's some more for you to chew on. Big Jake's girlfriend—who is Gwen Cosgrill, by the way—is fucking both Jake and Concho."

Ashbaugh laughed out loud. "Are you kidding me? What the fuck?"

"Yeah. That's what I thought too. I'd sure love it if you could scoop his ass up and eventually we could nail him for the extortion charge. I know a state senator that would be relieved too. You do realize my guy can ID Concho, right? Martinez was the one who physically collected all of the blackmail money from my client."

"Damn. This gets better and better. Do you suppose your client could actually finger this Concho Martinez in a lineup?"

"No problem, except you would have to keep his name out of the papers, somehow. Know what I mean? He'd balk otherwise, I'm sure."

"Good luck with that. Tell you what though, Hawk, give me some time here. I want to pull Caldwell's sheet just to bring myself up to date. Martinez too. I'll get back to you ASAP."

"Yeah. Trouble is I don't want to fuck around with this too long, Harve. We need to move on it as fast as possible because they know I'm getting close to them. That's why they kicked my ass—to get me to leave this whole thing alone."

"Hey, I understand, Hawk. Damn! Do you think I got these bars on my shoulders from sitting on my brains? Leave me alone for a few hours. I'll get back to you. Meanwhile, take my advice. Stay out of parking garages."

"Again, with that friggin' joke."

"Who says it's a joke?"

"Right. See you later, Harve."

"One other thing, Hawk. I'll have to let the police chief in Oak Park in on this before we ask a judge for warrants or we make any serious moves. That would be a captain named, Al Cicotto. I'll see what shakes out here on our end before I alert him, though. As far as I know, he's a hard-assed straight shooter. He'll love the whole idea of a big takedown in his town, I'm sure."

"Roger that, LT. Perfect."

• • •

Cleve still hadn't called Mo and he was feeling more guilty with each passing hour. He was back home in his apartment when he started to punch her in on his I phone. Then he suddenly stopped.

What in the hell do I say? Anything I say will sound like an excuse. Let's face it . . . I'm just afraid she's going to kiss me off once and for all. I do have a legitimate reason for not calling, don't I? Of course I do. I had to find a place for my friend Deckle and follow some more leads in this extortion case.

He sighed and took another deep drag on the cigarette he had copped from his secret stash above the fridge. He had forgotten how many times he quit.

He heard himself say, "I'll just tell the truth. That's always best."

When he stepped into the hot shower, he saw there was still bruising on his rib cage, but there was no bruising on the side of his face, he noticed, when he cleared the steam off the mirror to shave. His skin still felt tender near his right ear, though.

After opening an ice-cold bottle of Nehi orange pop, he called Mo. It rang four times, and he was about to hold off and try later when she picked up.

"Is this Detective Sam Spade calling?"

"Hi, babe. Sorry it took so long to call."

"Oh, that's okay. It's nothing new, right?"

"Right."

"Want another shot, big guy? Is that why you're calling?"

"Nope. That's the truth and nothing but, sweetheart. I come with my hat in my hand. Are you disgusted with me...or just plain pissed off?"

"Actually, believe it or not, I am not as pissed off as you might think." He heard her giggle. "I know you've got your hands full. Jeebers called me yesterday."

"Really? Why did he call you?"

"It seems he couldn't get your friend, Deckle, to eat or talk. He wondered if I knew any of your secrets to get along with the little guy."

"What did he mean?"

"It's like I said, Deckle just plain clammed up. Jeebers thought maybe he was doing something wrong with him...or he was sick."

Hawkins grinned from ear to ear. "So, what did you tell him?"

"I told him, good luck. I said he's probably just missing Cleve." She giggled again. "What else could I say? I did tell him I would try to get hold of you and ask if you had any ideas."

"That's not like Deck. He usually likes to talk. Hard to shut him up, in fact, once he gets started. And he'll eat anything that doesn't walk."

"Maybe you should call Jeebers and see what's up."

"I will, but right now I want to talk to you. I miss you, Mo."

"I've been missing you too, honey. When will you be able to come by?"

"I want to do better than stop by, babe. If you could find a way to schedule some vacation time, I thought we could slip away for a couple of weeks. Just the two of us. What do you say?"

"I'd love that. Where would you like to take me, you big galoot?"

"You name it, but I was thinking Vegas would be a good place to hang out for a while. Suck up some sun, you know, take all of their money. Eat at all those great buffets, make love and sleep as long as we want every day. What do you think?"

"Oh, Cleve, it sounds great. When can we leave?"

"Just as soon as I wrap up this case I'm on. I've about got it done. I'd say it will be all over in the next couple of days...if everything goes according to plan. Okay?"

"I hope you are being extra careful with those bruised ribs. Are you?"

"Of course. They're fine. I'm fine. Come on. Let's plan on it, okay?"

"Well . . . as long as we don't have to wait another three months, I guess. And . . . and if you don't get hurt again. When you hurt, I hurt, Hawkins. Remember that."

CHAPTER THIRTY-NINE

Hawkins wasn't able to sleep for several days, at least not in any restful sort of way. He closed his eyes and tried to meditate, but with little success. His brain was too occupied trying to sort out and make sense of everything he had experienced in the past couple of months.

Now that things were all coming to a head, revenge crept back into his thinking each time he remembered the beating he had endured at the hands of Caldwell's men. They would have to atone for that bullshit, he thought.

I'll make damned sure they pay.

He considered how he had been pulling at threads since that first day, when Big Russ Maclam hired him to find the senator's blackmailers. Since then Maclam had been murdered and Cleve's homeless friend, Deckle, had been assaulted twice. He, himself, had been involved in two physical altercations with Caldwell's thugs. His bruised ribs still reminded him of the last time he was assaulted.

The November dawn came much too early on the fifth day after the meeting with Ashbaugh, just a bluish-pink promise on the eastern horizon when Hawkins awoke. The pale morning sun was low in the east, and its soft gray light was coming in almost horizontally across

Chicago's landscape. The sun was definitely in the deep well of winter, and it was brutally cold.

Hawk reluctantly rolled out of bed while the sun was still low in the eastern sky. More sleep was out of the question. The idea of finishing the Albers case was enough to get him up onto his feet and into the shower that morning.

After drinking two cups of black coffee, he got dressed and perused the *Chicago Sun Times* before holstering his .357 magnum and slipping on his winter coat. He decided to strap his .22 caliber Beretta to his ankle, as well. He was aware that he felt anxious, but he also knew he would be prepared when the call came from Ashbaugh.

Who knows what'll go down after that?

The lieutenant had assured Hawkins that he would be given the heads up as soon as the stake-out and surveillance teams had been lined up to sit on Caldwell's place in Oak Park.

Big Jake Caldwell had always been as elusive as smoke. Long suspected of any number of criminal activities, he was still suspected of doing most of his business in extortion, loan sharking and money-laundering. Lately, word was, he had even made a modest move into the gun trade.

In addition, Caldwell was known to be hand-holding at least a couple unsavory politicians and other, high-level connected individuals who were able to influence his business concerns in a positive manner.

He lived by the old adage that "Money talks and bullshit walks."

•   •   •

Hawkins was having steak and eggs at Emma's Breakfast Place on North Avenue when his phone vibrated at eight-forty-five that morning.

"Hawk, this is Ashbaugh. I wanted you to know I'm all set on our end. Sorry I didn't call sooner. I've been busier than a whore in prison with a fistful of pardons. Anyway, I've already got two of my people sitting on Caldwell's place. And—not to worry—they have been told to make no moves of any kind on that house until they hear from me."

"Really? Alright, Harve! You sure can surprise a man when you have a mind to. I appreciate the call. I'm on my way out there then. Damn, you moved awful fast on this, considering everything that was involved. Good man."

"Well, it didn't take much checking to pin down Jake Caldwell's story. He has a sheet a mile long, everything from domestic abuse and bank fraud to assault with a deadly weapon. Good lawyers, though, of course, so he's never served any time, believe it or not. But this cutie has been in and out of criminal court more times than Perry Mason."

"He's just been lucky, that's all. Were you able to get the warrants, lieutenant?"

"Damned right. Judge Hunnicut was all too happy to give us a search warrant for probable cause. He said he would love to see Caldwell finally go down, whether it's for harboring a fugitive or anything else we can find. He thinks Big Jake is way overdue for a fall."

"So, when do we make our move, lieutenant?"

"Not sure yet, but we're ready. The mayor and police chief in Oak Park are on board with this, too, but they're going to keep their distance and let us handle everything. They will follow up and be available if we need them. Damn decent, considering this is all going down on their turf."

"Roger that, lieutenant."

"Andrews tells me they haven't seen anyone resembling Martinez approach Caldwell's place yet. They're beginning to wonder if your boy was already holed up in the house before we began the stakeout. They feel they might have missed him actually going in, know what I mean? That is possible, you know."

"That's entirely possible, of course, but as I told you, Concho is a creature of habit. He shacks up with Gwen behind his boss's back, but he'll need to touch base with Caldwell pretty soon. That asshole's playing a dangerous bed-hopping game. I figure after he gets some nookie from his honey, he'll float back to Jake's place. That should be fairly soon, I would think."

"Agreed. Sounds about right."

"Yeah, we just need patience here—as you know—but it will pay off, I'm fairly certain of that, LT."

"You don't have to convince me. Me and my people are in on this deal for the long haul, Hawk. You can count on that."

"Good. Meanwhile, I have to get rolling and get closer to the action. When you do go in, I'd like a piece of two of those assholes, myself. So tell me where your guys are located and tell them I'm on the way, okay?"

"You've got it." Ashbaugh gave Hawkins the specifics and said, "I'll call Andrews right now. I think he's planning on hitting their front door before dinner. Anyway, get moving, my friend, and good luck."

"Thanks, lieutenant."

On the way out to Oak Park, Hawkins pulled over to call Senator Albers and bring him up to date.

"Good, God, Hawkins, that's great. I'm overjoyed. You mean to tell me you have actually identified the man who was blackmailing me? Are you going to turn him in to the police now or what?"

"Slow down, senator. Right now I just need to ask you something very important. I need a straight answer with no ifs, ands, or buts attached. Understand?"

"Certainly, Hawkins . . . go ahead, shoot."

"As I told you, we are ready to make arrests and they may involve a lot more than your case. We will probably need you to review a police lineup and pick out the man you gave the two big money payments to. Are you ready for that?"

Albers hesitated. "Oh, God. I don't know about that now. I mean, I can pick him out, I'm pretty sure of that, but I cannot afford to have my name dragged into something as nasty as this, you know what I mean? It would be crippling to my career, you understand?" He paused. "Isn't there some way to arrest this man without having me appear in court?"

"I don't know about court. That's a long way down the line, but right now we need you to finger the men responsible for the extortion so they can be locked up. We will try to keep it as low key as is possible, but I cannot promise you anything. We both know how tenacious the press can be, but you need to help us with this, Senator. Either that or these clowns may skate. We don't want that, do we?"

Hawkins heard a long, hard sigh on the other end.

"You know I want to help in any way I can, Hawkins. Just please promise me you will do everything possible to keep our names out of the papers."

"Damn it! I said you have my word on that, senator. Just help us out with this line up, okay?"

"Very well. I guess I could help you and the police with this line up of yours. I will expect you to be a man of your word, though. Spare me and my Trish any unnecessary embarrassment. Please?"

"I'll do my best. Remember, I did not cause this situation to come about as it has, Gerry. You folks did that. You and Trish brought this whole thing on yourselves." He paused. "Sorry, I've got to go now . . . I'll keep you posted. Okay?"

"Well, yes, please do. But quite honestly, I don't mind saying I'm a nervous wreck and I'm scared silly, detective."

"Go have a double scotch and relax, senator."

Hawkins jumped on the Eisenhower Expressway and took it west to Highway 43 in Oak Park. The four lane road leading out to Ridgeland Avenue was lined on both sides by expensive homes, but also the occasional small strip mall.

Hawkins would rendezvous with detectives Andrews and McCurdy at the location of their stakeout, which Ashbaugh had given him earlier, on Augusta Avenue, almost directly across the street from Caldwell's property. The two men were set up in a small, empty building that was formerly occupied by a Domino's Pizza outlet. It was after four P.M. by the time Hawkins joined the two detectives.

"Hey, Hawk, glad you could make it," said Andrews. "I sure as hell hope you brought some chow and drink with you or we're sending your Dick Tracy ass right back to Wells Street...where you belong."

"Yeah, I've got you covered, sarge. I kind of figured you guys would be getting hungry about now, so I picked up some sliders from White Castle. I got two sacks full, so there's plenty. Go ahead, dig in."

"Hey, you're alright, Hawkins. I don't care what they all say," McCurdy said.

"Gee, thanks, Mac. Sorry if the Cokes are a little watered down by now. I've got a two liter of ginger ale in the car, too, if you want, but you'll still need ice."

"I really don't give a shit about ice," said McCurdy. "As long as that stuff is wet, I'm happy." He used a foot to shove an empty milk crate in Cleve's direction and took the bags from him. "Cop a squat, buddy."

Hawkins settled in, taking a seat on the crate, and then took the binoculars Andrews handed him. He zeroed in on Caldwell's huge front yard on the other side of the road.

"You guys seen anything worthwhile over there?"

"Not really," said Andrews. "Just the usual in and out the front door by some of the ugliest motherfuckers I ever seen. One of those assholes drove up in a '65 Caddy about an hour ago. He parked on the left side of the driveway. You can see it over there." He pointed. "Anyway, he parked and went to the front door. Talk about ugly, this asshole must have fallen out of the ugly tree and hit every fucking branch on the way down."

"But that Mexican dude, Concho, is a no show so far," said McCurdy. "Are you sure he hangs out over there?"

"As sure as I can be. Hell, you think I want you guys sitting over here waiting for nothing? Martinez is bound to show. It being the weekend and all, he should be on the move, know what I mean?"

"Yeah," Andrews said. "But for all we know, this Caldwell character has a poker game on Friday nights somewhere else. His sheet says he likes cards. So, we'll see."

McCurdy now had a mouthful of burger, but managed to say, "When this Concho dude shows up and goes inside, are we making our move right away, sarge?"

"That's the plan," said Andrews. "I'll call Ashbaugh and let him know we're on the move. Then we go in and he'll be sending backup immediately...just in case."

Andrews eyed Hawkins as he continued.

"Now, you do know you'll have to be strictly an observer in this deal, Hawk. You understand that, right? It would be a real clusterfuck if you were in the middle of an official bust and some strange shit went down we couldn't explain. We just never know. You know that, I'm sure, but I just had to tell you anyway."

"I understand, Andrews. No problem."

"Good. So, we'll arrest Concho immediately for parole violations. We'll read him his rights and cuff him, first thing. Then we'll get in Caldwell's shit for harboring a fugitive. He'll pitch a bitch and swear he didn't know anything about Concho being a wanted man, but we'll do the same with him, read him his rights and into the cuffs. Are we clear, so far?"

Hawkins and McCurdy both nodded. "Sounds good," said Hawkins.

"We'll search the place and check out any other yahoos who happen to be in there. They'd best have proper ID and so on, or they get cuffed too. And, who knows what else we'll find? Maybe we'll get lucky and find some white powder or meth. Wouldn't that be perfect?"

"Yeah," said Hawkins. "But the main thing is we will eventually get Concho to open up about the Albers blackmail by offering him a sweet deal. Hopefully he'll turn on Caldwell to save his own ass."

"The other fireworks should be something to behold when we inform Jake that Concho has been fucking his girlfriend, Gwen," Andrews added.

"And maybe I'll spot the two assholes who left me in the parking garage. I hope they give us a hard time so I have a chance to get my payback."

"Easy, Hawk," said Andrews. "I know how you feel, but we have to play this one strictly by the book. You'll get your chance when the coast is clear. Don't worry. I'll turn my back when the time is right."

McCurdy had been looking through the glasses, but suddenly said, "Hey . . . guys, don't look now, but I think I saw a Spanish-looking gent just pull in. He's getting out of a new Ford Mustang. Shit! He's on his way up to the front door."

Hawkins grabbed the binoculars out of McCurdy's hands. "Let me see, Mac."

He watched for a fleeting moment, just long enough to see Concho, wearing his trademark brown bomber jacket, saunter up to the front door.

"That's our boy, alright. Hot Damn! Go ahead and call Ashbaugh, Andrews. Tell him we're on our way in."

CHAPTER FORTY

Cops started swarming all over Caldwell's house right after Concho arrived, in the early evening hours that Friday in November. Detectives Andrews and McCurdy led the charge while Hawkins followed their lead. He knew he had to keep his personal feelings in check during the forthcoming action, but he still was relishing the upcoming scene.

Just as the detectives crossed the street around four P.M., a paperboy whizzed down the sidewalk on a bicycle and smacked a newspaper against the front step of Caldwell's porch with the eye of a marksman. Somewhere in the distance a bell chimed four times, a harbinger to begin the action.

Hawkins cursed under his breath as he watched the kid pedal away, unaware of impending danger.

Cleve remained alert as they approached Caldwell's front door. He had his .357 drawn, as he and Andrews both stepped on the front porch. McCurdy worked his way around to the back of the house to cover any attempted escape by the people inside.

With everyone in place, Andrews stepped to one side of the front door and knocked hard, the cop knock, Bam! Bam! Bam!

He barked, "Chicago police! Open up!"

Hawkins had his ear flush to his side of the door and listened. His pulse jumped. Adrenaline and frustration pumped through him in equal amounts. Andrews' announcement had sent a chill from the crack of his ass to the nape of his neck and he heard muffled voices inside.

He whispered to Andrews, "Somebody's coming."

Andrews nodded. His right hand rested on top of his holstered .45 pistol, immediately available, if necessary.

The man called Truck yanked the door open, but then pushed it closed again, leaving only a slight opening to talk through.

Andrews flashed his badge at Truck and waved the warrant. "Chicago police. I'm Detective Andrews. That is a warrant authorizing us to search these premises. I need to speak to Jacob Caldwell immediately."

Truck squinted. "Cops. Jesus! What's up with you people? You got nothing better to do than snoop in people's houses . . . their homes, for Chrissakes?"

He weighs at least three hundred pounds, Cleve thought, and with a neck as thick as a utility pole. A nasty gash over what was once a right eyebrow left him with a mean-looking, telltale scar. His smile was harrowing.

"That is a legal search warrant, sir. Just open the door and step aside so we can do our job and talk to Mr. Caldwell. This should be a relatively easy procedure, provided we have complete cooperation."

Truck stepped back.

"Who the fuck says you can just search this place? You know who Jake Caldwell is?"

"Yes, and I'm not impressed. Step aside. I'm not going to ask again."

A man's voice bellowed from somewhere inside, "It's okay, Truck. Let the officer in."

Truck called over his shoulder. "You sure, boss?"

Another man suddenly appeared behind Truck.

"What's going on here, Truck? What do they want?"

This man was a lot younger than Truck, with a head shaped like a bowling ball and eyes like the finger holes, and just about as close together. He had an olive complexion and an unattractive, blackened front tooth.

Truck rolled his eyes and said to the other man, "I got this, Tollie."

The boss shouted again. "It's okay, Tollie. I said show the man in. Bring that paper with you, too."

The two thugs slowly backed up and allowed Andrews to pass. Hawkins suddenly appeared from the other side of the door and both Truck and the one called Tollie were caught off guard.

"Jesus! Another fuckin' cop?" said Tollie. "What the hell!" He glared at Hawkins and shook his head. "How many fuckin' cops do you guys need to carry a piece of paper out here, anyway?"

"Not your concern, Tollie," Hawkins said. "Don't get your panties in a snit, okay? There's gonna be a lot more cops before we're done, so just relax and let fatso here give Jake the warrant."

Tollie led them through a spacious front room that boasted a cathedral ceiling and stylish, comfortable furniture. Oil-on-canvas paintings were mounted on the walls and displayed with tasteful, recessed lighting.

A baby grand piano and expensive antiques had been purposefully placed around the room. Oriental rugs covered several areas of the high gloss wood-finished floor and the furniture included industrial chic tables, black leather chairs and a huge black leather couch that faced a 69 inch widescreen TV.

Hawkins and Andrews spotted Martinez on the couch at about the same time, but acted as if they were surprised to see him there.

Concho appeared relaxed, with a can of Budweiser in one hand and the TV remote in the other. His legs were extended out in front of him with his ankles crossed. ESPN highlights flickered on the TV screen in front of him and he made no attempt to move when the two cops entered the room. He didn't even look up.

Andrews removed a set of cuffs from his belt and said, "Jesus, Martinez, You're under arrest. Get on your feet and keep your hands where I can see them."

"What the fuck? What did I do?" asked Concho. He drew his legs in and stood up as Andrews continued.

"I have a warrant for your arrest. You have the right to remain silent, anything you say can and will be used against you in a court of law."

Concho's eyes widened.

"You have got to be kidding, asshole. What the fuck?"

"You have the right to have an attorney present before and during the questioning. If you have none, an attorney will be appointed for you. Do you understand these rights as presented here, Mr. Martinez?"

Jake Caldwell had been sitting behind a mahogany desk in the adjoining den. He stood, came around through the arched doorway and eased into the living room.

"What the hell!" he said. "Are you people nuts? Why're you arresting my guest? I thought you were here to search my place. What does this man have to do with that?"

Andrews ignored Caldwell and said to Martinez, "Turn around and put your hands behind your back. Now!"

Concho glared at him with his signature lopsided grin, but slowly complied and turned. Andrews cuffed him.

"Now, I repeat, do you understand these rights as presented to you, Mr. Martinez? A simple yes or no will do."

"Si."

"Yes, well, 'si' will work, too."

He turned to Caldwell. "You're right, Caldwell. That warrant in your hand is for your premises only, and we will be conducting our search momentarily. I have one of my men posted at your back door, Jake. Have one of your men show him in, immediately."

He glanced at Hawkins. "Hawk, go ahead and follow him, so we can be sure to get Officer McCurdy in here and get this show on the road."

Andrew's eyes focused again on Caldwell.

"Like I was gonna say, Jake, as luck would have it, we also have a bench warrant for Mr. Martinez. He is in violation of his parole on numerous counts, but more importantly he is also wanted in connection with a couple of homicides."

He began to frisk Martinez, running his hands across the man's shoulders, over his back and waist, then down his front, as well as both legs, front and back. He suddenly stopped and held up a gun.

"Well, lookee here what we've got." He held a small .22 caliber pistol he had found strapped to Concho Martinez's ankle.

"Well, now, Concho, you being a felon and all, I'm sure you're not allowed to carry, are you?" He glanced over at Caldwell. "How about that? We're lucking out all over the place today, Jake, wouldn't you agree? Breaking that little law trumps all the other shit we've got on your friend here. I'd say your Mr. Martinez is now totally fucked, for sure."

Concho recognized Andrews and Hawkins from his interview in the box at police headquarters months before, and he couldn't hide the shit-eating grin on his face when that old experience registered.

"I remember both of you assholes now. Fuck you. I want my lawyer." He turned to Caldwell and said, "What the fuck is this, boss? You gonna let these pigs come in your place and slap your people in cuffs? Are you really going to let this shit happen?"

McCurdy came into the living room.

"I just heard from Ashbaugh," McCurdy said. "He said the cavalry is on the way and should be here in just a few."

"Good," said Andrews. "You can go ahead and start upstairs, Mac. I'll be down here with our friend until the troops get here." Turning to Hawkins, he said, "Why don't you go with him, Hawk. Be sure to turn everything upside down and inside out. You know what we're looking for, right?"

"Yeah, but I don't," said Jake. "How about letting me in on your little game? It's my fucking house and I have a right."

Andrews eyed Caldwell and then changed the subject.

"You know, I can't say as I blame you for not helping this asshole, Jake. If some mug was banging my girlfriend, the way Concho has been bragging about banging your Gwen, I'd be pissed, too. I'd probably kill the sonofabitch...if I had the chance. You can believe that."

Andrews shoved Concho down onto the couch.

"Don't look so fucking guilty, Mex," Hawkins said. "You look like you've seen a ghost. I'm sure Jake will be very forgiving...as long as you keep quiet about the blackmail money you picked up from Senator Albers for him on two occasions."

Andrews glanced at Hawkins and grinned. His eyes shifted back and forth between Caldwell and Concho.

Martinez became squirmy and began to shift this way and that on the couch.

"I don't have to hear this bullshit from you or anybody else, pig," he said.

"Stop moving around," Andrews told him. "Jesus. Just stay put until I say otherwise. And keep that trap of yours shut, you hear me?"

Jake Caldwell's eyes had widened and his jaw had dropped.

"What is this bullshit about Gwen, detective?" he asked Hawkins.

Hawkins acted like he didn't know what the man was referring to.

"What are you talking about now, Jake?"

"You know damned well what I'm talking about." He pointed to Martinez. "You said this man has been fucking my Gwen. That's one damned lie I won't abide, and I don't believe it. Explain yourself and do it right now, detective."

CHAPTER FORTY-ONE

Hawkins studied Caldwell.

Now in his sixties, Jake's face had collapsed long ago into a pile of gravity-ravaged tissue that pulled his eyes, nose and mouth downward into a permanent scowl. His mind still seemed to be all there even though his damaged body appeared to have deserted him.

"You fuckers will say anything to stir shit up, won't you?" Jake said and looked around at each man in the room, one at a time.

Hawkins felt smug when he saw how anxious Caldwell was to hear an explanation – from either the cops or from Concho—about Martinez and having an affair behind his back.

"Just sit back and cool your heels, Jake." Hawkins said to him, clearly enjoying Jake's discomfort. "It'll all become crystal clear to you before too much longer."

Hawkins noticed the gold bracelet that clung to Jake's left wrist, just below his diamond Rolex. On his right wrist a tasteful gold chain rattled when he moved back a few steps toward the den.

Detective McCurdy edged over to the living room windows and parted the drapes with his fingers.

"We've got company, sarge, but they're not our guys."

Hawkins flexed his hand and repositioned it on his Glock, ready for whatever might come through the door. He moved over to the window.

"Yeah, he's right. It's those two assholes from the Dearborn garage. One's name is Jeff. I'm not sure of the other one. I think it's Mike, but who cares?"

Mike was the taller of the two and wore the same black beret he'd worn that day in the parking garage. Jeff was short with a huge gut that hung over his belt. The two men appeared to have noticed the strange cars parked in the driveway, but after a slight hesitation they kept walking toward the front door.

"How about it, Jake? What's that other dude's name?"

"I don't know who you're talking about." Jake moved over and sat down in one of the black leather chairs, his head down, looking defeated. "You think I should know everybody's name in Oak Park just because I live here?"

"Yeah...if they work for you, why not?" said Andrews. "So, cut the shit." As the two thugs outside moved closer to the front door, Andrews added, "Never mind. They'll tell us soon enough."

When the two men stepped onto the porch, one behind the other, McCurdy yanked the door wide open before they could touch the knob. He flashed his badge.

"Get in here, assholes. Get over against that wall."

Mike began to back up, but stopped when he saw MaCurdy's badge.

"Cops? You've got to be shitting me!"

Jeff squeezed in right behind his buddy and saw Hawkins.

"What the fuck are you doing here, Snoopy? I thought we parted your hair for you back in that garage downtown? Guess not, huh?" He grinned. "Some people just have thicker heads, I guess."

McCurdy grabbed both men by their coat collars and jerked them inside. He kicked the door closed with the heel of his shoe and shoved the two men against the wall.

"Put your shit hooks on that wall, gentlemen, and don't move."

Jeff balked. "What in the hell is this?" he whined.

Hawkins, who had been assisting Andrews with Caldwell and his crew, now saw Andrews give him an unmistakable "okay" with a wink and slight nod of his head.

"Go ahead, Hawk. Give McCurdy a hand. I'll take care of these other yayhoos."

Hawkins edged over to assist McCurdy with the two new arrivals.

Jeff eyed Cleve, smirked and said, "You got some balls, Snoop. You ain't even a real cop, for Chrissakes."

Hawkins grabbed him by the lapels of his overcoat, whirled him around, and shoved him face first into the wall.

"You don't listen so good, Jeffrey. Now, stay turned around, facing that wall, and spread 'em."

Jeff did as he was told. Hawkins immediately thrust his knee between the man's legs, and with one powerful action brought his knee straight up and slammed it into the man's scrotum.

"Aarrrgh! Owwww! Owwww!" Jeff coughed two or three times, covered his package with both his hands, groaned, doubled over, and fell to his knees.

He began was having difficulty breathing and his mouth was opening and closing like a goldfish pecking at the surface. The smirk had slipped down and left his face. Strings of slimy spittle and puke dangled from his nose and mouth.

"Sorry about that. Damn. I slipped. What's the matter? Did you forget to bring your piece of pipe today, Nancy?" He leaned over Jeff's heaving form and added, "That's really too bad, you know?"

Hawkins clasped his hands together and brought the coupled mass of his fists down like a sledge hammer between Jeff's shoulder blades.

Jeff coughed and wheezed more and Hawkins said, "Yeah . . . I was looking forward to shoving every inch of that pipe straight up your melon-shaped ass, my friend. Now, get up!"

Jeff spat on the floor and wiped his mouth with the back of his hand. He was still fighting for breath when Hawkins grabbed him by the hair on his head and yanked.

"I said, on your feet!"

McCurdy stepped in and grabbed Cleve's arm.

"Okay. That's it, Hawk. I think this dude gets it now."

Mike turned away from the wall and watched his pal choking. He reared back, took a roundhouse swing at Hawkins and yelled, "You sonofabitch!"

Hawkins ducked.

"Oh, Mike! Say it isn't so!"

Hawkins heaved a sigh and his lips curled in tight as he drove his fist into the man's face and felt Mike's upper lip split against his teeth. Mike smashed into the wall and hung there like a broken doll for a second before he slumped to the floor and gasped.

He rolled to his side and scrambled to get up. Blood oozed from the corner of his mouth.

"Maybe you just want some more of what your buddy is currently enjoying, eh, Mike?"

Hawkins allowed the man time to get up as well as take another ineffective swing at him before he slugged him again, this time, square in the snot locker. Mike landed on his back, blood gushing from his nose. Clive saw that Mike evidently didn't realize it was hard to be scary while stemming a bloody nose with one hand.

"Maybe you'd better keep those crossed eyes of yours staring straight at that wall now, asshole. I won't tell you again."

Mike's mouth hung open and he was snorting like a broken diesel.

"I think you busted my fuckin' nose."

"So, sue me, Michael."

McCurdy turned and looked out the front door just in time to see three blue and white Chicago police cruisers pull into the driveway. They purposely parked to block all the other vehicles from leaving the scene. Two Oak Park police cars, marked with black and gold lettering, pulled in behind them. Four uniformed cops piled out of each of the Chicago vehicles.

"Sarge, our back-up is here," McCurdy called out to Andrews.

"Good. Go out there and bring them up to speed, will you, Mac. Get them all in here. I want every available swinging dick helping to turn this place upside down."

Andrews walked back into the living room. Caldwell looked up at him from the sofa, but still seemed too dejected to stand up. There was anger in his voice, but not much.

"This is such bullshit, detective, and you know it. You assholes come charging in here like Kojak and company with a warrant in your mitts, but instead of doing your job, you just continue to fuck over my people. And now you're fucking with me? If all you wanted was Martinez, why not just go ahead and take him. I could care less about that Mexican shithead. Just leave me and my people alone. I've had enough. You're setting the city of Chicago up for a big fucking lawsuit, Andrews."

Concho now glared at his boss.

"What the fuck are you saying, Chico? You hanging me out to dry after all the shit I've done for you? Huh?" He looked at Andrews and Hawkins. "Alright, fine. You cops been looking for the one who's been shaking down that senator, right?"

Andrews shrugged. "Maybe."

McCurdy came back in with twelve uniformed Chicago cops and four members of the Oak Park Police Department behind them. Andrews spoke as soon as they were all inside.

Tollie looked over at Caldwell.

"Boss. We must have the whole fucking Chicago police force here."

Andrews spoke,

"Men, I want to thank you for your cooperation. The main thing here is, of course, that we want a thorough search. I'm sure Detective McCurdy has briefed you. So, if we are all set, four of you can work the upstairs rooms. The rest of you can come with me and help cover this floor, the basement and the out buildings." He looked around the room. "No questions? Alright then, let's get started."

Andrews turned back to face Martinez.

"It's good you're ready to cooperate, Martinez, but what makes you think we need your testimony? You're going straight back to jail, regardless. Why do we need anything from you?"

"Amigo, you need to be real," Concho said. "I'm saying you need a statement from me...and you damned well know it. I'm ready to cut a deal with you guys, ya know, on that blackmail shit."

"Shut the fuck up, Mex," Jake shouted. "It's still not too late. If you know what's good for you, you'll keep that filthy lying taco chute of yours shut, right now, hombre." He glared at Concho. "I mean it."

"You in no position to threaten me, you old gringo fuck. What are you going to do? Raise my rent? You make me laugh. You're so fucking old. We all know you can't even get your dick up no more."

Jake flew off the sofa in a rage. He screamed and lunged forward trying to get to Martinez.

"You lying Mexican fuck! I'll slice your sneaky ass, hey-zoos."

"Back off old man," Concho sneered. "You had a chance to bust me out of this shit, but you wanted to fuck me over. I heard it. We all heard you. Okay, we'll see who gets screwed now, eh? I got nothing to lose, hombre."

"And I'm clean, you sonofabitch," Caldwell growled. "You actually think anybody is going to listen to your lying ass now...or believe anything that comes out of that lying mouth? After all the shit you've pulled? How about that Maclam dude you took off the board in the park? Come on. Yeah. Let's spill all that shit, homes."

Andrews held up a hand like a traffic cop.

"Hold it, dammit. Both of you!" He pointed to Martinez. "You just keep your mouth shut, Martinez."

Andrews turned to Caldwell.

"Jake, he may be lying through his teeth, but facts are facts. Either way, right now you are under arrest for knowingly harboring a fugitive. You know the drill. So turn around and put your hands behind your back while I read you your rights."

He cuffed Caldwell.

"Jacob Caldwell, you are under arrest for knowingly harboring a convicted felon and fugitive from the law. Anything you say can and will be held against you in a court of law."

Caldwell interrupted him.

"Wait! Hold it. Just one fucking minute here. I had no idea this man was a felon, or wanted by the law, for that matter. You can't pin that phony shit on me, Andrews. Now cut me loose before I get my lawyer in on this and have both of you assholes tagging parking violations tomorrow."

Andrews shook his head no.

"You'll get your phone call, but ignorance of the law is no excuse, Jake. Even your lawyer knows that. Harboring a fugitive has always been against both state and federal laws. Martinez here is a felon and a wanted man. He's wanted for a number of parole violations along with questioning about an ongoing homicide case in the city."

Jake snickered.

"Are you totally nuts, Andrews? I wouldn't have that asshole living here. You've got to be kidding. He just dropped by to pay some green he owes me for the ponies at Arlington. I had no idea he was a wanted man."

"That's horseshit and you know it, Jake. That warrant, signed by Judge Hunnicut, is for probable cause. We got a call and we had reason to believe you were keeping Martinez on your premises. Looks like that tip paid off. You had this asshole sitting right here in your living room."

Andrews finished reading Caldwell his rights.

"Tough break, Caldwell," he said when he was done. "Sounds to me like this is something the courts will have to straighten out. Martinez being here sure doesn't help your story, though."

"We'll see, detective. It's all about respect, you know. It all comes down to that in our world. Respect. Or lack of respect. Or earning respect. Or avenging the lack of respect, does it not?"

He paused. "Give that some thought, Andrews."

He pointed to Hawkins.

"He knows."

EPILOGUE

Hawkins was not completely satisfied with the way the case of the blackmailed senator was reported in the newspapers. He believed in the First Amendment, but had little use for the press. In his mind their reporting was a catch 22 situation. In his experience, the press caused more harm than good to most investigations by reaching for the most sensational headlines, leaking details that should have been held back, and reporting rumors and half-truths.

Worse, Cleve thought, the public snapped up their bullshit like Godiva chocolates.

The media had even helped sway Hawk's decision for quitting the Chicago police force five years earlier. As later developments took shape, though, he felt more assured than ever that his case had come to a logical conclusion and that justice had been done as well as was possible.

So, too with Senator Albers' case.

Less than forty-eight hours after the arrests had been made of Jesus Martinez and Jake Caldwell, a police lineup was held in the old city jail building on the south side of Chicago. Martinez and five other miscreants were included in the lineup, a total of six.

Senator Gerald Albers was on hand and identified Martinez as the individual who demanded cash payments from him on two separate occasions for a total of a quarter million dollars cash. With those payments, he was allegedly guaranteed that neither the press nor any other media would be made privy to the senator's extra-marital sex life, which included threesomes as well as some private pictures and videos.

Jake Caldwell's scheme had been to channel the blackmail in such a way as to ruin Albers politically and get the mob's own candidate elected as Illinois Governor in November. None of it had worked. The Senator and his wife were not exposed, thanks to the help of Cleve Hawkins.

All of the culpable parties involved with the elaborate scheme were arrested. Hawkins also made it clear that Caldwell had hired two other men to threaten and assault him on two separate occasions, and he had as a result suffered serious injury.

As it turned out, Martinez was also a prime suspect in two homicides—those of Russell Maclam and Raymond Glick. Both homicides were unsolved, but Martinez would eventually be charged based on data gathered by criminal experts about blood type, fingerprints and DNA gathered at both crime scenes.

The trials for all the people involved in the case would be put on the docket, but wouldn't be in line for the courtroom for at least three months from the date the accused were incarcerated in the Cook County jail.

Neither Caldwell nor Martinez were granted bail, and they would sit in the lock-up until their trials came up the following spring.

In the meantime, Chicago detectives would follow up on the two homicides and continue to gather evidence for the Illinois District Attorney, Harold Darwin, for both subsequent trials.

The senator and his wife, Trish, sued each other for divorce three months after the people involved in the extortion were jailed. Both parties filed based on grounds of "irreconcilable differences." Neither of them fought the other's suits, and their seventeen-year marriage was dissolved with everything settled equitably within a year of filing.

With the unfavorable publicity regarding the divorce, Albers lost his bid for another term in the Illinois Senate two years later. His best friend, and wife-swapping pal, Kent Collier, took the seat vacated by him. Albers was reported to have said, "That's just one more thing that sonofabitch swiped from me."

Deckle continued to be a lost soul. After Hawkins wrapped up the Albers case, he called his pal Jeebers to see how Deckle was faring. Jeebers was not home, and Deckle was not anywhere to be found either.

A couple of days later, when Hawkins caught up with Jeebers, his friend explained that Deckle had "clammed up" and wouldn't talk to him for one full day after Cleve had left him there.

Jeebers told Cleve, "Your pal acted like a lovesick schoolboy, I tell you. I think it was partly just because he was in a strange place. But then, to tell the truth, I think he just plain missed you, Hawk. He was missing your companionship, that's for sure, buddy. Who knows with those homeless people, right?"

In answer to Cleve's question about Deckle not eating, Jeebers said, "He was okay after that first couple of days when I couldn't get him to eat. After that, he ate anything and everything I had in the fridge and cupboards. Strange. He never touched my supply of booze though. So, go figure. I thought he was a drunk. Couldn't prove it by me. Not only did he not raid my stash, he never smelled of booze while he was here."

Jeebers said he had no idea where Deckle had wandered off to, though.

"Remember, I told you I couldn't be here every minute of the day to babysit him. One morning when I got home from the job, your guy was gone."

"Just like that, eh?"

"You've got it. It's been about four days since I've seen him. Sorry, Hawk."

• • •

When Cleve finally called Mo, his stomach was in knots with just the thought of holding her in his arms again. It had been so long. She wasn't home, but instead of leaving a message, he decided to just stop by that evening after she got home from work.

He wanted to surprise her.

Months before she had given him a key to the front entrance of her building, as well as the key to her apartment. He would wait on the landing by her door. Knowing Mo would be home from work between five-thirty and six that evening, he timed everything just right and had a bottle of champagne and a dozen roses with him when he arrived.

Wanting his hands free, he set the gifts on the floor next to his feet.

He heard her close the downstairs entry door and listened to her steps padding softly up each of the carpeted stairs. When she approached the landing, he inched forward and spoke in a throaty whisper.

"Honey, I'm home."

Mo jumped back.

"Oh, my God, Cleve Hawkins! You scared the hell right out of me."

She dropped her purse on the top step and wrapped her arms around his neck.

Cleve held her and kissed her just like Rhett had kissed Scarlett, he hoped, only with even more passion. It was a long-lasting one that caused a moan to rise from somewhere deep inside her.

When they finally moved apart, he said, "Good God, I missed you so much, Mo."

They gazed into each other's eyes and kissed again.

"Let's go inside," he whispered. "Your cheeks are cold. We need to warm you up some."

"Oh, yes," she murmured in his ear as he unlocked the apartment door and lifted her up in his arms. "Oh, yes. I need that so much, lover."

He nudged the door closed behind them.

•　　•　　•

Cleve was a man of his word.

Three weeks after he had given all his information to Lieutenant Ashbaugh and the prosecutors for the Martinez and Caldwell cases, he and Mo were checking in to their eight room suite at the MGM Grand Hotel on the strip in Las Vegas.

They would spend four weeks together getting spoiled by Sin City hospitality, roaming and romancing in and around the Entertainment Capital of the World. They knew that what happened in Vegas stayed in Vegas.

Hawkins was glad he had left his badge home.

NOTE FROM THE AUTHOR

Word-of-mouth is crucial for any author to succeed. If you enjoyed the book, please leave a review online—anywhere you are able. Even if it's just a sentence or two. It would make all the difference and would be very much appreciated.

Thanks!
R.C.

ABOUT THE AUTHOR

R.C. Hartson began his writing in 1967 when he attended Columbia College in Chicago. Three years later he was in the business sector working for Gulf Oil Corporation. He didn't take up his writing again until 1994 when he met his wife, Lynie. She encouraged him to follow his path as a writer. The winner of numerous awards for his short stories and poetry among those, a poem *Shadows of Iwo Jima* was published by the Marines in their Leatherneck magazine in 2003.

His other novels are Detective/Crime genre featuring protagonist, private detective Cleve Hawkins. *Fatal Beauty* was released in 2015 and *Triple Crossed* followed in 2016. A third novel, a family saga titled *Falling Up the Stairs* was released in 2017.

A retired U.S. Marine, R.C. is married, with five children and eight grandchildren and lives with his beautiful wife, Lynie, in gorgeous Western Michigan.

Thank you so much for reading one of R.C. Hartson's novels.
If you enjoyed the experience, please check out our recommended
title for your next great read!

The First book in the *Clive Hawkins Detective Series*

Fatal Beauty by R.C. Hartson

"A first-rate crime novel told in the classic noir tradition of
Raymond Chandler, Jonathan Cain and Dennis Lehane."
–Best Thrillers